RACHEL CUSK

Arlington Park

Rachel Cusk is the author of the Outline trilogy, the memoirs *A Life's Work* and *Aftermath*, and several other works of fiction and nonfiction. She is a Guggenheim Fellow. She lives in Paris.

ALSO BY RACHEL CUSK

FICTION

Second Place

Kudos

Transit

Outline

The Bradshaw Variations

In the Fold

The Lucky Ones

The Country Life

The Temporary

Saving Agnes

NONFICTION

Coventry

Aftermath: On Marriage and Separation

The Last Supper: A Summer in Italy

A Life's Work: On Becoming a Mother

PRAISE FOR RACHEL CUSK

"There is nothing blurry or muted about Cusk's literary vision or her prose . . . She is one of the smartest writers alive."
—Heidi Julavits, *The New York Times Book Review*

"[Cusk] has that ability, unique to the great performers in every art form, to hold one rapt from the moment she appears . . . A stark, modern, adamantine new skyscraper on the literary horizon."
—Dwight Garner, *The New York Times*

"In her effort to expose the illusions of both fiction and life, [Cusk] may have discovered the most genuine way to write a novel today."
—Ruth Franklin, *The Atlantic*

"Cusk has glimpsed the central truth of modern life . . . She moves through it as a blasted centre full only of instinct and super-human hearing and hackles."
—Patricia Lockwood, *London Review of Books*

"Cusk, like the best artists, has renovated her work from its deepest interior—the self—transforming her private crises into an expansive aesthetic vision."
—Meghan O'Gieblyn, *The New York Times Book Review*

"Quietly staggering and intellectually entrancing . . . [Cusk's] writing is silvery and precise, navigated by elegant syntax that steers its speaker toward revelations of great depth."
—Martha Schabas, *The Globe and Mail* (Toronto)

"[The Outline trilogy] can now be appreciated—and will surely be looked back on—as one of the literary masterpieces of our time."
—Sebastian Smee, *The Washington Post*

Arlington Park

RACHEL CUSK

Picador

Farrar, Straus and Giroux

New York

Picador
120 Broadway, New York 10271

Copyright © 2006 by Rachel Cusk
All rights reserved
Printed in the United States of America
Originally published in 2006 by Faber and Faber Ltd., Great Britain
Published in the United States in 2007 by Farrar, Straus and Giroux
First Picador paperback edition, 2007
Picador paperback reissue edition, 2021

Grateful acknowledgment is made for permission to reprint lines from
"Going, Going" from *Collected Poems* by Philip Larkin. Copyright © 1988,
2003 by the Estate of Philip Larkin. Reprinted by permission of
Farrar, Straus and Giroux, LLC, and Faber and Faber Ltd.

The Library of Congress has cataloged the Farrar, Straus and
Giroux hardcover edition as follows:

Cusk, Rachel, 1967–
    Arlington Park / Rachel Cusk.
        p. cm.
    ISBN-13: 978-0-374-10080-3
    ISBN-10: 0-374-10080-2
    1. Parents—Fiction.   2. Middle class—Fiction.   3. England—Fiction.
I. Title.
PR6053.U825 A89 2007
823'.914—dc22

                                                                2006007952

Picador Paperback ISBN: 978-1-250-82818-7

Designed by Jonathan D. Lippincott

For Penny, with affection

Arlington Park

All night the rain fell on Arlington Park.

The clouds came from the west: clouds like dark cathedrals, clouds like machines, clouds like black blossoms flowering in the arid starlit sky. They came over the English countryside, sunk in its muddled sleep. They came over the low, populous hills where scatterings of lights throbbed in the darkness. At midnight they reached the city, valiantly glittering in its shallow provincial basin. Unseen, they grew like a second city overhead, thickening, expanding, throwing up their savage monuments, their towers, their monstrous, unpeopled palaces of cloud.

In Arlington Park, people were sleeping. Here and there the houses showed an orange square of light. Cars crept along the deserted roads. A cat leapt from a wall, pouring itself down into the shadows. Silently the clouds filled the sky. The wind picked up. It faintly stirred the branches of the trees, and in the dark, empty park the swings moved back and forth a little. A handful of dried leaves shuffled on the pavement. Down in the city there were still people on the streets, but in Arlington Park they were in their beds, already surrendered to tomorrow. There was no one to see the rain coming, except a couple hurrying down the silent streets on their way back from an evening out.

"I don't like the look of that," said the man, peering up. "That's rain."

The woman gave an exasperated little laugh.

"You're the expert on everything tonight, aren't you?" she said.

They let themselves into their house. The orange light showed for an instant in their doorway and was extinguished again.

On Arlington Rise, where the streetlamps made a tunnel of hard light and the road began its descent down into the city, the wind lifted stray pieces of litter and whirled them around. Further down, the black sky sagged over the darkened shop-fronts. An irascible gust made the signs rattle against the windows. From here the city could be seen, spread out below in the half-splendour of night. A brown haze stood above it. In its heaped centre, cranes and office blocks and the tiny floodlit spires of the cathedral stood out in the dark against the haze. Red and yellow lights moved in little repeating patterns as though they were the lights of an intricate mechanism. All around it, where the suburbs extended to the north and the east, brilliant fields of light undulated over the blackened landscape.

In the centre of the city the pubs and restaurants were closed, but people were queuing outside the nightclubs. When the rain started to fall, a few of the girls shrieked and held their handbags over their heads. The boys laughed uneasily. They hunched their shoulders and put their hands in their pockets. The drops fell from the fathomless darkness and came glittering into the orange light. They fell on the awning of the Luna nightclub and twisted in the beams of the streetlamps. They fell into the melancholy, stained fountain in the square, where men in T-shirts sat with cans of lager and hooded boys made graceful circles in the dark on their skateboards. There were people milling in doorways, shrieking girls in stilettos, boys with sculpted hair, middle-aged men furtively carrying things in plastic bags. A woman in a tight raincoat tick-tacked hurriedly along the pavement, talking into her mobile phone. One of the men by the fountain took off his T-shirt and rubbed his startled chest in the rain while the others cheered. The traffic moved slowly through the spray. A group of men in a passing car blared their horn at the queuing girls and shouted out the windows as they went by.

The rain fell on the tortuous medieval streets and the grimy Victorian streets and on the big bombed streets where shopping centres had been built. It fell on the hospital and the old theatre and the new multiplex cinema. It fell on multistorey car parks and office blocks. It fell on fast-food restaurants and pubs with Union Jacks in the windows. It fell on newly built blocks of flats whose windows were still in their plastic wrappers and whose foundations stood in mud, and it fell on their hoardings. Along the river, commercial buildings—insurance buildings and banks—stood one after another, geometric-shaped, and the rain fell in their empty, geometric-shaped plazas. On the black river, under the bridge, swans sheltered from the dark drops amidst the floating rubbish. All along the rain-blackened High Street people were waiting at bus stops: people from desolate parts of the city, from Weston or Hartford, where the rain fell on boarded-up shops and houses and the concrete walkways of insomniac estates. They crowded into the bus shelters, a man with a giant sheaf of dreadlocks, a man with an enormous suitcase, an old lady neatly parcelled into a tweed coat, a couple in tracksuits who kissed and kissed beneath the plastic roof where the rain beat down, so that when the bus came in a great dark arc of water the old lady had to tap the boy on the shoulder and tell them to get on.

The bus went through the rain up Firley Way, which passed from the centre all the way through the suburbs to the retail park, where rain fell on featureless warehouses and superstores and tumbled down in sheets over their empty car parks. It fell on the roofs of darkened garage forecourts. It fell on car showrooms and builders' merchants. It battered the plastic verandas where supermarket trolleys clung together in long, chattering rows. It fell on the business park, and on the shrubs adorning its desolate roundabout. It fell on the black, submissive fields from which the new places were unrepentantly carved. Over Merrywood shopping mall the rain fell hard on the giant neo-classical roof, so that water streamed down its indifferent façade.

On Arlington Rise the rain was running downhill in the gutters. Below, a kind of vapour hung over the city, muffling the red and yellow lights. The sounds of car horns and a siren rose up the hill from the glittering, steaming heap of the city.

A little further up, around a bend in the road, the vista disappeared. The darkness deepened. The buildings grew more graceful and the pavements more orderly. As the road ascended to Arlington Park the big, brash shops down below were succeeded by florists and antique shops: the off-licences became wine merchants, the fast-food chains became bistros. To either side tree-lined roads began to appear. In the rain these roads had the resilient atmosphere of ancient places. Their large houses stood impassively in the dark, set back amidst their dripping trees. Between them, a last, panoramic glimpse of the city could be seen below: of its eternal red and yellow lights, its pulsing mechanism, its streets always crawling with indiscriminate life. It was a startling view, though not a reassuring one. It was too mercilessly dramatic: with its unrelenting activity it lacked the sense of intermission, the proper stops and pauses of time. The story of life required its stops and its pauses, its days and nights. It didn't make sense otherwise. But to look at that view you'd think that a human life was meaningless. You'd think that a day meant nothing at all.

The rain fell on Arlington Park, fell on its empty avenues and its well-pruned hedges, on its schools and its churches, on its trees and its gardens. It fell on its Victorian terraces with their darkened windows, on its rows of bay-fronted houses, on its Georgian properties behind their gates, on its maze of tidy streets where the little two-storey houses were painted pretty colours. It fell joyously over the dark, deserted sward of the park, over its neat paths and bushes. It beat down, washing the pavements, sluicing along the drains, drumming on the bonnets of the parked cars. All night it fell, until with a new intensity, just before dawn, it emptied a roaring cascade of water over the houses so that the rain was flung against the darkened windows.

In their sleep they heard it, people lying in their beds: the thunderous noise of the water. It penetrated their dreams, a sound like the sound of uproarious applause. It was as if a great audience were applauding. Louder and louder it grew, this strange, unsettling sound. It filled the night: it rattled the windows and made people turn beneath their covers and children cry in their sleep. It made them feel somehow observed, as if a dark audience had assembled outside and were looking in through the windows, clapping their hands.

Juliet Randall parted her hair before the mirror and there it was: a thing like a cockroach, three inches long and two across, embedded in her scalp, waving its legs triumphantly. She showed it to her husband. Look, she said, look! She bent her head forward, still holding aside her hair. Benedict looked. Oh, how it itched! How revolting it was, how unbearably revolting! Was there no way of getting it out? Her husband didn't seem to think so. He was evidently glad the thing hadn't decided to make its nest in his hair. Do something! Juliet shrieked, or tried to, but it was one of those dreams where you tried to say something and then suddenly found you couldn't. She struggled in the shroud of sleep. Then, with a great effort, she tore it from her and opened her eyes.

What a horrible dream—horrible! Juliet clutched her head and frantically searched her hair. The cockroach both was and wasn't there. She was full of its presence and yet she couldn't touch it; she could only feel it, the hideous stirring of its legs, the crawling feeling of infestation. Oh, the way it had greedily moved its legs! And the terrible knowledge that there was no way of getting it out, that she would have to endure it for ever! The daylight began to break down that knowledge a little. She felt a measure of relief, and then another. But the thing, the insect, was still real to her, more real than the unharmed patch of scalp her fingers went over and over. Where had it gone? What was it, to remain so real to her? It almost infuriated her in its non-existence: it was maddening, almost, to be tormented by something that wasn't there.

It wasn't there! She acknowledged that it wasn't. Steadily the sense of it diminished. All she could think of now was that Benedict hadn't helped her. He had pitied her, but he had accepted her fate. He had accepted her future, as the host of a giant cockroach. He was glad it hadn't happened to him. She looked into the deep innards of the dream and searched them again for their information. The moment she had parted her hair and showed him: that was when she realised. She had realised the true significance of a fact that was well known to her. She knew it, and yet it seemed that only in that moment did she finally understand its significance. Only then did she see what it meant, that she and Benedict were separate.

The house was silent, except for the steady sound of rain at the window and the submerged roar of the traffic on Arlington Rise. It was early, yet already the streets were awake, subversively going about their business in the dawn. What were people up to at this hour? What illicit advantage were they pursuing in their cars, going to and fro along Arlington Rise? The room stood muffled in tentative, crêpey light. Juliet scratched the place where the cockroach had been. Benedict was asleep. She drew away from the lump of him, moving further to the other side of the bed. Upstairs, above their heads, the children were still silent in their room. She listened to the sound of the rain. During the night—earlier, before the cockroach—she had woken and heard the thunderous water in the dark. It had made a sound like the sound of applause. She didn't know why, but it had made her afraid: she had felt a

9

fear of something it was too late to prevent, something that had already occurred. It was as if she could have gone and stood at the window and seen it standing there in the garden in the rainy dark, completed.

The indistinct light proceeded with its modest inventory of their room. There was the brown wardrobe and the inelegant chest of drawers; there was the ladder-backed chair with two rungs missing, the framed map of Venice, the chipped gilt mirror with its opaque oval of glass, all having survived the darkness unaltered. At the window the sagging curtains began to show their ancient folds and formations. Beside her, on the floor, her clothes lay in a heap: she had stepped out of them where she stood the night before. They had got back late and she had shed them, uncaring, and got straight into bed.

What an evening they'd had! It was the sort of evening that left a bitter taste in the mouth, that sat on your chest in the morning with its feeling of shame. It was an evening, in a sense, to which the cockroach had been the conclusion—the cockroach and the realisation that she and Benedict were not joined but separate. She couldn't even summon up a clear sense of outrage about it: she had drunk too much, and the feeling of shame sat on her chest. The bitterness lay in her veins like lead. Apparently, she had been slightly obnoxious. Benedict had told her so on the walk home. She, Juliet, aged thirty-six, mother of two, a teacher at Arlington Park High School for Girls—a person regarded in her youth as somewhat exceptional, a scholarship student and at one time Head Girl—had been slightly obnoxious to their hosts, the Milfords: Matthew Milford, the vilely wealthy owner of an office supplies company in Cheltenham, and his horse-faced, attenuated, raddled wife, Louisa.

She thought of their house, into whose kitchen alone the whole of the Randalls' shoddy establishment in Guthrie Road would comfortably have fitted. What had they done to deserve such a house? Where was the justice in that? She recalled that Matthew Milford had spoken harshly to her. The lord of the manor had spoken harshly from amidst his spoils, from his unjust throne, to Juliet, his guest. And Benedict called *her* obnoxious!

What was it he'd said? What was it Matthew had said, sitting there at the table like a lord, a bull, a red, angry bull blowing air through his nostrils? *You want to be careful.* He'd told her she wanted to be careful. His head was so bald the candlelight had made it shine like a shield. You want to be careful, he'd said, with the emphasis on *you*. He had spoken to Juliet not as if he'd invited her to his house but as if he'd employed her to be there. It was as if he'd employed her as a guest and was giving her a caution. That was how a man like that made you feel: as if your right to exist derived from his authority. He looked at her, a woman of thirty-six with a job and a house and a husband and two children of her own, and he decided whether or not she should be allowed to exist.

Beside her Benedict sat up.

"Right," he said, ruffling his thin, downy hair with his fingers.

Today it annoyed her, the way Benedict came to life in the mornings: as though life were a river he had rested beside, before climbing back into his one-man canoe and paddling off upstream. Benedict had not defended her from that man Matthew Milford, any more than he had removed the cockroach from her scalp.

"You were on the sauce last night," he observed.

He got out of bed and went to the window. Juliet still lay there with her head on the pillow and her hair spread around her in a fan.

"We all were," she said.

11

"Not me."

"Everyone except you, then."

Benedict was naked. In clothes he looked very slightly effeminate, but naked he did not. His freckled chest had a burly, bunched-up look. Benedict's nakedness had an extrovert quality, like that of people in nudist colonies.

"Incredible house," he said, parting the folds of the curtain a little with one finger and then letting them fall back again.

"Ridiculous," Juliet said.

"Ye-es, I suppose it was, in a way."

"It was," Juliet asseverated. "How can people who are so idiotic be so successful?"

"I thought you thought it was ridiculous."

"It was! All those hunting prints—and the antlers in the loo! Who do they think they are—the aristocracy? All he does is sell photocopiers to secretaries in offices!"

Benedict tutted.

"It's true," Juliet said bitterly. She was determined to exonerate herself. "I hate the way men like that think they're important. They expect you to defer to them, just because they run a business! What's so important about a business? It's just selling things for your own personal profit. It's just greed, dressed up as usefulness."

Benedict withdrew to the bathroom. Juliet lay and listened to the rain, and the muffled sound of the traffic going through it.

"Who is he to go around telling people to be careful?" she called. "He should be careful himself. People might decide to stop using photocopiers. I hope they do decide to stop using them," she added, though there was no reply.

She scratched the place where the cockroach had been.

"How dared he!" she resumed when Benedict returned.

"Who?"

"Matthew Milford, last night. *Women your age can start to sound strident,*" she mimicked. "Who does he think he is?"

"I don't suppose he meant any harm," Benedict said vaguely. "It was probably nothing to do with you."

"That wasn't what you said last night."

"Wasn't it?"

"You said it was my fault. You said I'd been obnoxious."

She saw he had forgotten that he'd even said it. In fact, he wasn't really attending to her at all. He was thinking about the coming day. He was thinking about school, where his ravenous classes awaited him. Last year his classes had attained exam results unheard of in the annals of the comprehensive's grim history. It had made the front page of the *Arlington Gazette*, the miracle of Benedict's results. Boys with knives and shaved heads, boys who were more than slightly obnoxious, boys with drug problems and drink problems, commended for their essays on Shakespeare's late plays! It was extraordinary. Juliet's classes got results that were entirely in line with the high school's reputation. But at Benedict's school the boys were searched for weapons before they were allowed on the premises. Benedict's results were extraordinary.

Juliet never thought about school until the moment she walked through its wrought-iron gates. It was Benedict who thought, in order to be extraordinary. He ran off their joint life as if it were a generator fuelled by Juliet, and then he separated himself and thought.

He unhooked his dressing gown from the back of the door, put it on, and with a rueful expression returned to the bathroom.

"Bloody photocopiers!" she exclaimed to the empty room.

She lay and looked at the ceiling. She could hear movements from the children's room above her head. In a minute she would have to get up and deal with them. Benedict wouldn't go. It was Juliet who did everything. Everything! She would put them in their uniforms and take them out into the rain. Then she recalled that it was Friday, the last Friday of the month, the day Benedict collected the children from school.

Juliet and Benedict did not know the Milfords well. Louisa Milford always seemed very fractured and busy and *distrait*, as though she had some difficult secret, some difficult burden at home she was unable to tell you about. It might have been her husband, it was hard to tell: he ran his own business and was hardly ever seen. They lived in one of the Georgian houses on the park, in Parry's Place to be exact, which Juliet was told—she liked to pretend not to know that sort of thing—was the most expensive address in Arlington Park.

Though they did not know them well, Louisa's invitation—"supper in the kitchen at Parry's Place, just us, *totally* informal"—did imply knowledge of a kind: Louisa's knowledge of the Randalls as a level at which an invitation could be pitched. Juliet and Benedict walked, and once across the park began to pass grand houses, standing behind Bath-stone walls and closed gates. By night they had the monolithic appearance of temples, rearing up from the shadowy mass of grass and trees, their façades fabulous with a particular kind of amber light. It was strange, to be amidst this little aristocracy of houses. In Guthrie Road, as elsewhere in Arlington Park, the solid, bourgeois, profitable ordinariness of life was generally ascendant. But here things existed at a pitch of striking ostentation. It was hard to know exactly what it signified. Juliet felt at one minute that she and Benedict might be eaten, or enslaved; and at the next that some form of reward awaited them. It was exciting, in a way.

But then, glimpsing the armoured forms of the big, expensive cars crouched among the shadows in driveways all along the park, she had a sort of oceanic sense of malevolence, of a great, diffuse evil silently undulating all around them in the darkness. In the Milfords' own driveway an enormous glittering Mercedes crouched on the gravel on giant, ogreish tyres. Its tinted windows seemed to cast on everything their shuttered, annihilating gaze. Juliet had felt a force of pure aggression emanating from its metal surfaces. It was the car of an assassin, a killer. Louisa Milford opened the panelled front door and looked at the Randalls rather blankly. Was she a killer? Juliet wasn't sure.

"Did you walk?" exclaimed Louisa. "You *are* marvellous."

The hall was full of amber light. There was a smell of flowers, and of cooking, and of wax polish, and Juliet was overpowered by a new realisation, the realisation that life was meant to be wonderful. She felt she had known this at some point before, but had inexplicably forgotten it. Benedict handed over the bottle of supermarket wine and Bendick's mints, which his sense of irony permitted him on such occasions.

"Oh, you *are* marvellous!" said Louisa, examining her booty and then smiling at them with her head on one side, as though they had just made a donation to some charitable cause she was supporting.

People like the Milfords invariably thought the Randalls, both teachers, were marvellous. ("I really think you two and the work you do are just *marvellous.*") Of course, it was Benedict they meant. They would never have dreamt of sending their own children to Hartford View Comprehensive, famed centre of violence and anomie; but it was thrilling to have contact, however indirect, with those whose misfortune it was to do so. Juliet's afternoons at Arlington Park High School for Girls gained a referred lustre of significance from Benedict: the denizens of the temples on the park found it a satisfying evening's entertainment, this little drama of male force and female sensibility. Also, people of the Milfords' sort preferred to think of the Randalls as non-materialistic, a condition they seemed to regard as being in some way irresponsible, as though materialism were an aged parent they liked to rail about while believing themselves bound to it by chains of honour and duty.

The four of them sat in a kitchen like a ballroom, around a heavy, square dining table with carved feet. When Louisa Milford smiled she disclosed a sinister jumble of grey teeth like a bouquet of tombstones. Her daughters went to the High School: it was on their account that she thought Juliet was marvellous, and might cease to think it. Her husband, Matthew, was a big red man, as plump and sleek as a seal, whose teeth were white and prominent and even; he kept them continually a little bared as though to refute his wife's inferior set. He had folds of pink skin at the back of his neck. He was like a big sleek seal sitting barking on its rock, or so Juliet thought. He and Benedict talked, and Louisa and Juliet fed on the scraps of the men's conversation that fell to them. Benedict sat twisted around in his chair: the more Matthew spoke, the more contorted Benedict's posture became. It was a sign, recognisable only to Juliet, that he disagreed with Matthew; or rather, that he was listening to him with studied detachment, which was as close as Benedict generally cared to come to conflict. Louisa repeatedly sat down and got up again from the table, moving around the vast kitchen in bemusement, like a woman whose servants have been given their first evening off. She was attentive to the candles, and kept lighting new ones, placing them fancifully all around the room as though she could never tire of this trick of making light. Matthew brought out bottle after bottle of wine. Each time he carefully wrapped a white napkin around the neck with his thick fingers before he poured.

Juliet drank, with a prodigiousness that at first seemed like a response to the prodigiousness of her setting, a need to equalise herself with it. It all seemed to invite her to cast herself off into a sea of wine. But as she drank, the evening grew tarnished. Life did not seem to be meant to be as wonderful as it had done earlier. Wherever she looked she saw the sheen coming off it.

Louisa kept saying, "I do think Matthew's got a point."

Matthew talked on and on. He talked about politics and taxes and the people who got in his way. He talked about people who were lazy and people who were dishonest. He talked about women. Every time he employed a woman, he said, he spent a year training her and sending her on courses and getting her up to scratch, and then she promptly got pregnant and went off on maternity leave. Well, he wasn't going to employ women any more. Flatly refused to. Didn't care if it wasn't politically correct. Wasn't going to do it.

"I *do* think Matthew's got a point," Louisa said to Juliet.

"You ask your boss," Matthew said to Benedict. "He'll tell you the same thing. It's the same story everywhere. And don't start saying that a school isn't like a business. A school is exactly like a business. You don't need to tell me that yours is different. They're all the same in one respect. What they're interested in are results."

The headteacher of Hartford View was a woman. Last year, encountering him in a crowded school corridor after Benedict's exam results had come in, she had apparently gone down on her knees in front of him, in full view of the passing pupils and teachers.

"They're certainly interested in them," Benedict said. "They just can't get them."

"Well, I'll tell you why they can't—half the staff will be on long-term maternity leave!" Matthew said, looking virtually ecstatic.

"Tell them about Sonia," Louisa urged him.

Matthew nodded and raised a hand to stay her.

"I had a girl phone in the other day," he said. "*Mr. Milford*, she says, *Mr. Milford*." He put on a silly, high-pitched voice as the girl. "*Mr. Milford, I'm afraid I can't come back when I said I would*. Why not, I say. *Well, Mr. Milford, the thing is, my baby needs me*." He paused, and pantomimed bemusement. "I need you, I say. *But it's not the same*, she says. *It's not the same thing, Mr. Milford. All I'm asking for is a little more time*, she says. Darling, I say, how much time do you think you'll need? Will eighteen years be enough? See him off to university? On second thought, send him here when you've finished and I'll give him a job!"

Matthew laughed loudly.

"But did you let her have more time?" Juliet asked shakily.

Adrift on a sea of wine, she had not prepared herself for the unexpected necessity of setting herself apart from him. She had let the wine carry her away, and then she found she was not prepared, for the coldness of life.

"Of course I didn't. I'm not running a bloody NCT group. I told her she could come back when her three months were up or not come back at all. No hard feelings, I said. As far as I was concerned she could spend the rest of her life folding nappies if that was what she wanted to do with that fluff between her ears. As I say, no hard feelings."

"People don't *fold* nappies any more, darling," said

Louisa. "They buy them from the supermarket." She winked at Juliet. "That tells you how many *he's* changed."

"She could stay at home playing happy families," resumed Matthew. "Or she could come back and work for me on the day and time we agreed. End of story."

"That's illegal," said Juliet.

There was a silence. Matthew stared down at his own powerful arms, folded across his chest. A dark red colour rose into his neck and face.

"I don't think you can really say it's actually *illegal*, Juliet," said Louisa.

"I can. That's exactly what it is."

"But you can't blame *Matthew*!"

Louisa looked around at them all with an air of gracious incredulity.

"Look, sweetie," Matthew presently said to Juliet. "I'm not saying I don't value all the wonderful work you women do. It's a big job, running a family. It's hard work. I know because it's all Lou ever talks about, how hard it is managing the kids and the house and how tired she gets all the time. I'm the last person to say it's an easy job, making a home and raising the next generation. What I do say is that sometimes you don't think about how it's all going to get paid for. I pay for the house, the cars, the school fees, the au pair, the cleaner, the holidays, the gym membership, Lou's wardrobe"—he counted it with his thick fingers in front of Juliet's face, as though she ought to be grateful—"and most of the time I'm not even here. So when the girl phones in and says she wants to spend more time with baby, and she wants me to pay for that too, I'm going to tell her where to get off."

"You have to admit he's got a point," said Louisa, while Matthew took a long, bellicose swallow from his wineglass.

"She could take you to court," said Juliet.

He lifted his head a little with predatory alertness.

"She won't," he said steadily.

"Well, she should."

And that was when he said it.

"You want to be careful," he said. She saw how close she was to his hatred: it was like a nerve she was within a millimetre of touching. "You want to take care. You can start to sound strident at your age." He wiped his mouth with the back of his hand and looked at Juliet as though she were naked. "The problem with women like you is that you don't know how to play to your strengths."

It was now that she felt herself to be drunk; now that her aversion to him wanted to be born in all its intensity but could not be, tied up as it was in imprecision, in paralysing layers of numbness. Benedict was staring at the tip of his shoe, where it nearly touched the white damask hem of the table-cloth. Juliet watched as he moved it carefully until it touched the hem and then moved it away again.

"Actually, Juliet's got a fine pair of strengths," he said, craning his neck a little to see his shoe.

There was a silence, and then Matthew laughed explosively.

"A fine pair!" he shouted, rocking back in his chair and laughing deliriously at the ceiling.

Juliet was astonished. Never, in all the time she'd known him, had Benedict said such a thing. Louisa gave a little reproving, shrieking laugh of her own. Matthew flung his arm across the table and grasped Juliet's hand.

"A bloody fine pair." He laughed, squeezing her fingers, his eyes fixed on Benedict.

All men are murderers, Juliet thought. All of them. They murder women. They take a woman, and little by little they murder her.

Now Juliet lay still and looked at the map of Venice that hung in a frame on the wall opposite their bed. She looked at the intestinal canals all held against each other in a knot. Now, just as the stone walls of Venice endured the dark water that lay between them, and the water endured its confinement in the twisting walls that held it there, and as their eternal involvement was something that had a name, a being, a kind of beauty, so Juliet could endure the coming day.

And it was Friday, the last Friday of the month! Juliet taught English part-time at Arlington Park High, and in the normal course of things her last lesson concluded at half past three. At the same time, half a mile away at Arlington Primary, the white-faced teachers were opening the doors, releasing great waves of used air while the children—Katherine and Barnaby amongst them—crushed in the doorway in their coats. Over near the park, at the sound of the bell, Juliet would run. She would leave her fair-haired, faintly astonished class and run down the waxed corridors, run out into the grounds where well-dressed women stood in groups, run through the gates and into the street. She would run along the pavements clutching her bag of exercise books. Seven or eight minutes later she would arrive, breathless, sweat cascading down her sides. Katherine and Barnaby weren't always the last. There was usually at least one other child there, following the teacher around. Juliet didn't hit the bottom, quite: there was always one child resignedly helping put things away, like a ward of the state, apparently without hope of ever being collected.

But still, it required her to run.

On the last Friday of every month, however, Juliet took the school Literary Club. These Fridays were like a dividend from which she eked out a whole secretive life. She was a giant organism depending for its life on the single capillary that issued from her Friday afternoons. The Literary Club was open to the whole senior school, and was quite popular. It commenced at four o'clock and lasted an hour. On those days, Juliet did not run. Benedict collected the children. They had to get a supply teacher in to cover for him, because Benedict's school was down in the city and it took him an hour to get back to Arlington Park. Normally, what with one thing and another, he was never home before six. Juliet, convening the Literary Club on the last Friday of the month, would think of that supply teacher. She felt that he—she always saw him as a man—and she were linked in some strange way. Together they made a little mechanism, of the sort that might be used to bypass an organ. It was a complicated arrangement that ensured the continuance of life. While the supply teacher taught, Juliet chugged into a siding of time and Benedict collected the children from school.

All through that leaden hour, the hour when children were released from school and manacled themselves once more to one's breathless form, she sat and discussed literature with fourteen or so privileged girls of assorted ages. Or at least, she gave the appearance of discussing it: there was always something else that crept in, an element of display, almost of exhibitionism. It was as if, in this atmosphere that was at once less formal and more rarefied than the classroom, she displayed herself to them in all her textured humanity. Look at me, she said, a woman, a woman journeying, manacled, to the shrine of art. She presented herself to them as an artefact of human drama, a sculpted piece of life, almost as an artwork herself. In the classroom, teaching one form after another by rote, it was not generally possible to appear to them thus: she was an oddity, an adult in the child's world of school. They saw her, even the sixth-formers, as an isolated figure, a sort of lone pillar in their midst who for one reason or another had elected to support the roof above their heads. They could not imagine her married, or as the mother of children; and to impute humanity to her—lust or sinfulness or plain subjectivity—was, she knew, a kind of joke. She knew because she had felt the same way about her own teachers, that they were like strange little gods in their benevolence and fury, their fixity. They weren't human at all: rather, they were like carved figures that symbolised human attributes.

At the Literary Club, however, for an hour, Juliet took a human form. She displayed herself to fourteen girls, aged thirteen upwards, who had gathered in their own time to discuss matters of a higher order. She showed herself to them, half warning, half enigma. You will never understand me, she seemed to say; and at the same time: This is what one day you might become.

She rose from the bed and went out onto the landing. Benedict was emerging from the bathroom in a voluminous, smock-like shirt.

"Are you going to London today?" she said.

He looked at her as if she were mad. "To *London*?" he said.

Murderer, she thought.

"It's just for some reason I remembered you saying you were going to London. For a conference or something. And it's Literary Club today."

"I'm here today," he said. "Why, were you hoping to have me out of the way so you could have your lover round to breakfast?"

She turned to the window that gave a view out to the side of the house. There was Guthrie Road in the rain, at the junction with Arlington Rise. A delta of brown water obscured a whole section of pavement at the corner. A woman stood by it holding an umbrella, hesitating. Just then a car passed and unearthed a great root of brown water from the puddle, which toppled and crashed at her feet. Going the other way, into town, the cars stood end to end, not moving. Clouds of vapour rose from their exhausts. Their lights glowed through the grey atmosphere with a sort of diabolical suggestion. The spinsterly rows of Victorian houses looked puny, dreary, next to the rows of expensive, obstructed cars.

"Funny kind of lover you'd have round for breakfast," she said.

Arlington Park in the rain: a maze of grey, orderly streets with cars passing through them like private thoughts. This was what it boiled down to, all of history: a place of purely material being, traversed by private thoughts. She had never expected to find herself here, where women drank coffee all day and pushed prams around the grey, orderly streets, and men went to work, went there and never came back, like there was a war on. She had thought she would be in a university department somewhere, or on the staff of a national newspaper. Other people had thought so too. At school she was the exceptional one. She was the one everybody talked about. She came top in all her subjects; she got a scholarship to university. They even made her Head Girl. It was funny, in a way, that she had ended up as a teacher, back at school. It made it seem as though school was her natural habitat. It made it seem that she wasn't bright or gifted or exceptional at all. She was merely good at going to school.

On her last day in the sixth form her English teacher, Mrs. Mountford, had hugged her with tears glittering in her hard, unhappy little eyes and said, "Well, I expect I'll be hearing about you." Juliet should write her a letter. Dear Mrs. Mountford, just to let you know that I found another school that was kind enough to take me in. Dear Mrs. Mountford, just to let you know what I did with all that education you gave me. I found some other girls and gave it to them. That was good, wasn't it, Mrs. Mountford? Dear Mrs. Mountford, you may have been wondering why you haven't heard from me in all these years. The thing is, I was murdered, Mrs. Mountford. My husband, Benedict, murdered me. He was very gentle about it; it didn't really hurt at all. In fact, I hardly knew it was happening. But I'm all right now, Mrs. Mountford. You'll be glad to hear that I'm being careful.

Behind her, Benedict touched her hair. She shrank from the feeling of his hand. She turned around so that he couldn't touch her any more and his hand was left suspended in mid-air. There was his face, smooth and red-cheeked like a baby's face, with his little knowing eyes in the middle of it. In his smock, with his red cheeks and his eyes that were like the twinkling eyes of an old man, he looked like an illustration from a fairy tale. He looked like a woodcutter, or a shoe-maker. She did not want to be touched by a shoemaker from a fairy tale. She was prepared to acknowledge his magical qualities, but she didn't want him touching her.

"It's so long," he said.

She realised he meant her hair. It was nearly down to her waist. Since childhood she'd had long hair. Year in and year out she'd kept it, though it had vexed her mother. It was un-practical, her mother said. In those days, Juliet had had no in-tention of being practical. She had defended her hair against her mother's punitive, twice-yearly appointments with the hairdresser. She would sit in the chair and cry, so that the woman didn't have the heart to take off more than an inch. It's just a form of attention-seeking, her mother would tell the hairdresser: she seemed to be referring to the tears, but re-ally, Juliet knew, she was talking about the hair itself. It's not like it's particularly special hair, her mother used to say. It's one thing having long hair if it's an unusual colour. But yours is mouse. It looks strange, having all that mouse-coloured hair. I like it! Juliet would shout. It wasn't so much that she liked it, more that she regarded it as a kind of symbol, a sign: it was the outward growth of the inner conviction she held about herself, that she was exceptional.

Benedict had loved her hair. He had loved it so much that he had climbed all the way up it, like the man in the fairy tale. He had climbed up it to the top of the tower, to Juliet's place, and somehow he had made it more his place than hers.

"Don't forget we're going out tonight," she said, ducking her head away from his hand, which was still hovering near her face as though looking for somewhere to put itself.

Benedict looked displeased.

"Are we? Again?"

"We're having dinner with the Lanhams."

He frowned. He didn't know any Lanhams. How could he be expected to know about Lanhams when another day awaited him at Hartford View, where giant sixth-formers threw tables across the classrooms and people got down on their knees before Benedict in the corridors?

"Christine Lanham," Juliet said. "She was at school with me. I told you, I met her in the street."

She had met Christine Lanham on her way back from the supermarket. Juliet was carrying her shopping in plastic bags. She had Katherine and Barnaby with her, and she was carrying her shopping because Benedict took the car to work. How are *you*, Christine said, amazed. She hadn't known Juliet lived in Arlington Park. Had she just arrived? Juliet said she'd been here for nearly four years and Christine was amazed again. In fact, she was more than amazed, Juliet saw: she was disappointed. I don't know why, Christine said, but I always thought of you in London. Isn't that funny? Juliet didn't think it was particularly funny. Actually, it was one of the least funny things she'd ever heard. She wanted to say that personally she hadn't thought of Christine at all, not once in all these years, and that if she had ever thought of her for even one second she'd have seen her right here where she was, in Arlington Park. She hardly knew Christine, but still, she would not have been mistaken, because she, Juliet, remained in some sense exceptional. So how *are* you, Christine said, opening her eyes very wide, wide enough to accommodate the shopping, the two children, Juliet's clothes that were the clothes of someone who no longer cared. How *are* you, Christine said, and Juliet nearly replied, Actually, I'm dead. I was murdered a few years ago, nearly four years ago to be exact.

"Oh yes," Benedict said now, nodding, with the vague look of a person encouraging her to go on so that he could think about something else.

"Christine Lanham and her husband, Joe," Juliet said. She emphasised *Joe*. Benedict had the unnerving habit of confidently addressing people by names that did not belong to them.

"Joe," he said. "Right you are."

Benedict's hand hovered and then with an awkward movement laid itself once more on her hair. He looked at her half-beseechingly out of his little eyes. Where on earth had he got that smock? How did he get away with it, facing down the giant sixth-formers in that smock?

"I've got to get the children to school," she said.

He twined his fingers in the mouse-coloured tresses. He wasn't even thinking about it, she realised. He had forgotten why his hand was there in her hair. He just wound it absently round and round his fingers, forgetting what he had felt only a minute earlier. He had felt that she was remote from him. She knew it: he had caught sight of her there on the landing and remembered that she kept herself far away from him. It was like when Juliet sometimes stood in front of the television with the remote control, switching channels to find something for the children to watch, and a fragment of news would come on the screen. She would see a war or an earthquake, the faces of people in pain or people holding guns, see regions of dust and mountains far away. She would see it, a few instants of turmoil on the other side of the world, and then she would switch over.

Upstairs there was the sound of feet running to and fro and a door slamming.

"Get dressed, you two!" she bawled, so loudly that Benedict, whose face was six inches from her own, was forced to take a step back and let go of her hair.

What she'd actually said to Christine Lanham was: We came here for my husband's job. She'd explained it to her, every detail. She'd said, My husband likes to move around every few years, you see. He's a teacher, she'd said. He specialises in failing schools. He sounds *fascinating*, Christine had said, so that a bitter feeling of pride had risen into Juliet's mouth. Well, she'd said, laughing, I suppose he is. As I say, he likes to move around and find new challenges. So I— She'd tossed back her mouse-coloured hair and moved her shopping to the other hand. She'd acted as if it was no concern of hers what she did. So I usually just find work locally, she'd said.

She was in her room getting dressed when Katherine came in. Katherine was in her school uniform, though she'd done up the buttons wrongly over her tubby chest. Only five years old and she got herself dressed when she was told to. What a good girl she was, sensible and good.

"Where's Barnaby?" Juliet said.

"He's upstairs," Katherine informed her. "Barnaby's being stupid. He says he won't get dressed."

"Does he?"

Katherine was good, but Barnaby would win. Katherine would toil and try, but in the end he would defeat her.

"And he's taken all the things off his bed," Katherine said. "I told him not to, but he did. I told him you said not to. He's taken all the sheets off and everything. He made a mountain with it."

"Damn him," said Juliet.

She brushed her hair in front of the mirror. Behind her Katherine sat down on the edge of the bed. Juliet could see her in the glass. In her navy-blue uniform she made a sort of dark ellipsis in the pale covers. It was strange, that she had created these uniformed beings. The uniforms were like another exam certificate: they seemed to certify the private, tangled strain of her achievement. It had grieved her at first, to clothe Katherine's unfinished little body in uniform. She had felt that she wanted to keep Katherine for herself.

"Mummy," Katherine said.

Juliet gathered her hair at her shoulder and brushed the ends until they were straight.

"What?"

"At school they taught us a song."

"Did they?"

"They taught us a funny song. Shall I tell you how it goes?"

"All right."

Katherine sang it in a clear little voice:

> *Mr. Clickety-Cane*
> *He plays a silly game.*
> *And all the children in the street*

29

They like to do the same.
Wash your face with orange juice!
Wash your face with orange juice!

"Mummy—it says wash your face with orange juice!"

She rolled around in the covers with mirth.

Juliet had wanted to keep Katherine for herself, but instead she'd had to surrender her, as though called upon to make a sacrifice to her own implacable gods. It was hard, harder than she'd expected it to be, to take the vigorous, joyful, wild body of Katherine and clothe it in a school uniform. Until that moment the possibilities for Katherine had seemed endless. Katherine's femaleness had seemed like a joyful, a beautiful thing. It had seemed invincible, even in its half-formed fragility. She had not realised what she was. She had only delighted in it, in her female being. Now, though, she was different. She knew she was a girl. She returned from school full of a kind of programmatic agony. Her soul was in training. They had told her what she was, and now she knew. She didn't play with the boys in the playground, she told Juliet. Juliet asked why not, and Katherine shrugged. None of the girls do, she said.

"Let's go and find Barnaby, shall we?" said Juliet, holding out her hand.

Immediately Katherine jumped off the bed and came to her. Now, when Juliet spoke, Katherine answered. She heard in her mother's voice the call of her sex and she replied with her answering femaleness.

It had to be admitted that Juliet didn't know what she'd have done with Katherine, had she been allowed to keep her. She only wanted to protect her, that was all. As she had made Katherine with her body, so she could only think of her in terms of a physical expense. She wanted to protect her. She wanted to throw herself in her path. She wanted to shield her, from the bullet of an ordinary life.

Upstairs, Barnaby was standing on his mountain, naked, with his dressing-gown cord tied around his head.

"Time to get dressed," Juliet said. "Time for school now."

Barnaby did not seem to hear her. He was holding a little horse in his hand, brown, plastic, tanalised in mid-gallop with its mane and tail rippling out behind. He was making it canter. Up and down it went in his hand.

"Barnaby, did you hear me?"

Up and down went the horse, oblivious to all but the gods of carefree cantering, so preferable to those of Juliet's ugly, autocratic regime. She began to pick things up off the floor. She worked closer and closer to him, and when she got close enough she grabbed his bare arm and yanked him off the mountain.

"Get dressed," she said.

"I was playing," he protested.

"I don't care what you were doing. Get dressed."

She gathered up all the bedclothes and hurled them onto the bed. Oh, how differently she felt when it came to Barnaby! How punitively she yearned to have him in uniform, to have him straitjacketed! When he played, as he was playing just now with the little horse, it felt as if he were stealing something from her. She started to make his bed.

"In this house, Barnaby," she said, "we don't have servants."

"We do," he said. "You're our servant."

Tightly she strapped the sheets beneath the mattress. Tightly she tucked the covers round.

"You're stupid, Barnaby!" Katherine cried.

31

Juliet shook the pillow until it made a sort of blur before her eyes. Then she flung it into place with everything else.

"You can tidy up the rest," she told him.

He looked at her with round blue eyes.

"I can't," he said. "I've got to go to school."

It was what Benedict said, at least a dozen times each week.

"I'll ring the school," she said. "I'll ring them and tell them why you're late."

His eyes grew a little rounder. Would she? Would she really? She could see him wondering. The problem was that the next time he would wonder a little less.

"I'll ring and talk to Mr. Masters about it."

Mr. Masters was the headteacher. She imagined talking to him about the state of Barnaby's room. It would have a certain finality, that conversation. It would be in a sense the last, the final conversation. Where would you go, after a conversation like that? What would you have to live for?

"No, you won't," said Barnaby. He appeared to have decided. "You wouldn't dare."

"Wouldn't I? He's not *my* headteacher, you know. He's just another adult, like me."

"He's more important than you," Barnaby said.

"Perhaps he is," said Juliet.

"You're stupid, Barnaby!" Katherine shouted.

"Perhaps he *is* more important. And that's why," she continued, making her way to the door, "you're going to have to explain to him that you couldn't come to school because you wouldn't put your uniform on."

Outside the room she stood for a minute with Katherine and listened. There was silence, and then the sound of drawers being opened.

"He's doing it," Katherine said to her mother, half satisfied and half, Juliet felt, afraid. She wore a little look of discomfort. She seemed to be digesting the politics of the situation. She seemed to be chewing on their tough, inedible fibres and extracting the bitter juices.

When they came downstairs they found Benedict in the hall, putting things into a cardboard box. He put in some books, and his portable CD player, and a handful of discs in their cases. Outside, the rain fell. A cliff of shadow seemed to lean over Benedict where he stood at the bottom of the stairs.

"Purcell today, I think," he said, flinging another disc into the box.

Benedict took his things to school in a box every day. He wouldn't leave them there in case they got stolen. He liked to play music during his lessons. He liked to bathe the giant sixth-formers in the sound of the early English composers. He felt it enhanced their understanding of the period.

"Hello!" he said to Katherine—rather, Juliet felt, as though he hadn't specifically met her before. In his shoemaker's smock he was a red-cheeked man who loved children generally, and was pleased to see another one coming down the stairs.

"Daddy," she said, "Barnaby's being stupid."

"Is he?" Benedict filleted out a disc and put it to one side. "Well, boys *are* a bit stupid, don't you think?"

"He said he wouldn't get dressed. He said Mummy was his servant. Mummy said she was going to tell Mr. Masters."

"Did she now?" Benedict gave a bark of laughter. "Did she really?"

"Yes," said Katherine.

"*That* would have been funny, don't you think?"

Katherine did not reply. She didn't seem to think it would have been funny. She stood beside him and waited, as if for a more satisfactory response.

"I hope she doesn't tell Mr. Masters about me," Benedict said. "He might give me detention."

At this, Katherine laughed. Benedict handed her the disc he had kept out of the box.

"Let's put this on now, shall we?" he said.

"All right," she said. "What is it?"

"It's a beautiful lady singing."

"Oh."

She followed him into the sitting room and Juliet stood at the door. The rain fell at the window. It was so grey, so grey and unavailing! It was like sorrow: it seemed to preclude every possibility, every other shade of feeling. Benedict put the disc into the machine and the room filled with music. She recognised it as a song by Ravel. It was the Melanie Barth recording Benedict had bought last year. The sound of it brought tears to Juliet's eyes. It was the voice, that woman's voice, so solitary and powerful, so—transcendent. It made Juliet think she could transcend it all, this little house with its stained carpets, its shopping, its flawed people, transcend the grey, rain-sodden distances of Arlington Park; transcend, even, her own body, where bitterness lay like lead in the veins. She could open somewhere like a flower. She could find a place less cramped, less confining, and open out all the petals packed inside her.

"Her French is just exquisite, don't you think?" Benedict said to her.

He was reading the sleeve notes, where a photograph showed Melanie Barth standing in a green ball-gown on a beach, gazing out to sea. Juliet wanted to tear it from his hand, tear it and destroy it, rip Melanie with her exquisite French to shreds. Of course her French was exquisite! She hadn't had to spend her life looking after Benedict, buying food for him, washing his clothes, bearing and caring for his children! Instead, she had thought about herself: she had brushed up her French and then she had gone down to the beach in her ball-gown.

Juliet did not feel transcendent any longer. She felt angry, dense and angry and dark, compacted, like lead.

"Daddy," said Katherine, "would you like it if this lady sang to you?"

Benedict smiled, a trifle forlornly, and ruffled her shining hair.

"I'd like it very much," he said.

She walked the children to school through the rain. All the way up Guthrie Road and Arlington Rise, all along Bedford Crescent and Southfield Street, the cars stood stationary in lines. Their lights glowed like devilish pairs of eyes. The rain fell on their impervious metal roofs. Heat came in great sheets of steam off their armoured bonnets. The arms of their windscreen wipers went back and forth, back and forth. In each one sat a man in a tie and an ironed shirt, warm and dry, his suit jacket hanging from a peg beside the door. These men glanced at Juliet as she went by, one after another through their beaded windscreens. She went along the grey pavements holding her umbrella. Katherine was holding her hand. Barnaby was walking behind, with his hood up and his hands in his pockets. Juliet carried their lunchboxes and their schoolbags. The children were wearing Wellingtons, but the water had soaked Juliet's tights nearly up to the knee. She laboured along the pavement, burdened, bedraggled, while the men looked at her from their cars.

It was a mysterious place, Arlington Park: it was a suburb, a sort of enormous village really, yet even here the force of life came up strong, dealing out its hard facts, its irrepressible, universal dimensions. It was all so vigorous and uncrushable, the getting and having, the putting forth, the relentless, war-like assertion of one thing over another. It was civilisation, and yet to Juliet it seemed uncivilised to the core. What was there here that brought about such a rude growth of life? It lacked art: worse, it lacked any conception of justice. It was just getting and having—look at them all, backed up in their cars all the way to the park, jostling, fighting to get and to have! And as for the women, they were even worse! They were harsh, compassionless, driven by that rude force away from anything that smacked of failure or difficulty, driven headlong, and riding roughshod as they went over justice, over art!

The girls Juliet taught were self-satisfied little creatures who came from the mould of their mothers, came out with a plop and quivered there, naked and pink, with no sense whatever of their own vulnerability. Did they not fear that something might rise up, rise up and smite their jellied forms? Did Matthew Milford not fear it? Did the men in those cars not await it in terror, the possibility that one day they would be interrogated and smitten down where they stood? You could not live your life in flagrant disregard for justice, Juliet thought. You couldn't live like that and get away with it for ever.

She crossed the road with the children and went up the High Street. There were the shops, with their windows still dark and their shutters down. There were shops selling cush-ions and scented candles, shops selling women's clothes, shops selling jewellery and silver and antiques; there were nail bars and hairdressers, beauty salons and boutiques, and a shop with a single vast cream leather sofa in the window. They passed a coffee shop and the three of them automatically turned their heads in the rain towards its gorgeous aroma.

36

Juliet gave a pound to a man sitting in his sleeping bag in a doorway. He lifted his plastic cup to her in a gentlemanly salute.

Barnaby thought she shouldn't have done it.

"That's our money," he said. "You shouldn't have given it to him."

"He needs it more than we do," Juliet said.

"Then why doesn't he get some himself?" Barnaby said.

"We could give him more things we don't need," Katherine said. "We could give him our house."

Juliet laughed. "But we do need our house!"

"We could have a smaller house," Katherine said.

"That's true," Juliet said. "We could all have less of everything."

Barnaby kicked a lamppost and muttered something under his breath.

"What was that?" Juliet said.

"Nothing."

"No, go on, tell me what you said."

"It was nothing."

"You said you hated Mummy," Katherine told him quietly.

"I did not."

"You did! Mummy, he did! I heard him!"

When they reached the school Juliet put the children in their classrooms and returned outside. The rain was falling abandonedly into the grey playground. Huddled figures ran everywhere, their coats over their heads. She stood beneath her umbrella and watched them. Oh, how it moved her, strangely moved her, to see people running, scattering, fleeing this way and that with their heads covered! They were most of them women, though beneath their hoods you couldn't really tell. That was what moved her, the veil, the disguise: it brought her into a great sympathy with her own kind.

More women were emerging behind her through the doors, unencumbered by children. Always, they came through the doors into the daylight, and they looked around, as if to verify that they were really alone. They always seemed, for an instant, utterly bereft. Then they fell to the business of chatting, making plans, reattaching themselves to life. They made battle plans for their first coffee, for lunch, for a trip to the park with the children after school. They did not include Juliet in their plans, though she stood no more than three feet away from them. They didn't mean her any harm, but they didn't invite her to join them for coffee. In its way it was a religious ceremony, and she was not of their religion. With her job, her Ph.D., her air of bitterness, she was an outsider.

Slowly she walked away from the school. Her first class wasn't until eleven. She lost herself in the grey streets, walking vaguely back towards the shops. She thought of Benedict in his smock and the fact that she couldn't let him touch her. She thought of his fingers winding themselves further and further into her hair. Really, she should love him. She didn't know why she couldn't. It was unclear to her whether she could love anybody. When she was away from him she saw love from a distance and it seemed easy, an easy climb up to the sunlit peak. Yet when she was there, closer, it seemed impossible. What would become of her if she couldn't love?

She walked along the High Street in the rain and saw that the shutters were coming up. The shops were opening themselves to another day, putting their lights on, flinging themselves into the stream, into the great rude current. If only she could sing, like Melanie Barth! If only she could open her mouth, open her throat, and let herself out! Then she, too, could be borne along, go forward down the river, lighter, alive! Instead, she was heavy, full of lead. She sank like a stone through the onrush of time. Why shouldn't Barnaby hate her?

Why shouldn't he, when she hated herself? No, not hated herself; not that, quite. It was only that she was so heavy. She was full of the deposits of wasted days. If only she could open her mouth and let out a great sound; but the truth was she had never expressed herself, in any native act. Not in sex, not in love, not even in childbirth, when she had ensured she was numbed from her neck down to the soles of her feet. She had expected to find expression by a different route. She had expected to find it carefully, patiently, by a system of reward.

And that was how it had got her, this strange life; that was how it had reeled her in. She had forgotten she was a woman. She had forgotten she was a native creature, a thing of flesh. One day she had met Benedict and it had risen up before her startled eyes, a great vista of challenges like a mountain range: things she didn't have, things she'd never even thought of! Really they were only the dreary lineaments of her mother's life, a husband, a house, children—but to Juliet they seemed mysterious, full of foreign, ineluctable glamour. She had never thought of how she would go about getting those things. She had thought only of how long she would have to wait before her chance of expression came: her university job, her newspaper by-line. And Benedict was so clever that he seemed somehow allied with all that. When he came climbing up her hair, she didn't detect him as a threat, not at all. She saw him as a prize, her first, in the strange new field of endeavour known as human relationships.

It almost made her laugh now, to think of it. A woman a hundred years ago knew her life would be over the moment she got herself pregnant. But Juliet had thought it required a degree of cleverness, that there was something difficult about it. For a while she prized the idea of a house and a husband and children, as though these things were uncommon, as though they represented some new refinement of human experience. Then she got them, and the feeling of lead started to build up in her veins, a little more each day. The time she realised that if she didn't go and buy food herself there would be none in the house; the time Benedict returned to work a week after Barnaby's birth and she realised she would be looking after him alone; the countless times a domestic task had fallen to her, so that she became experienced and preferred to do it because it was easier than asking Benedict—it was all surprising to her, outrageous almost. With her sense of justice she expected that at some point the outrage would be detected and addressed, but of course it was not. She made the mistake of complaining to her mother. Oh, the joy, the harsh, vitriolic joy in her mother's face! She could almost hear her mother thinking, That's showed you. That's told you what's what. Juliet remembered her mother when younger as a rather loud, passionate, untidy, and unbridled person. Now she was a vitriolic woman who kept a house full of dustless ornaments, sparkling glass paperweights, and little ivory boxes in which she took a strange, voluptuous, almost demented pleasure.

Yet she could imagine her mother, as she could not imagine herself, saying to Matthew Milford, "You want to be careful," and frightening him a bit.

She stopped at a shop window and, pretending to look inside, stared at herself in the rain-streaked glass. The window wouldn't reflect her properly. She was just a shape, an amorphous shape with water running down her. She realised she was looking into the window not of a shop but of a hairdresser's. She saw the rows of empty white leather chairs, the mirrors, the neat arrangements of implements, ready for the day. A girl was in there. She was walking about, aligning hairbrushes, making little adjustments to things. Juliet pushed open the door and went in. The girl looked up. She was wearing tight black trousers and a white T-shirt that showed a stretch of plump brown stomach. She had a nose ring and hair extravagantly tinted and feathered, shaved on one side and on the other fluffed up like a parakeet's tail feathers. Juliet gazed at her. What was this creature doing here, alone in this room in the rain? Where had she come from?

"Can I help you?" she said. She looked about eighteen.

"I wondered if you had any free appointments," Juliet said. She felt old. Her voice was old. It seemed to come out of a cave, somewhere on a desolate mountainside.

"When were you thinking of?" said the girl, leafing through a ledger on the front desk.

"I was wondering—well, now," said Juliet. "Are you busy now?"

It was evident from the empty salon that she was not, but nevertheless she looked through her ledger.

"We've got a space at nine-fifteen," she said.

Juliet looked at her watch. It was nine-ten.

"Fine," she said.

"Would you like to come over?" the girl said, proceeding to one of the white leather chairs and pulling it out a little.

Juliet sat down while the girl fastened a synthetic cape around her shoulders. She lifted Juliet's hair in handfuls, inspecting it, first one handful then another.

"Just a trim, is it?" she said.

"No," Juliet said. "I want you to cut it off."

The girl instantly looked alarmed. She looked as though such a thing had never happened to her before. For a second Juliet hated her. What else did people come to hairdressers for, if not to have their hair cut off?

"What, all of it?" she said.

"All of it," said Juliet.

"Are you sure? Are you sure you don't want to just think

about it? There's a coffee shop over the road," she persisted unexpectedly. "You could go over there for half an hour and have a little think."

"I don't want to think," Juliet said. "I've thought enough."

That shut her up.

"Any particular style?" she said. "We've got lots of magazines you can look at. You can find a photo of something you like and I can copy it."

Juliet rested her hands on the sides of the chair. She drew herself up before the mirror and looked herself right in the eyes.

"I don't care what you do," she said. "Just cut it off."

The women had said they might come to Amanda's house for coffee.

She was in her car, cruising through the rain along the High Street while the turbid seas of Arlington Park parted before her. It was nine-fifteen. Her husband had left the house punctually at eight, and her daughter Jessica was at school by nine; she had a feeling of rapid ascent, as though the members of her household were sandbags she was heaving one by one out of the basket of a hot-air balloon. Only Eddie remained: Amanda could see him in the rear-view mirror, self-absorbed and slightly shifty. He kept looking up, apparently to check for unwelcome developments, such as a turn off the High Street to the right that might signify he was being taken to nursery.

Eddie didn't go to nursery on Fridays, but he didn't really know that. Amanda kept him at home as a matter of form. It was a disorderly area of the week that she disciplined herself to tolerate. She looked forward to the time—September—when he would start school, and their Fridays could be packed up and put away, as his outgrown clothes and tricycle and high chair had been put away, at the correct and proper moment. These things were not her true companions. They were bumps on the surface of life that fretted and jolted her as she was forced to go over them.

Her car was her true companion: it was clean and spacious and mechanically discreet, and it did her bidding powerfully, efficiently, and with silent approval of her style of command. When she was in her car she had a feeling of infinite passage. She felt she could go anywhere; more than that, she felt she didn't need to. Driving through Arlington Park she experienced a sense of consummation, a feeling that to live and to desire were indistinguishable. High up in the seat of her silver Toyota she desired herself; her soul was combusted and life, motion, were produced.

And there was something else, too, something to do with time, with the fact that while each hour—on her Fridays with Eddie, for instance—was like a boulder she had to single-handedly lift and move laboriously out of her path, in her car time seemed to pass at a remove. It passed on the other side of the windows. She drove along, and through her windows she saw people burdened by time, while she herself remained free.

Now, for example, in the High Street, in the grey, slanting rain, the shop-fronts stood in an imprisoned row with water running down their canopies, and there were roadworks where men picked and jabbed hopelessly at the earth, fenced in by tattered lengths of incident tape, and a van was trying to reverse out into the resistant traffic, and people were walking along the wet pavements with bags and umbrellas and pushchairs, bowed over, drenched, encumbered; and this spectacle was entirely the work of time, which moved irresistibly, mercilessly, through everything and turned it to chaos, like a plough moving through the ground and churning up great furrows of rock and roots and mud.

Through her window Amanda saw a plastic bag blown this way and that on the pavement by wet, random little gusts of wind. Why did people expose themselves, to the casual cruelties of a Friday morning in the rain? The woman walking past her now, soaked to the skin, with a baby in a pram and a child Eddie's age dangling by the wrist: what was she doing? Amanda was waiting at a traffic light while this woman plodded by like an ox in harness. When the lights changed she surged past her, so that her miserable diminishing form was trapped in the wing mirror.

Outside the butcher's she commanded the localised bureaucracy of the street to yield to her: immediately a car prised itself out of the parking bay right in front of the shop and went slouching and blinking off down the road, dismissed. Sometimes Amanda was able to evoke perfect subjection in the world around her and sometimes she was not. Her writ ran through the centre of the day like a single wire on which she maintained an unpredictable balance. Destiny stemmed from her in a constant stream on that wire. There were times, as now, when it was channelled in an orderly, forward-going current that recognised no obstruction; and times when her confidence fell away, when the oncoming stream of minutes and hours broke its banks and flooded out sideways, on and on, until she seemed to be disgorging a force of pure catastrophe. Then the car no longer flew, the seas of Arlington Park no longer parted before her. There were mornings when she had driven around weeping, sweating, palpably distressed, with her feet shaking on the pedals so that the world would come surging alarmingly towards her through the windscreen and then jolt to a quavering standstill; when she had lunged for traffic lights and parking spaces while human bodies and the great metallic forms of other cars revolved inchoately around her in a white haze of danger. She never knew how or when these frightening interludes would end, or why they had come at all.

Today, however, she drew to an irreproachable halt outside the butcher's in the rain and turned around in her seat so as to reverse into the parking bay. Eddie, who was strapped in behind her, also turned around. Together they looked out of the rear window at the grey, wet vista of the road. The car behind had stopped too close for Amanda to be able to reverse into her parking space.

"Oh, for Christ's sake," Eddie said.

Amanda regarded the car with predatory patience. Her hands remained on the steering wheel; her body was twisted so that she could feel her form, as though it had grown out of the seat beneath her. She was all steel today, all determination. The car behind reversed a few feet. She raised her hand in general-like acknowledgement and in two manoeuvres brought the car to a standstill six inches from the pavement, where she sat in the muted aura of the lavishly cooling engine and regarded the butcher's window. Rain ran down it in thick, viscous-looking channels. Behind the glass the pink and red display made its lurid statement.

Amanda felt that if she were not married, it would not have been required of her to go to the butcher. These visits seemed to emanate from a core of physical embroilment, from a fleshly basis that sought out other flesh by which to feed itself. It all seemed somehow grotesquely related, the conjoining and making of bodies and the dismemberment and ingestion of them. She imagined that if she were alone she would have eaten only food that was white. A vegetarian friend of hers used to say that she never ate anything "with a face." Eddie had a face. Amanda looked at it in the rear-view mirror.

"It isn't nice to swear, Eddie," she said.

Then she got out of the car.

Inside, the butcher's shop was cold and smelled rankly of blood and sawdust. Eddie stood beside the refrigerated glass cabinets and stared uneasily at the cuts of meat with their white rinds of fat and the flesh-coloured sausages in twisted heaps on metal trays. Carcasses hung lividly from hooks in the window. A customer left the shop, and when the door closed the carcasses turned a little on their hooks. Red ledgers of bacon stood in rows in one cabinet, with an assortment of ribs and limbs and shoulders that seemed to have a strange, angry, autonomous life. Chickens sat in anonymous lines like parked cars, their pimpled, denuded flesh tightly wrapped in plastic: they sat, identical in their ranks, in an infinity of waiting. There was a fresh mountain of pork chops dotted with sprigs of parsley. Pieces of lamb were dealt out in a fan shape. There were some smaller, yellow, old-looking birds, like elderly relatives of the chickens. In front of them a group of tiny black-speckled eggs stood in an open carton. They had a monochrome, embryonic prettiness. They seemed to have come from some particularly malevolent factory of death.

Behind the cabinets the butcher and his two assistants, in their green aprons, stood in their tiled enclosure. They had a long sideboard with knives and trays and weighing machines on it, and a machine with a big circular blade. They were laughing at something, down at the far end. Amanda saw them laughing while the white, muscled arm of the butcher rose and fell, as he hacked the bone away from a joint of meat with a cleaver. He held the soft red part of the meat in his fingers. The men's deep voices were indistinct, and they moved around while they talked and laughed. Their white crescent smiles moved around too, as though unbodied in the murky, meat-coloured light. One of them looked up and saw her and said something to one of the others.

"Sorry to keep you waiting," he said, coming towards her. "What can I get for you today?"

He was still smiling. Amanda noticed that his arms ended

at the elbows. His two small, misshapen hands came out of them at right angles, like feet. She looked at them and then she looked at his face. She made herself look only at his face, at his eyes and mouth, which dragged down slightly at the corners. He had freckled skin and coarse, light-red hair that grew vigorously from his scalp.

"I'll have some mince, please," she said.

She moved her eyes to the window, as though there were something in the milling road outside it that was of particular significance to her, something she'd forgotten or thought of escaping from.

"How much would you like?" said the man.

"Oh," she said, "half a kilo or so."

"Half a kilo of the mince," he said.

The smile had gone from his face. He seemed to wish to return to a world of plainness and exactitude. Normally she was served by the butcher himself, amongst whose liberal gallantries she could stay afloat in this blood-smelling place: he would ask her what she wanted the mince for, and how many she intended to feed with it; he had a concerned and tutelary air, a kind of complicity with her position, in the darkly secretive work of feeding her family. The man took a metal scoop and bent down into the glass cabinet; and she could not prevent her eyes from following him, from looking uncontrolledly at his strange, twisted little hands as they rapidly scooped the pink, mottled meat into a plastic bag. He had to bend far into the cabinet to reach it; he emerged with the bag dangling from the blind hook of his elbow, and placed it with a movement of his whole torso on the scales. Eddie stood beside her. He said, "Why doesn't that man have any hands?"

Of all the members of her household Eddie was the one who most often led her into the senseless, run-down parts of life. Two or three times a day he put her close to the concept of failure and meaninglessness. As she could think of no appropriate answer to his question, she decided to ignore it and wait for the embarrassment to pass. She stood on her wire, swaying, while the turbulence of the situation moved slowly around her. The man weighed the meat and with his eyes on the scale shook a bit more off his scoop. His impassivity was like a wall in front of her.

"Four twenty," he said, placing the bag on the counter.

She gave him the money, while Eddie stood and fingered the glass so that the spectacle of dismemberment behind it seemed to expand itself, to incorporate him. She saw his parts arrayed on metal trays, in fans and pyramids of flesh fringed with parsley.

"Mummy," he said indignantly, "I asked you why—"

"Shut up," she said.

In the car on the way home she kept looking into the rear-view mirror at the road behind her. Each time she saw the butcher's rueful, enquiring expression, as he lifted his head when she called goodbye.

She and Eddie turned off the High Street and drove along the deserted park, then down St. John's Avenue, where the trees looked bowed over in the rain, then down Bedford Road, and finally into Western Gardens, whose air of empty seclusion was complete, as though they had been folded further and further into the creases of a thick, unpeopled insulation through which the attrition of the outside world could no longer be felt.

"Mummy," said Eddie, for she had explained to him as they drove the tragic effects of the drug thalidomide on a generation of babies, "it's lucky *you* weren't born without any hands."

Amanda was surprised by this reaction: when she was with Eddie she forgot she ever *had* been born. She had told him the story in the belief that he might relate its menace, punitively, to himself.

"I suppose you could say that, Eddie."

"They were stupid to take that medicine."

"They weren't stupid. Mothers aren't stupid. The doctor gave it to them. They didn't know what would happen. They only knew when the babies were born."

"Oh."

"It's lucky *I* didn't take it, because then *you* would have been born like that."

She was speaking to the gravelled drive, on whose uncritical expanses the car was parked.

"Did the doctor want you to take it?"

Eddie sounded concerned at the idea that his fate had rested, even momentarily, on the precarious peaks of his mother's mist-shrouded judgement. Anything could happen up there: it was a place of unpredictable danger and occasional savagery.

"No, Eddie. He didn't want me to take it."

Through the car window she could see her neighbour Jocasta Fearnley, dressed in a big man's raincoat, doing something in her front garden on the other side of the wall.

"He didn't give it to you because now he knows it's bad," Eddie concluded, as though trying to collate the various aspects of what he'd been told.

Something raised itself swiftly in her like a club, a desire to disclose to him the truth of herself. She wanted to hammer him over the head with it until his understanding of her was complete.

"The point, Eddie, is that I would have had hands. The man in the butcher's shop had hands. They didn't look like your hands, but they were still hands. It was his arms that were wrong. So when you keep saying, Why doesn't that man

50

have any *hands*, Where have his *hands* gone, It's lucky, Mummy, you weren't born without *hands*, you make people think you're not really paying attention."

"Oh."

"When you said in the butcher's shop, Why doesn't that man have any *hands*, you were putting me in a difficult situation, because I couldn't say, He does have hands, look! I couldn't say that, could I? Because it would have been rude. It's rude to talk about people when they're standing in front of you. And it's especially difficult if what you've said is wrong, because people can't correct you without being rude as well."

She was aware, staring at the gravelled drive, that she would continue to speak for ever unless she got out of the car. The rain came patiently down over the front lawn. Jocasta was still bent on her task on the other side of the wall. Water was dropping heavily from the bare, unruly branches of the Fearnleys' birch tree on to her back. Her head went up and down—it appeared over the wall and then vanished again. It looked like she was repeatedly stamping on something.

Amanda was intimidated by the Fearnleys: it was as though they conducted their lives in a language that was unfamiliar to her, so that she had to translate everything they did into her native vocabulary. And yet there was no mistaking the fact—she had mistaken it at first—that this language was the sovereign tongue of the well-appointed principality in which James and Amanda Clapp now lived. Western Gardens, crescent-shaped, spacious, staffed by magnificent trees, was home to a race of whose existence Amanda had until relatively recently been ignorant. They went skiing and had houses in France or Italy. Their children went to private schools and were wild-looking and unkempt and had eyes that—unlike Eddie's and Jessica's—seemed actually to observe her as she went by. More perplexing, their houses and gardens were distinctly shabby, in spite of the fact that they had paid a fortune for them. Sometimes she thought they wanted to disguise this fact, for reasons that were unclear to her. They gave the impression that no ordinary transaction had brought them to Western Gardens: that they had somehow received it, or that they had always been here.

Amanda and James had trained their sights on Western Gardens in the earliest days of their marriage. They had tracked it through the thickets of Arlington Park's property market, with diligence and a sort of prideful patience—it had taken them three years—and they had brought it down between them with a single bullet. They had studied this market at length, and had amassed a strange, compendious knowledge of it. They knew the ranking of every street—each *side* of every street, the direction of sunlight being a factor in establishing the desirability of a property—in Arlington Park's canon of propitious places for a family to live. They knew how big the gardens were in Guthrie Road, how low the ceilings in Southfield Street, how restrictive the planning regulations on the Georgian properties that stood along the park. They knew so much that they could automatically conjure up from a bare address a picture of the life that was lived there, and its limitations. They had, in a sense, lived little aborted lives there themselves.

They had concluded, all things considered, that Western Gardens was Arlington Park's first—or least flawed—address; and so it had surprised Amanda to discover that its reality could not be contained by her conception of it, learned as it was. Since they moved there, a feeling of colourlessness had stolen steadily over her, as though in the act of being made manifest the object of her desire had eluded her. In the lavish wrapping of their highly prized, ardently sought, thoroughly refurbished new home, Amanda felt strangely naked. She began to suspect some inadequacy in herself and James, a lack of substance that made redundant all her knowledge of what she had—or, at least, returned it to its dry, correct dimensions.

She sometimes thought it was people like the Fearnleys who caused her to feel this sense of inferiority. They spoke in loud, aristocratic voices and treated everything as a joke, except for their social lives, in which they were as commanding and conniving as a pair of politicians maintaining office. At the weekends their drive was packed with cars, their house and garden filled with a riotous, secretive commotion. Unless they were away, of course—then the place was silent, a silence almost as distracting as the noise, in that everything seemed to fall into the void of absence next door. They had violent arguments in which the whole family was engaged. Amanda heard them, even through the capacious defences of their respective houses. She would sit in her kitchen, and the sounds of slamming doors and full-throated screams came to her ears and made her feel that she was at the boundary, at the very brink, of everything disturbing and unsatisfactory that had happened in her life. She felt herself to be at the front line of the possibility that things might not turn out for the best.

"I'm digging a grave," Jocasta called, raising her spade in greeting through the rain.

Amanda was lifting her shopping out of the back of the car. A feeling of precariousness had been steadily besieging her on the wire, ever since they left the butcher's shop: it crystallised now into the belief that it was a human grave Jocasta was digging, for a member of her family she had either already killed or meant to. Hadn't Max Fearnley been ill recently? Come to think of it, she hadn't seen him for a week or two.

Jocasta drew close to the boundary wall. "Poor Samson," she said. "Lydie found him in his cage this morning."

Lydie was the name of the Fearnleys' au pair, an etiolated Polish girl who came and went melancholically in her black leather jacket beneath a white wedge of peroxided hair. Amanda gave a shrill laugh and Jocasta looked at her snappishly. This was evidently one of the things that was not funny.

"Don't let Sadie hear you laughing," she said, glancing back at the house. "Samson was really her best friend. She said to me, Mummy, I know he's only a rabbit, but I loved him more than I love some *people*. I said to her, Well, let's give him a proper burial, shall we? At least we can give him that. Actually, she's made him rather a lovely coffin. She used all the tester pots we got for doing the drawing room to paint it. It's a sort of symphony of taupe. I said to her, Darling, how *fashionable*!" Here Jocasta gave a snort of mirth and raised her red-veined eyes to the grey heavens. "To be quite honest," she said in a low voice, "I'm not altogether sorry he's gone. I'm not sure it helps at fourteen for one's best friend to be a rabbit. And she was terribly severe with him. She seemed particularly to enjoy the locking-up part."

She delivered this last remark with her hands resting like a farmer's on the handle of her spade. Her fingers were dirty, with red, sore nails. She wore a ring with a big diamond in its tarnished gold claw.

"My sister killed her rabbit by hugging it too hard," Amanda said.

Jocasta looked troubled by this revelation. She did not seem to feel it belonged in the same ribald category as her daughter's fondly punitive experiments.

"Did she?" she said. "And was that . . . love? Or—"

The rain came steadily down on their hair and on their faces. Eddie remained strapped into the back seat of the car. Amanda could see his white, accusatory face through the window.

"Oh, she loved him," Amanda said. "She just forgot that

he was fragile. She's the same with men. She loves them so much that they run away."

Beneath her raincoat Jocasta was wearing a stained blue smock-like garment and a pair of tracksuit trousers that had been trodden into the mud around the hems. Her hair hung in dirty-looking tails around her face. She wore no make-up except for mascara, which appeared old and made her lashes stand out in clotted spikes. She was looking at Amanda's house. She seemed to be accusing it of something, or Amanda herself; something suspicious that arose from their mutual association.

"How are you getting on in there?" she said. "Are you getting on all right?"

"We're fine," Amanda said.

"I often say to Max, you know, those *Clapps* are very quiet, what *can* they be up to in there? We decided that you must have a secret life. Max thought your husband might be a spy, but I said no, that's not nearly fun enough, and anyway, spies are always telling people that that's what they are. No, I thought it must be something much naughtier than that."

She gave Amanda a raffish smile with her yellowed teeth. Her small blue eyes in their striated pockets of skin twinkled with suggestion. Sometimes Amanda had seen her and Max going out for the evening and Jocasta looked beautiful. The sight of her then caused Amanda to feel that there were certain people she lacked the ability to perceive, just as she often failed to see in famous paintings what it was that they were famous for. It gave her a sensation of instability, like vertigo.

"We're just boring," Amanda said.

Jocasta looked astounded and slightly embarrassed by this reply.

"Oh, darling!" she cried. "You're not *boring*—nobody's boring! I didn't mean to suggest that at all, you poor thing!"

Faint cries could be heard from the car where it was

parked on the drive. Amanda turned her head. Eddie had got out of his car seat; his face and hands were pressed against the window. His mouth was open and his pink tongue was crushed against the glass.

"Look, we must arrange a time for you and your husband to come round and have a drink," Jocasta said. "It seems ridiculous that you've been living here all this time and— Oh dear, *someone* doesn't look very happy."

Amanda went to the car and opened the door so that Eddie fell forwards on to the gravel. By the time she came back, with Eddie bawling and holding his hands to his face, Jocasta had returned with her spade to the foot of the birch tree.

"We'll get out our diaries!" she called, waving her arm.

Inside the vault of her house Amanda felt secure, though the prospect of fresh sieges remained a possibility. Eddie wandered away from her, crying noisily, into the sitting room, where the large, pacific eye of the television enfolded him, unblinking, into the sky-blue-bordered depths of children's programming that it had been relaying like a dream into the empty house all through the hour of their absence. Amanda went the other way, into the kitchen. There she pondered the arrival, in twenty minutes' time, of any or all of the five women she had seen standing in the rain outside Jessica's school and had invited back for coffee. She left the kitchen and made a wordless foray into the sitting room, in order to remove Eddie's wet shoes from his insensate feet and place them in the closet in the hall. There she saw her shopping bags. She transported them into the kitchen and removed the little white sack of meat. It was small and obscenely heavy, like a bladder. She carried it dangling in her fingers and placed it in the fridge.

She had asked people back for coffee before, but it always seemed that her invitation to Western Gardens had the effect of reminding them how much else they had to do; that her suggestion of coffee spoke to them reprovingly of all the other coffees, awoke in their consciences a shamed awareness of how much time they had spent drinking coffee when they might have been doing something more productive. Amanda did not believe they were shunning her: it was almost as though she inspired them, to reapply themselves to the job of who they were. She could evoke, in other people, a type of self-consciousness, a reconnection with themselves. In her last months at Pembroke Recruitment before her marriage, she had won the firm's Manager of the Year Award 1998 (Southwest Region). James used to tell people that Amanda was evangelical about work. He still did, though now he would shake his head and say, "She was just *evangelical* about it," so that they would feel it was a good thing she had stopped and represented no immediate danger to them.

It was her impression that the women she knew did nothing but drink coffee at each other's houses all day, yet she had never succeeded—the facts could not be prevented from speaking for themselves—in attracting them into her own domain. Amanda and James held their domain in such high regard that the situation mystified and grated on her. Her kitchen, for example: like the pyramids or the New York skyline, more people knew about her kitchen than had seen it for themselves. Recently, over coffee at Christine Lanham's house, Amanda had referred to Jessica's enthusiasm for rollerskating around it and one of the assembled women had said, "That must play havoc with your lovely oak floors." Amanda did not know this woman well; certainly she had never been to the house, or seen the floors in question.

Looking out of her windows at the sodden, motionless

spectacle of the garden, Amanda felt the melancholia of a cu-
rator of neglected works of art. The windows were the
kitchen's most dramatic feature. They went from floor to ceiling all along the back of the house. James and Amanda had
installed these windows after having the dividing walls torn
down to create one vast room. They had decided to do this
long before they bought the house itself: in the science of
property, knocking things "through" was the tenet in which
they most passionately believed. Their conversations on the
subject of knocking through were so numerous and so energetic that by the time they moved into Western Gardens, they
had gained so much velocity from them that the walls seemed
almost to fall down by themselves.

Sometimes Amanda remembered the quavering places that
had stood where her kitchen now was: the sinister little toilet
with its tiny window of marbled glass, the cold, abject wash-
room, the austerity of the original kitchen itself, with its air of
denial, almost of castigation—there had been a helplessness to
these rooms that at the time had inflamed the Clapps' urge to
destroy them, but which now occasionally caused her to wonder what had become of them and what their true nature had
been. For days the men had gone back and forth to the skip
with metal wheelbarrows full of rubble, in which shreds of the
thick vinyl paper with which every wall had been covered
made strange forms, as though in attitudes of torment. Sometimes she had the inexplicable desire to bring those rooms
back to life: to reunite those torn, tortured shreds, to build
the rubble into walls again. This ambition fatally lacked the
drive of the desires that had brought the walls down in the
first place; it might have been that she entertained it only as a
consequence of those efforts, a kind of run-off of energy, like
a wheel continuing to revolve after the motor has been
switched off.

But there was a moment, like a new soul, that had flickered into life when Amanda's kitchen was created. It occurred on a winter's day when heat surged in the radiators like blood in clean, vigorous veins and the warm air blazed with electric light, and the appliances thrummed steadily like the engine room of a majestic ship around which the grey, cluttered world outside churned like a roiling sea; and in summer, when the french doors were open and the light lay in golden, quiescent panels on the oak floors. These moments came and they were beautiful, fragile pauses, like bubbles, in which Amanda experienced a feeling of summation, almost of symbolism. They were representations: they were advertisements, for something that lay half-way between the life that was lived here and her own feelings about it. It irked her that more people were not there to witness them.

Recently Amanda and James had invited two couples over for dinner, and when their guests left at eleven-thirty after lasagne, chocolate mousse, coffee, and a quantity of wine that fell somewhere between modesty and correctness, Amanda had felt an uneasy sense of completion, as though she had accomplished a reputedly difficult task with greater speed and facility than expected. A day or two later she met one of the women in the street: she had thanked Amanda profusely and then laughingly confessed that after leaving Western Gardens the four of them had gone back to her house and drunk a whole bottle of whiskey—her hand went ruefully to her forehead—and danced to music in her sitting room until three o'clock in the morning.

Like a settler in a new, uncharted country, Amanda was aware of movements in her terrain: of the deep habits of herds migrating and convening across the reaches of Arlington Park, engaged in the unconscious business of their own survival. She was aware of them passing and feeding and gathering in groups to graze or rest, but try as she might, she could not bridge their distance from her. When she worked for Pembroke Recruitment these things had not concerned her. She spent most of her time in her car, neat and powerful in her suit, driving from one regional office to another. But the stationary life of Western Gardens required a different knowledge. It was not enough to have subjugated the rooms of her house, to have mastered the weekly disciplines of shopping and cooking, to have penetrated her husband, her children, her possessions with such sanitary force that their very natures seemed to recur, like laundry, in a transfigurative cycle of cleanliness; it was not enough—sometimes she wondered if it was anything at all—to be in control.

Today the women standing in the rain outside the school had looked lost, unfocused, like a demoralised troop of soldiers in the middle of a long, obscure campaign. She had discerned in them an unusual vulnerability, an exposure of flank, and she was right: for the first time, her offer of coffee aroused their interest, or at least silently generated the possibility of obedience. It might have been that they merely forgot to oppose her, as Jessica sometimes did when for no particular reason she did what she was told. She said she would be back in Western Gardens by ten, and she saw this information pass into their sense of the coming day. She had bought pastries on the High Street: their flaky, disastrous forms were sealed in a plastic bag which she placed ambivalently on the counter. There were crumbs there, and a smear of butter, which James had left behind like the small, modest mark of his indelible masculinity. She put on her yellow rubber gloves and with an aerosol gun of Flash she annihilated it. Then she went over all the worktops and doors, as well as the hob, oven, and fridge.

There was nothing in the hall for her to neutralise, or in the sitting room either, except for Eddie, who remained motionless on the cream sofa with the determination of someone playing a party game from which even the smallest movement would disqualify him. Amanda went soundlessly up the beige-carpeted stairs to Jessica's room, where the bed was already made and all the toys and clothes put away, as though there were some doubt over the question of whether Jessica would ever return to it. On her wall Jessica had a large framed poster of a lion's face. Its amber eyes met Amanda's with a look of godlike enquiry. She returned to the kitchen and dismantled the coffee machine in order to wash all the separate parts. Her yellow-gloved hands were immersed in foam when the telephone rang, like the first, startling clarion call of the coming invasion. She removed her gloves in order to answer it.

"Mandy? Is that you?"

It was her sister Susannah: no one else called her Mandy any more. Mandy Clapp—it was the name on the badge of someone working at a supermarket check-out—did not exist; and as for Mandy Barker, she had been left behind on the day Amanda married James, left behind like someone standing on a pier waving at the departing ship, abandoned with all her dubious habits, her liking of ready meals and red carnations from petrol stations, her scarlet fingernails and ankle chain— she had been left to go her own ignorant way in the irretrievable past.

"Oh my God, Mandy!"

Susannah was crying. Amanda could hear her gasping and sobbing in the distances of the telephone.

"What's the matter?" she said. "What is it? What's happened?"

"It's Gran—she's dead, she just died. Oh my God, Mandy, she died right next to me—I was holding her hand!"

Amanda saw her grandmother, a white, wordless slip of a woman in an institutional armchair.

"Are you at the hospice?"

"Yes—I—Mum asked me to call in while she and Dad were on holiday, and I came last night and they said she'd had a s-s-stroke—" Susannah receded in a paroxysm of sobs. "So I stayed the night here," she said, more clearly.

"You stayed the night?"

"I thought, I can't leave her alone, I can't let her die all alone! So they made up a bed for me and I stayed, and in the morning I was sitting with her and she opened her eyes and looked at me, just looked and looked at me, and then she started to let out these great big breaths. It was like all the air coming out of a balloon. Oh, Mandy, it was awful! Then she took one of these breaths and she didn't take another one, she just didn't take another one, and she was holding my hand and I felt her die—"

Amanda looked around the room with frantic eyes while her sister wept. It was ten to ten. The dismantled coffee machine lay in the cooling water.

"It must have been horrible," she said.

"No," Susannah said faintly, coughing, "it wasn't horrible, it was—sad. It was so, so sad. One minute I was in this room with her and the next it was empty, she was still there, but it was empty, and I was so alone. And I knew. Suddenly I knew then, for certain."

"Knew what?"

"That there's nothing else. That you just die and that's all there is. I felt it—I was sitting there looking out of the window at the car park, and I thought, this is all there is."

Amanda could have guessed that Susannah wouldn't take a straightforward view even of the death of a ninety-three-year-old, but nevertheless she said:

"She was ninety-three. I expect she wanted to go."

"She didn't!" her sister cried. "She didn't want to—she was sad, and frightened, and she looked just like a little child lying there, like a child with nobody to protect it—"

Amanda wondered why her mother hadn't asked her to call in on Gran while they were away on holiday—she was the eldest, after all. And she had always been the responsible one, with Gran and with everyone else. She was the one who sent cards and presents, who called in with bits of shopping while Susannah was in London, out of touch for weeks at a time, living a life whose emotional peaks and troughs she expected everyone to take account of, as though they were geographical features that presented exceptional challenges to those brave enough to scale them.

Susannah had never bought red carnations in a petrol station. Since childhood she had distinguished herself cheerfully but unfalteringly from the suburban dogma of the family home. She was an actress: she had been on television a few times, but mostly she acted in plays in London. Amanda did not like her sister being on television: it tainted the river of anonymity that she liked to have flowing steadily through her house from the screen. It made her think that she ought to switch the television off, and then what would she be left with?

For a while Amanda had lived in fear of Susannah becoming famous, but she was thirty-five now and Amanda felt she could take her eye off her sister, though every time she saw her it seemed that Susannah had found a new way of being beautiful. She reverberated amidst the stringencies of the Clapp household long after she had departed: she left behind her the suggestion that life should tend less towards a killing orderliness and more in the fruitful direction of risk and whimsicality. She would sit in Amanda's kitchen and shout "Oh, *stop*!" as Amanda washed the floor or wiped down the cupboards; as she exercised what was nothing less than her entitlement to perform the daily task of being herself. In Susannah's presence Amanda discovered that her perfectionism was a compulsion. She hoovered in front of the sofa so that

Susannah had to raise her feet, even though she knew her sister would laugh at her for it.

James always looked at Susannah with an expression of indecision on his face, as though Susannah and Amanda were two things in a shop he thought he had to choose between. He was petulant and slightly rebellious when she was around: he would go along with her brazen critiques ("Oh, *stop*!") of the situation, giving them a weak, spiteful twist of his own. "It's so *tidy* here!" Susannah always said when she crossed their threshold; once, in Amanda's hearing, James had replied, "Well, you know what they say—clean house, boring woman," and then looked around at them all as though expecting them to laugh at his wit.

It was Susannah who had first pointed out to Amanda the fact that Jocasta Fearnley was beautiful, or had been. She liked—no, loved—famous paintings, for reasons that appeared to be her own. She would pick up a fat, racy paperback from Amanda's bedside table, read the back cover, and then fling the book with a groan on to the immaculate covers.

"My life will never be the same," she said now in a low, sonorous, breaking voice. "Nothing can ever be the same."

"Of course it can," said Amanda. "You'll feel better once you get home."

"I can't go home. I can't. I couldn't stand it."

"Is Marcus there with you?"

Marcus was Susannah's boyfriend.

"I don't want Marcus. I don't ever want to see him again. I want to be on my own. I want to change everything."

It was one minute to ten.

"I can't be the same, not with this—this *knowledge*. If I go home I'll forget it, I'll forget the way I feel right now and I'll have missed my chance, you know, the chance to discover what life really is, to see death in life, actually in it—"

Amanda recalled what she had said to Jocasta Fearnley about Susannah and the rabbit. It was a lie: Susannah had not killed her rabbit. It was Amanda who killed it. She felt that she had only just realised that she had. At the time, what she had said to Jocasta Fearnley seemed true. But Susannah's weeping reminded her: it insisted on itself in the very teeth of her confusion. She looked out of the window at the garden, as though expecting to see her grandmother there, with her face at the glass.

Then the doorbell rang.

Through the mullioned window panes she could see them standing in the rain. There were four of them.

"*This* is nice!" Christine Lanham exclaimed when Amanda opened the door.

The rain fell on the path. One of the women had a pushchair and water ran down its plastic cover. Through it Amanda could see the blurred, fleshy folds of a child. The spongy green rectangle of the lawn lay behind them, silently absorbing water.

Amanda looked at her car, which stood with silvered fidelity on the gravel. It occurred to her to get in it and drive away; or perhaps not even drive. She felt she would have liked merely to live in it, within the confines of her provable successes.

In the hall she took their wet coats and bags and umbrellas. They prised their water-stained shoes, muddy, perilously garnished with soaked leaves, from their feet. It was messy work, the unending struggle to maintain separation between outside and in.

"This is nice," Sally Gibson said to Christine.

"Isn't it? They had such a lot of work done. I'm just saying what a lot of work you had done on the house, Amanda. It took them nearly a year."

Sally Gibson raised her eyebrows.

"*That* must have been a strain."

"Oh, it was all done by the time they moved in. They kept their flat in Fenton Road while the work was being done."

"Fenton Road's lovely," said Sally, mollified.

"I'm just saying how sensible you were to keep Fenton Road," said Christine. She removed her coat and shook out her brown hair. "When I think that Joe and I had the builders in for six months when Danny was three and Ella was still in nappies! What were we like? I used to go round all the beds every night and shake out the covers before they got in, and you could hear all the nails hitting the floor. Ting, ting, ting!"

The women laughed.

"I'm not being funny," said Christine. "We were in Casualty so often they knew the children's names. It was a sort of race to paint everything off-white before we got divorced."

The women laughed again, all except Liz Connelly, who was manoeuvring the rain-drenched form of the pushchair over the front step. She lifted the plastic hood.

"There," she said sourly, to the child who was revealed.

"Isn't this nice?" said Dinky Smith, bunching up her shoulders with pleasure. "Lovely house!" she added, straying into the kitchen.

It was Dinky who the week before had inferred havoc from Amanda's description of Jessica roller-skating on the kitchen floor. As it happened, the floors were sealed and tanalised and entirely scratch-proof; all the same, Amanda disliked it when Jessica put on her roller-skates. The thumping sounds delivered hammer-blows to her nerve ends. She wondered whether this was what Dinky had meant.

"Do you want to get out?" Liz Connelly was enquiring of

her son, who was writhing and making noises of protest in the pushchair. "Do you want to get out or don't you?"

"*What* an enormous kitchen!" cried Sally Gibson, following Christine and Dinky in.

In that moment Amanda knew that her kitchen was too large. She would not have thought such a thing was possible, but entering it now she knew that it was true. They had knocked through until they had created not space but emptiness. They had gone too far: nobody had told them to stop.

The three women stood looking around them, apparently bewildered. All of them looked upwards, as people in churches look upwards, to ascertain the height of human folly.

"There must have been four or five rooms here!" exclaimed Sally. She appeared to find something concerning in the disappearance of these rooms.

"Jesus!" said Liz heavily, coming in behind Amanda. "You could fit a jumbo jet in here. Not that I can see why you'd want to do that," she added, apparently for the sake of politeness.

"Are you two *fantastic* cooks?" Dinky asked, smiling at this delightful explanation to the conundrum.

Amanda realised Dinky was referring to herself and James. She tried to imagine the life this suggestion invoked. It appeared that they could have devoted themselves to the production of extravagant meals, instead of allowing their urge for knocking through to run away with them.

"It's a nice colour," Sally conceded.

"You can't go wrong with neutrals, really, can you?" said Christine.

Amanda expected the women to laugh again, but it seemed Christine was speaking in earnest. Of the four of them Christine was the only one she could correctly call a friend. She had felt before the surprising milk-white disclosure of her benevolence, all the more unexpected and believable for the fact that Christine was often what Susannah would have called ironic.

The others were wandering around the room as if it were a shop. They had the unself-conscious look of people engaged in private, practical ruminations. Sally was examining the grain of the kitchen table—"Is this veneer?" she asked—and Dinky stood at the windows looking out at the garden with a dreamy smile on her face. Liz Connelly stood beside the mantelpiece and one by one took down the framed photographs of the children. She held each one in her hand and looked at it, back and front, as though comparing these children to the children she had at home. "Is this your husband?" she asked, holding up a photograph of James.

Amanda went into the sitting room to check on Eddie. Liz Connelly's son Owen had joined him on the sofa in front of the television.

"Are you two all right?" she asked.

Their somnolescence confirmed by silence, she returned to the kitchen and was strangely surprised to see the four women there, sitting in the vastness around the table. There they were in their jackets and scarves and jewellery, their fragrant silks (Dinky) and their severe blacks (Liz). They had come or she had captured them, she wasn't sure which. They inhabited her kitchen like exotic creatures habituating themselves to a new zoo.

"I just can't get over it," Sally was saying, her head in her hands. "I can't believe it. I really can't."

"We're talking about Betsy Miller," Christine informed her in a discreet voice.

"All last night I lay there listening to the rain, thinking, Where is she? What's happening to her now? When I *think* of Rosie at four—she was helpless! She was just completely helpless."

She looked around at them in appeal. Christine was nodding her head sympathetically.

"And now they're saying she isn't lost at all. They're saying someone actually *took* her—abducted her, whatever you call it."

Sally shook her head, as though the person responsible for these reports was vindictively bent on destroying her optimistic view of things.

"She's probably dead," Liz Connelly interposed grimly.

"Don't!" Sally shrieked.

Liz Connelly shrugged.

"It's not like you know her," she said.

Sally looked at her with her pert face.

"You know, Liz," she said, "I think that's a really heartless thing to say."

"None of us *know* her, Liz," Christine added. "That doesn't stop us feeling for her. That doesn't stop us thinking, Christ, what if it was Rosie, or Danny, or, or"—she glanced at Amanda, and added, as though not wishing her to feel left out—"or Eddie."

"That little girl," Sally said in a distant voice. "That poor little girl."

Amanda removed the tray of pastries from the oven with a pair of padded gloves and placed it in the middle of the table.

"What about the two million people who die each year from malnutrition?" Liz said.

Christine nodded thoughtfully. Sally looked stricken: not even two million people could distract her from the plight of Betsy Miller—they may even have made it worse.

"I take your point, Liz," Christine said. "What you're saying is that people are suffering all over the world. We're all fixated on this one girl when something worse might be happening somewhere else. It's just that we don't know about it."

Liz looked doubtful.

Christine continued, "But the thing is, you can't live your life feeling guilty. Look at us! We're all so lucky—wouldn't it be a waste if we spoiled it by worrying all the time about people who are less lucky than us? The fact is, it isn't our fault that people are dying of starvation."

"Talking of starvation—" Dinky gave an impish smile and reached out her hand for a pastry.

"I mean, what's *your* explanation for it?" said Christine. "I'm asking Liz why she thinks some people lead such rich and fulfilling lives while there are all these other people who've apparently got nothing. Don't you think there's something to the idea that they might just have brought it on themselves? I'm not being funny here." Christine folded her arms and looked challengingly around the table. "We've all worked hard for what we've got, right? None of us got given it on a plate, did we? I mean, look at Liz—she doesn't get an easy ride, she's a single parent with two growing, energetic boys."

"We all know what boys are like," Dinky said, with her small mouth full.

"She manages all by herself, with no help from anyone. And what's she doing? She's worrying about people on the other side of the world dying of starvation!"

Christine brought her hand conclusively down on the table and shook her head in despair.

"I'm sick of being made to feel guilty all the time," Sally agreed. "As if we don't all feel guilty enough already. I mean, I know that if I eat one of *those* I'll feel guilty all day."

The women laughed. Sally rolled her eyes ruefully.

"I will," she insisted. "I don't know how you do it, Dinky. You're like a stick."

Dinky shrugged with twinkling eyes, as though she didn't know how she did it either.

"I want to hear what Liz has to say," said Christine, calling order. "Liz, why are you worrying about people in African villages? Why can't they sort out their own bloody problems?"

There was a silence. Everyone looked at Liz, who was studying the table-top with a stubby white finger. Amanda went around behind them refilling their coffee cups, each of which bore the pink imprint of a lip around its rim, so that they seemed to Amanda to be grinning at her. The closing minutes of her conversation with Susannah were pressing against her consciousness. They leaned against her concentration as though it were a door they were trying to force. Susannah had said a terrible thing to her in those minutes. It was something Gran had said last night, apparently. She'd woken up and asked where Amanda was, and when Susannah had said she was at home, Gran said, Amanda's cold. She's always been cold. She's got no love in her heart.

I shouldn't have told you that, should I? Susannah had said.

"What I think," Liz said, "is that God has a plan for all of us." She looked at them with her small brown eyes.

"And you're saying," interposed Christine, "that this is His plan for you—to be an anxious person, is that what you're saying?"

Liz wore an expression of hesitant defiance.

"He's told me to accept myself the way I am, yes."

"He's *told* you?"

Christine took an urgent draught from her coffee cup.

"When did all this happen?" said Sally, looking around enquiringly.

"What about the two million dying of starvation?" Christine said. "Where have they got to? I'm wondering where they fit in with the concept of self-acceptance. I'm starting to get a bit worried about them."

"God has a plan for them too."

"Well, I'm glad I'm not part of *that* plan. That plan sounds distinctly"—she drank deep again of her coffee cup—"crap."

"I didn't know you *believed*," said Dinky, thrilled.

Liz reddened. "It's quite a new relationship," she said.

"When did it—ah—start?" Sally asked.

Liz reddened further. "Six weeks ago."

"And it just—what—started?"

Liz examined her jacket buttons. Then she leaned into the table, as though precipitating herself forwards from a height.

"I'd been asking," she said. "But it was the wrong question. I was asking why I had so many problems. All the time I was like why, why, why? Why me? Why did Ian leave me and the boys? Why is Alfie being kept back a year at school? Why has Mum got Parkinson's?"

"I don't think anyone could blame you for that," Christine observed. "We'd all ask ourselves those sorts of questions."

"Why Betsy Miller?" Sally proposed.

"Then I had my turning away. That's sort of the beginning of the relationship, apparently. I gave up on all of it. I thought, I don't care any more. I turned my back on God. And that's when He finally got in touch with me."

"That's exactly what they say you should do with men," said Dinky professorially. "Apparently it works every time."

"How do you mean, He got in touch with you?" Christine said sceptically. "What exactly do you mean?"

"I woke up in the middle of the night," Liz said, "and He was there."

"In your room?" said Sally.

"In my heart." Liz clasped her hands over her capacious chest. "And He said, I've got a plan for you. It's a wonderful plan, and it's yours. Not anyone else's—yours."

Liz relayed God's remarks in a gruff voice. Her cheeks were blazing.

"And He said this in your heart?" Christine turned it over. "That must have been exciting," she stated flatly. "I'm really pleased for you, Liz," she added presently. "I wish I could believe in God, but I can't. I just don't believe it."

Liz sat back in her chair. "That's His plan for you," she said, nodding. "For the time being."

"I'm not trying to be controversial here," Christine said, "but what's it all about? You do a fantastic job and everything, Liz, but let's face it, your life's not easy, is it? You've got two kids, no husband, no money, a parent who's a full-time invalid—why don't you tell God to stuff His plan? Why don't you put on some make-up, buy yourself some new clothes, and go out and have some fun for a change?"

Liz looked at her abjectly.

"Tell me if I'm going over the top here," Christine said.

"It's hard, isn't it?" said Sally sympathetically.

"I'll take the boys," Christine persisted. "You don't need to get a babysitter, I'll have them. It's no trouble to me at all. Just go out and have some *fun*."

"There are some advantages to being single," said Dinky.

"Don't we all know it," Sally said.

Liz shook her head and said, "That's just not the way I am."

"God!" expostulated Christine. "Why do we all *worry* so much? Here we are, drinking coffee, free to talk about fashion, or where we want to go on holiday, or whatever we like, and what do we do?" She put a hand to her forehead. "We spend our time debating the existence of God! It's not what you'd think, is it? I say to Joe, Look, it can get really heavy on a coffee morning, you don't believe me, but it can."

"Sam thinks we all sit around complaining about our husbands," said Sally, as though wishing to suggest the topic for consideration.

"What's *your* husband like, Amanda?" Dinky enquired.

"James is—" Christine started, then stopped herself, smiling. "No. Sorry, Amanda—you tell."

Amanda wondered what Christine had been about to say. James is the world's most boring man? Susannah had said this once, on the telephone, when she thought Amanda couldn't hear her.

"Well—he's very nice," she said.

"James," Christine resumed, now that his wife's contribution was out of the way, "is like one of those characters you always get in films: the very, very last person you'd suspect of having committed the crime. No matter how much you try and think of who you least suspect of doing it, he's the one you never think of."

This seemed to be more or less what Susannah had said.

"He sounds really fascinating!" said Dinky.

Amanda collected the stained coffee cups on a tray and took them to the sink. She turned on the taps and put on her yellow rubber gloves, and the sight of them reminded her of how death had entered her kitchen, how it had come in from the rainy day through the large windows.

Suddenly Eddie was standing beside her.

"Mummy!"

He yanked twice at her skirt.

"Mummy!"

"What *is* it, Eddie?"

"Mummy, that boy is drawing on the sofa. He got out my felt-tips and he's drawing on the sofa with them. I told him not to," he called after her, as she strode rapidly out of the room.

A big red patch like a stain of blood lay indelibly on the cream-coloured flank of the sofa. Amanda lifted the child bodily from amidst the cushions and tore the pens from his hand.

"How dare you?" she said in a savage whisper in his ear.

Pens were scattered all over the carpet. There were other, different-coloured stains there, where their inky, suppurating tips touched the beige fibres and bled into them.

"I could kill you!" she whispered. "I could kill you!"

She threw him back down on the cushions. His body felt unfamiliar—his whole being recoiled from her in its half-formed confidence. He was like a seedling she could have torn up, his established needs trailing from him like roots, and dashed to the ground. He did not cry, as Eddie would have done: he watched her from amidst the cushions with his round blue eyes. She picked up the pens and replaced their lids one by one with shaking fingers.

"Amanda!" someone called from the hall. "Amanda, we're—oh God, did Eddie do that?"

Christine Lanham stood over Amanda where she was crouched on the carpet. Amanda could see her shoes, which she had not removed at the door. A rind of mud ran along one of the soles. What did it matter now?

"Was it Owen?" Christine said in a low voice, when Amanda did not reply.

Amanda nodded.

"Blimey," said Liz loudly, appearing in the doorway. "It'll take more than a bit of Vanish to get that out."

"You'd better start praying," Christine said to her.

Liz seemed confused by this remark.

"I'm really sorry, but I've got to go," said Christine. "I've got to pick up Ella from nursery. Thanks for this morning. It was *great*! So nice to catch up. Bloody Owen," she added under her breath, once they were out in the hall. "It's just not on, is it?"

Sally and Dinky stood there smiling in their coats.

"Bye!" they cried.

The door opened and shut, and the three of them were gone into the rain. Amanda turned around and saw Liz Connelly, the black-clad hulk of her, still in the sitting room.

"Do you mind if I stay here for a bit?" she said ashamedly.

In an instant she saw Liz Connelly's life, saw it entire: her small flat, the unrelieved expanses of her days, the prospect of time going on and on, the burden of it to be carried on and on and on, with no hope of it ever being even for a moment lifted from her. She wanted it to be lifted from her: she was asking, like a beggar.

For the next hour Liz Connelly did not have a better place to be than Amanda Clapp's sitting room.

"Not really," Amanda said. "As long as you don't mind me getting on with things."

"I'll just sit here with Owen and watch the telly," Liz said. She parked herself on the sofa, as far from the stain as she could comfortably get. "It's a shame about your sofa," she said, fingering the material. "Children and white sofas—they don't really get on, do they?"

Amanda watched her.

"Will he get into trouble for that?" Liz said.

She meant Eddie.

"No," Amanda said levelly.

Liz lifted her eyebrows. "I suppose it was you who put the sofa there in the first place," she said meditatively. "And the pens. They're not to know, are they?"

This would not have been Amanda's interpretation of things, had Eddie actually been responsible for the disaster. She didn't know what she'd have done to him. The possibilities seemed fathomless. Yet she felt, beneath Liz Connelly's assumption of her benevolence, strangely transfigured: a sort of ghost passed through her that was both herself and not herself. It was like a momentary projection into the void of her heart, of a detailed image whose precious information she sought to store even as it faded again into nothingness.

Amanda realised that she did not have to tell Liz that it was Owen who had ruined her white sofa.

"That doesn't always stop you, though," Liz said. She turned to look at the screen so that Amanda was facing the indeterminate brown back of her head. "It doesn't always stop you."

In the kitchen Eddie was standing staring out of the window, just standing there, in the middle of the spot where the old kitchen had once stood. He was looking at the garden in the rain. He always wanted to go out there: Amanda wouldn't let him, except on perfect summer days, when the grass was dry and springy and unlikely to cleave to the soles of his feet. And even then, he wasn't content just to sit in it—he had to dig things up, and carry woodlice around in his fingers, and make structures out of stones and twigs and leaves for snails to live in. Amanda had seen something on television about children eating such things, in conditions of starvation: cockroaches, snails, even rats and mice. Now, as he stood in the neutral-coloured vault of the kitchen, apparently paralysed by its blankness, she imagined letting him out into the garden to fend for himself, to pick up wriggling woodlice in his grubby fingers and feed them into his mouth, to make a shelter for himself to sleep in out of stones and twigs and leaves. It seemed the only alternative, to the sterility that adhered to her, to her heart that had no love in it. And if it was true that she had no love in her heart, then what was the reason for it? Her life had been an ordinary life: her parents and grandparents were ordinary, they had said and done ordinary things together. They had all lived together ordinarily, in their ordinary home. They had gone to sleep and got up again and eaten their meals and done their work in an ordinary way. If there was a wrong, then it was an ordinary kind of wrong.

Yet Gran had said she was cold: Gran, a tiny, limp, flaxen-haired creature with skin that felt like dust and watery, receding eyes. She had been a tiny, harmless woman, but now Amanda felt her as an oppressor, a scourge. What was her knowledge? What vision had she seen on the shore of death? And how, if it was only a vision of ordinariness, had Gran extrapolated from it such sweeping, seigneurial disapprobation, such condemnatory power? Love! Was love the disguise a necessity wore in the moment you bowed down before it? Did Christine Lanham love her husband, actually love him? Did Sally Gibson love her daughter, or did she fear her, fear her daughter's ability to destroy her the way Betsy Miller—poor girl—was even now destroying her parents? Was love not, in fact, the first concession to death?

Amanda loved her silver Toyota: she was no fool. And she had loved Susannah's rabbit, whose soft white body had struggled frantically in her arms. The feeling of love had besieged her: she had burned in it and lived in it both. She remembered it clearly. She had wanted both to have the rabbit and to be it. She had wanted to be Susannah. The fact that she was not Susannah—it seemed possible that this was the reason love could never gain a foothold in her. When Jessica was born—dark-haired, lavishly screaming—it came round again, the possibility of transference. But there was too much work to do, too much disorder and incessant change, too much protesting reality, for this dark, burning, jealous love to make a channel through. So she made Jessica resemble herself instead, her nervous indifference, her prejudice against chaos, her unblinking soul.

And Eddie was the stultifying noon of her life's day, the

grind: he was all unvarnished, unmitigated work. He did not, could not reflect her: he merely went through the hours ahead of her, displacing things in order that she should put them back. He had a pure relationship with her worst self. Now he stretched out his hand as though to touch the garden and his fingers met the window.

"Don't, Eddie," she said. "You'll get marks on the glass."

"I saw Granny in the garden," he said.

"Granny? You mean Marlene?" Marlene was Amanda's mother, who lived in Kent. "What was Marlene doing in our garden?"

"Not her. Old Granny. The one who gives me sweets. She was in the garden. I saw her."

A shadow passed over Amanda.

"Old Granny can't have been in the garden," she said.

Eddie shrugged. "She was."

"Old Granny died. She died this morning. She died in the place where she lives."

"Oh," said Eddie.

"Auntie Susannah was with her. She was holding her hand."

Eddie considered this.

"Oh. Poor Granny. Will you tell her I like her?"

"I can't tell her, because she's dead. That's what being dead means. It means you can't tell people things any more."

Eddie turned away from the window and looked at her. His clothes were rumpled. His eyes were large and tremulous. His hair stood up in tufts, like grass. He came towards her. In his face she saw the realisation of her own mortality. He seemed to want her to comfort him for the fact that one day she too would die. It was another piece of disorder she was expected to attend to, another thing she was expected to carry; he would slip off the knowledge, slip away from it having handed it to her, and go away lighter. And who carried her own deadly revelations, her ordinary terror? Her mother, sitting in her slippers in Kent, or caravanning, as she was now, in Wales in the rain?

He rested his head against her thighs, and then he put his arms around her legs and hugged her. A faint, uneven warmth came from his vigorous little body. She looked out of the window at the garden, at the backs of the houses in Bedford Road that always looked so undignified somehow, with their drainpipes and their electric cables and their patchy bits of mortar. At the front, where they could be seen, they were faced with handsome masonry and the hedges were pruned. The fronts were seen by strangers, by passers-by, while Amanda had to look at the backs every day. What was it about intimacy that encouraged such vulnerability, such dilapidation? Why was her solemn undertaking to spend her life with James and Jessica and Eddie repaid in her husband's stained underwear in the laundry basket and his hairs from shaving in the sink, in her children's discarded emotions? She rested her hands on Eddie's small shoulders.

"I love you, Mummy," he said, into her skirt.

"Silly boy." She squeezed his shoulders.

"I'm always going to tell you things. For when you're dead."

"It's not very nice to talk about people being dead, Eddie."

She tried to disengage him from her legs, but he clung on.

"I don't mind," he said.

After all, she felt a little wave of recognition of him, a little sense of being overpowered by his small, forward-going nature. He rushed up and over her, a little wave going over a ridge in the sand.

Liz Connelly and Owen were still in the sitting room,

watching television. She had almost forgotten about them. From where she stood she could see the kaleidoscopic edge of the television screen and one of Liz Connelly's robust, black-trousered legs. She remembered the red stain, like a strange red flower, on the sofa and a bolt of sensation passed through her, a feeling of violence and confusion and shame. She had thrown the little boy on to the cushions. She remembered his soft, dry, appraising eyes.

Soon they would go; she would cause them to go. First, she would cause Eddie to let go of her legs. Then she would package the Connellys up and put them out in the rain, with the red stain remaining as a reminder of this day, this day of her life in which all the other days seemed to be coming together and showing themselves at last.

Then she would cook the mince.

The women drove to the mall in two separate cars.

Maisie Carrington went with Stephanie Sykes, in Stephanie's tidy slate-blue Alhambra. Christine Lanham took her own car in case of emergency, and because all of them piling into one car to go out to Merrywood Mall might have led her to feel like one of a troupe of secretaries on an expedition to the shops.

It was nearly midday, and the rain fell on Arlington Park.

Christine collected Ella from nursery on the way. She parked the car on a double yellow line and ran in through the rain with her coat over her head. It was the same nursery Liz Connelly's son Owen went to on Mondays, Wednesdays, and Thursdays. In his absence Christine raised with the supervisors the issue of Owen's aggressive behaviour towards the other children in the morning sessions, before tearing back outside, with Ella under her arm, to where Stephanie and Maisie sat waiting, parked in the Alhambra behind Christine's car with the engine running.

It was three miles from Arlington Park to Merrywood Mall. The road passed out through the lesser suburbs of Redbourne and Firley. It was here that the residential flank of the city succumbed by degrees to the motorway interchange, and the first forlorn stretches of naked countryside lay amidst the oceanic concrete of giant car parks and warehouses. Christine drove with music on and Ella writhing in the back, her mouth stoppered by a dummy, a prophylactic beaker of milk clutched in her hand. The suburbs of Redbourne and Firley, seen through the windows of a car driven from Arlington Park, had an undistinguished aspect of organised anonymity; they were expedient places whose only tangible function was to provide shelter for human beings, as though in the service of a strategy too universal to account for individual lives. For two miles the route to the mall passed through the cortex of these regions and afforded a view to either side of the unrelieved symmetry of their long, straight residential roads, which elapsed precisely, like measured time, each one briefly showing its vista of identical houses and front gardens and driveways protruding like little paved tongues. In recent years the main road had been widened to take two lanes of traffic each way, which increased the tempo of the passing houses and made them seem more stranded than ever in their ignominious version of living.

Redbourne and Firley had another purpose in Christine Lanham's view, which was to reacquaint those denizens of Arlington Park who passed through them with their own, more motivated condition; with the greater interest, variety, and refinement of their own habitat. There was nothing like going to Redbourne to remind you why you lived in Arlington Park, where too long a sojourn without the intrusion of contrasts could give rise to a strange, questing sense of having asked too much of life; of having taken excessive pains to seclude oneself from what was actually harmless and may even have been fruitful.

One look at Firley could cure you of that. Firley was a desert traversed by cauliflower-haired old ladies in motorised wheelchairs, and men who slowly washed the caravans parked in their front drives; by teenaged boys in baseball caps and headphones and hooded tops, their swaddled heads a V-sign to conversation, to life itself; by young girls in tracksuits that had seen no beneficial kind of sport, pushing prams the size of their own bodies and looking towards the road with expectant faces, as though thinking salvation might come to them by that route. There was nothing of any note in Firley, except for one house by the road which from mid-October proffered the most extravagant display of neon-lit moulded plastic Christmas decorations, including a giant Santa, sleigh, and reindeer on the roof which flashed on and off in a repeating pattern so that the reindeer seemed to gallop on luminous red legs. The children would strain at their seatbelts to see it as they went by, to see the reindeer spastically cantering and the riot of pulsing lights like a flashing fountain, a fountain of what seemed to them to be love, making its gaudy, eternal arabesques out there in the null redbrick obscurity of those straight, sempiternal streets.

At the traffic lights Maisie Carrington and Stephanie Sykes looked at the back of Christine Lanham's head in the car in front and at the densely graven piece of her face captured in the rectangle of the wing mirror, in which she could see their faces side by side behind her.

Christine Lanham had a black, private fear of Redbourne and Firley; of Redbourne more than Firley, proximate as it was to Arlington Park and hence more threatening. Firley stood on the threshold of the motorway, where the road widened and ascended in a great concrete arc of human aspiration, and the traffic sped away, liberated, from the last dejected houses toward Merrywood Mall. But Redbourne was denser and more constricting, and every time she passed through it, Christine felt a fear from which the plain unlikelihood of its realisation could not protect her. It was the same kind of fear she had felt in childhood, when pondering the secret possibility that she might not be the true child of her parents: a retrospective fear of inauthenticity which seemed to reveal to her the vulnerability of her grasp on the real, the authentic life. Redbourne reminded Christine of the insufficiency of her control of destiny, the fatal slightness of its degrees, where the smallest shift to left or right could produce a world altered in every particular. Half a mile apart, in some places less than half a mile, Arlington Park and this textureless suburb were the very illustration of this principle. Geographically, half a mile was the slenderest of threads: that was how close she had come to living in Redbourne. Its presence was a constant hazard, in that it sustained a distinction in the face of which she could never feel entirely safe. Generally she only went there on her way to Merrywood, looking at its residents from the safety of her car and despising them the more for her sense of how near she was to being one of them.

The two cars passed out of Firley and on to the overpass, over the motorway with its stampede of traffic making for the grey horizon, and up the new four-lane road that ran like a fast, broad river past fields and farmhouses which had the diminutive appearance of relics, of old bones. There were a few sheep in one of the fields, next to a great, glinting car showroom, and further along a little cottage in the lee of a petrol station where four horses stood in a paddock. They stood all in a group, by the fence. There was something vaguely human in their demeanour, the disquiet of personality, which seemed to have replaced their animal natures. Thirty-foot-tall streetlamps lined the road as it ascended the hill, where enormous, pavilion-like supermarkets and warehouses had risen up one upon another: Tiles R Us, a bathroom emporium, two DIY superstores, an electrical goods warehouse, and a brand-new supermarket to add to those already there, standing in a fresh swirl of tarmac. A huge new pyramidal roundabout, rising forty-odd feet at its concrete centre, took three lanes of traffic and dealt them out in four different directions. On the crest of the hill stood Merrywood itself, monolithic, temple-shaped, light flashing off its glass-plated sides.

Recently Christine had read a letter in the correspondence page of the *Arlington Gazette* that had described Merrywood as "a tumour on the constipated bowel of the motorway." She often wrote to this page herself. Once—her outraged response to a diatribe against mothers "ferrying around" schoolchildren and causing traffic congestion—they had put her sentiments in bold and called them Letter of the Week. Reaching for those same heights, she had given vent to a delirious, unconstrained anger. Did their correspondent wish them all to return to the Stone Age? Did he wish to inhabit an era in which freedom of choice and movement were the preserve of a privileged few? Perhaps he would prefer it if those who patronised Merrywood felt guilt and shame about their material prosperity—or better still, weren't prosperous at all, lest in the absence of Merrywood they were forced to come in their hordes to the exclusive little establishments where he did *his* shopping!

These remarks lacked a killer blow, which Christine had presently understood would be impossible to administer, and also unnecessary: for Merrywood did indeed possess a creeping, unstoppable, vegetable growth, and if the paper's correspondent wanted to see this as a bad thing, then that was nothing more than his choice.

The rain had stopped, and as they drew in formation into the car park the sun gushed through a rent in the sagging, dark-grey sky. The roofs of the cars, line after line of them, made a brilliant, undulating metallic field that stretched almost out of sight.

"Now why don't we do this more often?" Christine said, through Stephanie's lowered window.

"I don't *know*," Stephanie said suggestively, waiting to be told why they didn't.

"I mean, there we all are, sitting in our houses feeding our children pureed carrots—why don't we do *this* more often?"

The three women gazed upon Merrywood, whose vast plate-glass doors were opening and shutting mechanically all along its broad façade, ingesting and disgorging people.

"Perhaps we're just too damned scared of our husbands," said Stephanie, with a valiant, lipsticked smile which implied that this idea was something she'd heard of rather than experienced for herself.

"Oh, sod *them*," Christine said. "Though in fairness to Joe, he doesn't mind me coming here. In fact, I think he wishes I came here more. He's like, you know, for Christ's sake, get yourself some decent clothes. Don't just buy things for the children. Get yourself some nice things to wear."

"You always look great!" protested Stephanie.

"You know how it is," Christine said through the window. "After Ella was born I wore the same trousers for two years. It was like what they say about people when they get out of prison. In the end I didn't know how to take them off. I needed to be rehabilitated."

"Two years," Stephanie said. "That must be some kind of record."

"Stephanie never even needed maternity clothes," Christine said to Maisie Carrington, who was in the passenger seat. "The rest of us were trying to convince our husbands that it was perfectly normal to look seven months pregnant a year after the baby was born, and then they'd see Stephanie."

"I was huge after Jasper," Stephanie said.

"You were not."

"I was! I just covered it up."

"I love just *coming* here," Christine expostulated, surveying the brutal grandeur of the car park, where the sky still hurled down its unsteady shafts of light and the morning's rain stood in beads on the coruscating metal of cars and made them look reborn. There were lavish puddles in the new tarmac where fleecy clouds and pieces of brilliant sky were reflected. "I don't know, it just makes me feel good. It makes me feel that life is full of possibilities."

She opened the back door of her car, where Ella sat gazing upwards through the window, her thumb in her fleshy mouth. She gripped her toy rabbit, Robbie, in her fist. Her hot little lap was full of crumbs, and patches of wetness where her beaker of milk had capsized across her legs. The back seat of the car was strewn with toys and dirty remnants of children's clothing, and discarded cartons of juice and half-eaten biscuits. Occasionally Christine would sweep the litter out with a careless arm; it seemed to her that cleaning her car was a Redbourne thing to do. She put Ella in her pushchair and slammed the door, whereupon Ella began to wail and struggle furiously at the straps, holding out her arms beseechingly. Christine opened the door again, retrieved Robbie from his fallen position in the footwell, shoved him into Ella's lap, and once more slammed the door. Robbie was grey and worn out with Ella's need for him. He looked shapeless and insensate with the drudgery of love.

"Ready?" Christine said to the others.

Stephanie stood there in her little buttoned-up jacket and boots, with Jasper neatly in his pushchair, as though she were modelling her own life.

"Ready," she said with a little laugh.

Maisie Carrington was wearing old jeans with a skirt on top, a big, roughly knitted jersey of a marshy, indistinct colour, and a used-looking tweed jacket. She looked like she was wearing more than one outfit, as though in case of sudden destitution. Beneath her untidy black hair her face was solemn.

Christine pointed at her. "You haven't got a child!" she observed.

Maisie looked around her. She seemed dumbfounded.

"They're both at school," she said.

"I only just noticed," Christine said, thinking that the last thing she'd do if she didn't have children to look after was spend time with people who did. "Isn't that funny?"

Maisie Carrington had recently moved with her husband and two children to Arlington Park. They'd come from London. Every time she saw her, Christine felt a pricking desire to secure her, almost to neutralise her: there was something about her that raised again and again in Christine's mind the uncomfortable spectre of degrees, that caused her to wonder whether Arlington Park was to London what Redbourne was to Arlington Park. It was strange: she wanted to secure her and yet she was a little dismayed now by how easily she had succeeded. She had found that the easiest way to capture people was to get them at anchor, when they were tethered by children and their time was a kind of public commodity, an open space into which others were free to intrude. It surprised her that Maisie Carrington would elect to spend her own time with herself and Stephanie Sykes: it disappointed her a little.

Christine didn't have to think about what she would do if she was on her own, because she never was.

"I didn't realise how far it was," Maisie said, a little apologetically.

It was Christine who had invited Maisie to have lunch

with Stephanie and herself; and Christine who had claimed—she had sensed some early resistance to the idea—that Merrywood was just "up the road." It was Christine, reluctant now to back down at the impediment of Maisie's carlessness, who had urged her to come in Stephanie's car—with the result that Maisie was trapped at Merrywood for the next two hours with no means of escape, entirely at Christine's behest. She had a sense of her own brute strength at having achieved all this unopposed: perhaps Maisie, with her aura of London, was all fragility, all easily crushed sensibility. Perhaps fragility was what an aura of London was.

And on top of that, the Carringtons were coming to her, Christine's, house for dinner this evening, which might well be the end of them, which might be the last straw. They would return to London with terrible, hilarious stories of Arlington Park, and entirely through Christine's fault Arlington Park would have lost two of exactly the kind of unusual people that made it the interesting, vibrant place it was.

"I just meant, you know, how *amazing*. How amazing to have some time for *you*. None of us have enough time for ourselves, do we? Granted, you might not always choose to spend it here . . . But once in a while it's fun, isn't it?"

"Enough gabbing, girls," said Stephanie Sykes, raising her pencilled eyebrows impatiently to the heavens.

There were so many people like Stephanie Sykes in Arlington Park that you could have laid them end to end all around Merrywood car park and still not have accounted for them all.

"I miss them when they're at school," said Maisie, which deepened Christine's confusion still further. "I think it's because I can never resolve my relationship with them at home. They go away and I feel this sense of incompletion. Look at that," she added suddenly, stopping as they walked through the car park and pointing.

Christine looked. Maisie appeared to be indicating something at the far side of the car park, beyond the automatic barriers. There was a patch of rough ground beside the delivery and collection warehouse, where you drove to pick up large purchases. Cars were buzzing to and fro up the slip road. Beyond it Christine could see the shabby white shapes of what looked like three or four caravans. They had washing lines strung between them, with children's clothes hung out to dry.

"Gypsies," Maisie said. She shook her head. "What a place to have to live. Right where people come to pick up their sofas."

Christine pondered the caravans and tried to work out what Maisie's remarks signified. It wasn't the nicest thing to have a pack of Gypsies staring at you when you came to collect your sofa, she could admit, but it wasn't the end of the world either.

She sensed again the presence of the aura of London, like a fog through which she couldn't properly make anything out.

"I don't think they're really doing any harm," she said, trotting to catch up with Maisie and Stephanie. "I mean, when you think about it, it's not such a bad place to put them. At least they're out of the way here. I'm sure the police would move them if they caused any trouble."

"They're *people*," Maisie said quietly, so that Christine felt fretful and a little bellicose, and determined to defend the pleasures of Merrywood from the threat of spoliation, from whichever quarter it was coming.

They left the car park and passed through the great glass doors with their chrome portico into the atrium of the mall, where glass escalators ascended in constant rotation through three floors to the transparent dome of the roof, so that all the layers of the building could be seen from below. It was like an illustration of the chambers of the heart: people were carried upwards by the escalators, eventually to re-emerge, oxygenated by shopping. At the centre of the main hall a huge fountain steadily pumped out its jet of water amidst fronded networks of plants, and bunches of coloured balloons drifted silently around on their tethers as though they were suspended in liquid. A steady level of mysterious hydraulic sound filled the echoing, daylight-coloured spaces, though there was music running just beneath the surface of it and human noises, strangely muffled and indistinct, like a commotion heard under water: the rise and fall of voices that came in loops and sudden reports, the piercing, shrill call of babies, the syncopated hoots and shrieks of rubber shoes on the tiled floors, and the spontaneous mechanical birdsong of mobile phones. The place was full of people, on the escalators, all along the glass-fronted galleries, milling in the broad avenues that led off the main hall; yet the strange acoustics and saturating, glassy light deadened the sense of human congress, so that they seemed almost to be swimming or floating rather than walking. The conditioned air negated the smell of bodies. Instead, the atmosphere was divided into invisible regions of perfume, and a continuous odour of coffee and baking stood around the open-air cafés like a replacement for walls and language.

Maisie, Stephanie, and Christine paused at the fountain, in whose tiled shallow pool people had flung their spare change, and the children strained at the straps on their pushchairs to put their hands into the cold, chlorinated water, and to explore the foliage of the plastic plants in their pebbled tubs. On a bench beside the fountain a fat girl sat holding a little pink carrier-bag printed with the word *Me*, tied at the top with a pink ribbon, like a present for her solitary, gazing self. The people moving around the hall and up and down the escalators gave an impression of blinding whiteness: girls with white, toneless skin and pale hair drawn tightly back from their faces; large white women with the wobbling, creamy bodies of blanc-manges; men in clean white trainers and white, ironed T-shirts from which the chemical smell of washing powder briefly emanated before being drawn up into the air vents; teenagers in immaculate tracksuits and baseball caps, some of them thin as wraiths, with skin the white of shrouds and protuberant teeth and the eyes of starving children. There were tiny girls dressed like angels and poodles and show ponies, little boys dressed as miniature sportsmen or lumberjacks, girls with new babies in prams wrapped in blinding white blankets who raked the glass ceiling with their flimsy gazes, girls with jewellery and fake fur who shrieked with laughter. Here and there toddlers on leading reins bellowed and staggered about insanely in small, echoing chambers of noise.

"Where do we *start*?" Christine said, opening her eyes very wide.

The three women proceeded down the broad central avenue of the mall. An oncoming delegation of people in wheelchairs, some of them propelling themselves, others gazing off unseeing to one side with their chins in their chests, caused them to separate a little. They passed mobile phone shops and shops selling trainers, sports shops and jewellery shops and shops with headless white moulded mannequins standing conversationally in the neon-lit windows. Rotating billboards were suspended from the ceiling above them on long wires. A close-up photograph appeared of two laughing mouths about to kiss, then a photo of a couple lying on a laminated wooden floor like mating insects, she on his back, a glass of wine standing next to them. There was an image of a small pile of abandoned clothes on a beach, like the remains of a suicide, with the blue sea stretching beyond it to the horizon and the words Free Yourself above.

They entered the department store at the far end of the mall and were instantly engulfed by the cosmetics section. Women with painted faces and white coats, like actors playing surgeons, stood in their laboratories of beauty and pinioned passers-by with enquiring looks from beneath their narrow, arched brows. There was a buzz of excitement in the hot, scented hall. Stephanie and Christine rubbed lipsticks on to the backs of their hands and then rubbed them off again, and Stephanie bravely accepted the ambivalent compliments of the salesgirl for the youthful appearance of her skin—"given your age"—while Maisie shrank from the offer of a free trial colour-matching session, as though the woman had threatened to wrench her teeth out with a pair of pliers.

In Ladies' Fashions a small female crowd had gathered around a platform where a woman with a microphone was dispensing what a notice board described as a "Fashion Workshop." The white crowds did not by and large seem to have penetrated the sedate fastnesses of the department store, particularly not Ladies' Fashions. Here the heads were grey and the colours autumnal, as though their garments were the indication of an episcopal seniority, in the service of which they had gathered here to hear new interpretations of the gospel of discreet self-presentation.

"Let's see this," said Christine, in a low voice of seminary urgency.

"This look is very now, very this season," the woman said into her microphone, which was suspended in front of her lips by a headset, to enable her to put on and take off the items under discussion, "and it's particularly easy on those of you like me who are a little bigger around the hips than they'd like to be."

She removed one jacket, becoming momentarily entangled in the wire from her headset, and put on another. Her cream lace undergarment had come loose from the waistband of her trousers. The flesh of her arms and chest looked red and distressed.

"She hasn't got big hips," said one of the grey heads to another. "She's as slim as a flower."

"Some of you might be wondering, if you're too long in the body like I am, what you're meant to do with your spare tyre—I see we *all* know what I mean by that," she said into the generalised laughter. "What you're meant to do, if you're wearing this shorter kind of jacket, with that great wobbling band of fat around your middle—come on, ladies, admit it!"

"Oh, for Christ's sake," murmured Christine, her fingers resting critically on her chin.

"Let's face it, ladies, no one wants to see our flabby tummies and our flabby tits any more! And another thing—most of us don't want them to! We've all had enough of that, haven't we?"

Muted cheers of approval.

"I think she's very attractive," said a woman in front of Christine.

The woman removed her latest jacket and bared herself to the audience in her rumpled, ill-fitting cream lace. Her face was flushed and her blond-streaked hair tousled. She raised her arms to them in appeal.

"Mummy!" Ella shouted.

"What I want to turn your minds to—what I want to fix your attention on, ladies, are the magic three Ts." She lowered her voice. "Tailoring, tailoring, and tailoring!"

"Mummy! Mum! Mummy! Need the toilet!"

Maisie, Stephanie, and Christine were forced to descend to the basement in search of a toilet for Ella. In the furniture department Christine sat on the edge of a bed and said:

"I'm not being funny, but I found that frankly depressing."

"It was a bit over the top," Stephanie said.

"I mean, is that all there is to look forward to? Is that all there is on the other side of all this bloody hassle? Frigging tailoring? I'd rather be some fat old slag propping up the bar in her white stilettos—I would!" she insisted, when Maisie and Stephanie laughed.

They were sitting in a simulation of a child's bedroom. The white particleboard bed was tented in white netting suspended from a hoop overhead. The bed was neatly made with a pillow and duvet, on whose pink cover the word *Princess* was inscribed repeatedly in different fonts. One of the struts was coming out of the headboard, and it sagged where Christine sat on it. There was a white particleboard chest of drawers, and a wardrobe with a pink, plastic-framed oval mirror fixed to the door. *Mirror, mirror on the wall* . . . was written on the glass in scratched transfers.

"That woman made me want to slit my wrists," Christine added mildly, gazing off into the furnished labyrinths of the basement.

Extravagantly padded white leather sofas were arranged around a chrome and glass coffee table the size of a pond, and numerous sterile arrangements of dining-room furniture hosted their invisible meals for four and six and eight. At the far end there were rows of double beds, stark and unmade, like waiting graves.

"Why?" Stephanie smiled, shaking her shiny head. "Why did she get to you so much?"

Christine did not reply. Ella, released from her pushchair, was investigating the hostilities of her new home. She pulled open a drawer from the little white chest and it made a cracking sound as it fell to the floor. Silently Christine rose from the bed and shoved the drawer back on to its runners.

"I wouldn't like to shock you, Stephanie," she said.

"You can't shock me," Stephanie asserted, smiling.

"As I say," Christine reiterated, after a pause, "I don't want to shock you both, but it's things like that that make me think one day I'm going to have to do something desperate. That woman talking about flabby tits—I can't explain."

They rose, wheeled the pushchairs into the lift, and returned to the ground floor.

"The thing is, Stephanie," Christine said, "you probably never wanted to be a hairdresser."

Stephanie's pert, pretty face wore an expression of indecision, as though she was facing the fact that this possibility was excluded from her for ever.

"I mean, you probably always wanted to be a primary-school teacher, with a husband who makes lots of money and a gorgeous house and four lovely children."

They re-entered the echoing main concourse of the mall, where a large, shapeless woman with short hair brutally sculpted around her broad, doughy face was shouting "Savannah! Savannah!" and a tiny, pale, limp-limbed girl was wandering uncertainly towards the escalators.

"What I'm saying is that you're actually very lucky," Christine said. "We're all actually very lucky. Before I met Joe I was the sort of person who ate tinned fruit salad and bought Blue Nun for a dinner party. We were the sort of family that had all our meals in front of the telly. My mum used to go to the bingo on Thursday nights. That isn't to say she wasn't a lovely person," she added, steering the pushchair after Stephanie through the open doors of a shop. "She was a lovely person. She still is a lovely person, though she likes a drink and she won't have anything to do with her grandchildren."

The shop was a clothes shop, in whose windows the headless mannequins wore sequinned bikini tops and tight miniskirts and trousers so low in the crotch as to abrogate the power of suggestion.

"What do you think, girls?" Stephanie said over her shoulder, with a game little smile that made her mouth turn down at the corners. "Shall we risk it?"

"Why not?" Christine said.

"I love it here," Stephanie said. "I just *love* it. All these fabulous trashy clothes—it's fine so long as you don't wear them all at the same time," she qualified. "And everything's so *fantastically* cheap."

"Stephanie!" said Christine, raising her eyebrows. "I'm surprised at you. There you are at the school gate in your teensy little mohair wraps and your calfskin boots—we had no idea you had this other side!"

"Don't you find that sometimes you just want to wear something really *slutty?*" Stephanie said, reddening prettily as she raked through a rack of clothes and engaged the brake of Jasper's pushchair with her heel.

"I can't say that I do," Christine said, giving Maisie a wide-eyed, comical look. "As I say, all that stuff's a bit close to home for me, Stephanie. I might find myself reverting to type. I might just go home and find myself cracking open a bottle of Blue Nun."

"Where do you buy your clothes, Maisie?" Stephanie said.

Maisie Carrington was standing with her hands clasped in front of her and a vacant expression on her face, like an overgrown child awaiting collection.

"I don't know," she said. She shrugged helpfully. "Lots of different places."

"You've got a very idiosyncratic look," Christine said. "A very—what's the word?—eclectic look. Like what you've got on now. The skirt over the trousers. That's a very individual, eclectic look."

"Thanks," Maisie said.

"Bloody hell," Christine said, arching her eyebrows at a passing salesgirl. "She looks like she should be at school."

"You've got to try not to think about it," Stephanie said fervidly. "You've just got to think, you know, I've got a right to be here. I've got money, I'm female, and I've got a right to be here if I want to be."

"I'm just thinking, you know, what about the pushchairs? They're sort of blowing our cover, Stephanie, don't you think?"

"Half the sixteen-year-old girls who come in here have pushchairs," Stephanie said, a little impatiently.

"That's a sobering thought," Christine said. "Expressed with real feeling, Stephanie. I'm thinking, you know, maybe tailoring isn't so bad after all. I'm not being funny here. I'm thinking, what's so wrong with looking your age? What's so wrong with looking like what you actually are?"

The shop was narrow but deep, and broadened at its far end into a kind of cavern, where shoes and boots and sandals rested on innumerable Perspex stalks and jewellery in abundant gilded clusters hung from metal trees. All through the centre of the shop and high up the walls on both sides clothes were crammed on to rails, so that from the door they had the appearance of a silent, motionless crowd, or the categorised remains of one. The hordes of spangled tops and tiny jackets, of empty dresses and flattened trousers and ghostly, customised T-shirts, were like the lineaments of a lived existence, like the contents of a museum commemorating an elapsed era of rudimentary human intercourse, of social incidents so fleeting and voluntary that no one had bothered to come and flesh them out. They hung there in all their pernickety, suggestive design, tented in shadow, while loud music held them in its perennial moment of synthetic consummation, and outside, in the echoing, light-filled mall, motiveless people came and went as though they were traversing the fields of purgatory.

Maisie said, "I don't understand why they always play this music."

"What do you mean?" said Christine. "What's wrong with it?"

"Oh, nothing," Maisie muttered. "Except that it's full of hatred. It's all about people hating each other."

"I can't really hear it," Christine said.

"Oh, come on, girls," Stephanie exhorted. "Get into the spirit of things."

"What do you mean, it's about people hating each other?"

"The words," Maisie said, putting her hands over her ears.

"I quite like it," Christine said, swaying from side to side. "I'm getting quite into it. Stephanie, I'm feeling a dangerous purchase coming on. I'm thinking, you know, let's show some cleavage. I'm thinking, let's show our—what did she call them?"

"Flabby tits," Stephanie said loudly, and then put a hand over her mouth. "Sorry."

In the changing rooms, a girl with a long, white belly like a root and mournful kohled eyes gave them a plastic docket and said:

"There's room for the buggies in the one at the end."

"See?" Stephanie said as they hastened down the row of empty curtained cubicles. "I told you."

"We've been upgraded," Christine said, "to the teen pregnancy suite."

"Maisie, haven't you got anything?" Stephanie said, bending down to let Jasper out of his pushchair, holding the docket between her white, even teeth.

Maisie smiled and shook her head, and seated herself on

the padded bench in the corner of their cubicle. Stephanie stowed her bag and pushchair in another corner. Christine drew the heavy purple curtain and hung her clothes neatly by their hangers on a hook. They were like itinerant people arriving in a new, exiguous room.

"You're making us all feel trivial, Maisie," Christine said. "She's going to go home and tell her husband what a sad, trivial bunch of women we are. She's going to ring up all her London friends and tell them about us."

"Your husband's very handsome, Maisie," Stephanie said, with her smile that turned down at the corners.

"The thing is," Christine said, "I'm having the time of my life here. I mean, we're all so responsible, aren't we? Most of the time we're all such good people, aren't we? We're all such good *wives* and good *mothers*, and there we are feeding our families these healthy meals and taking our children to piano lessons and making our houses all perfect, and sometimes"— she lifted her shirt over her head and revealed her large, blue-veined breasts in their white wired bra—"sometimes you just want to have some fun, don't you? Sometimes I think, God, I could just bring all this down. I could just bring it all down around me. What do you think?"

She turned from side to side in a straining violet chemise tied with little strings at the back.

"Actually," Stephanie said, "that looks really nice."

Christine pondered herself for an instant in the mirror.

"Nice for pulling pints at the Coach and Horses," she said, unbuttoning it again. "God, Stephanie, that's fantastic."

Stephanie had put on a tight green dress with a Chinese collar and a slit all the way up the leg. She twisted around and looked at herself with her head over her shoulder.

"You look amazing," Christine said. "Doesn't she look amazing?"

Stephanie turned to the front again. Her face was excited.

"It's a bit over the top," she said.

"If I had your figure I wouldn't care what it was," Christine said.

Jasper stumbled over his mother's handbag and hit his head against the mirror.

"Oh, darling!" Stephanie cried, wading through the clothes in her green dress to pick him up.

He bawled with his small hand to his forehead as Stephanie resurrected him from the floor.

"Oh, sweetheart! Does it hurt?"

He roared and buried his face in her shoulder, running his hands up and down the unfamiliar silky fabric of her dress. Stephanie sat down with him beside Maisie on the padded bench. She cradled him and rocked him to and fro, ministrations to which her outfit imparted a kind of exotic theatricality. A moment later Ella also began to cry, regarding herself in the mirror.

"Don't you start," Christine said. "I quite like this," she added, turning to them in another top.

"Does it fit?" Stephanie said, over Jasper's laments. "It doesn't look like it quite fits."

"I really like it." Christine looked at herself from one side and then the other. "Oh, Ella, what *is* it?"

"Are you sure?" Stephanie said.

Christine's face was flushed. She rummaged in her bag and took out a beaker of milk, which she thrust into Ella's hands.

"There," she said. "No, I really like it. I really like the colour."

"You've got quite a few things in that colour," Stephanie observed.

"Have I? What, in purple?"

"You're often wearing purple."

"Am I? What, like a bishop? Is that what people say? Oh, look, here comes Christine in her bishop outfit."

Stephanie laughed uncertainly.

"No, not at all," she said.

"Here comes the vicar in drag," Christine persisted. "Here comes the fucking Purple Lady."

"Christine!" said Stephanie shrilly. "I was only talking about the colour."

"I like the colour." Christine regarded her reflection with narrowed eyes. "Ella, if you don't shut up I'm going to rip your tongue out of your throat."

"We should really feed them before long," Stephanie said. "Are you hungry, sweetheart? Jasper, sweetie, are you hungry? Shall Mummy get you some lunch?"

Jasper nodded and pawed her dress.

"Mummy's just going to try on one more thing. One more thing, all right?"

There was a momentary silence while the women removed their outfits. In their underwear they looked strangely destitute, abandoned, like women whose husbands have gone off to war. They moved their learned purplish limbs, their complicated breasts and bellies, as though they were a little thrilled at their freedom but on the verge of a killing knowledge of what it implied.

"I don't *think* so," Stephanie said, in a black cocktail dress held up by thin sequinned straps over the shoulders.

"Why not?" Christine shrugged. "I think it looks great. I think you should buy it."

"You're so sweet!" Stephanie cried. "You want everybody to have everything."

"That's what bishops are like, Stephanie. That's what men of the cloth are fucking into. Here comes the *puuuuurple* lady!" Christine sang, sweeping up Ella in her arms and dancing with her around the narrow cubicle.

Outside in the shop a sudden crowd had formed at the till, of girls with sunglasses pushed back on their heads and girls in tiny vests, girls with hair chemically coloured, curled or straightened, fat girls with white elephant's legs in short skirts, girls who were morose or screamed with laughter or talked into their mobile phones.

"This is annoying," said Christine. "There wasn't anybody in here when we came in."

They stood in the queue. Christine had her purple top draped over her arm. The children were strapped protesting into their pushchairs. Ella was leaning out over the seat and flinging herself sideways at her mother's legs. Christine looked at the others.

"Aren't you buying anything?" she said to Stephanie. "Aren't you going to buy that dress?"

Stephanie wrinkled her nose and shook her head. Christine looked straight ahead of her, into the fleshy, chattering forest of girls.

"This is annoying," she said.

The restaurant was on the top floor and had vast semi-circular windows on three sides that showed three grey views: one of the car park, one of the slip road and the distant motorway, and one of the grilles, pipes, and vents that characterised the domed roof of Merrywood when seen from above. There was a dead seagull lying in one of the gullies, its livid yellow beak flat against the roof, its oiled feathers moving stiffly in the wind.

Inside, a field of Formica-topped tables and chairs covered the carpeted expanses of a hangar-like space that seemed permanently on the brink of a generalised chaos. People threaded through displaced chairs and tables with laden plastic trays. Everywhere landslides of shopping bags spilled out into the aisles, and children's toys and coats lay unnoticed on the floor. Uniformed workers moved around the tables with big sacks, sweeping the discarded casings of dead lunches, the plastic cartons and cardboard and cellophane, the straws and water bottles and paper napkins, the entire packaged forms of the restaurant's Kids Lunchboxes like an unbroken set of geological remains, into their rustling depths. Big groups sat at some tables, their chairs pushed back, presiding raucously over the wreckage of food and trays and rubbish in their midst. Men sat with their arms folded over their swollen bellies, their heads erect, their scrutinising eyes moving around the room like silent searchlights. Elderly couples occupied tables for two, gazing off to either side of them as though watching facing television sets. Pairs of women in their fifties and sixties, dressed as if in preparation for a random event that might lead to their helpless forms being handled by strangers, talked steadily, with their heads close together, large, glossy shopping bags at their feet like well-behaved pets. Here and there a solitary person sat with a book, ingesting a sandwich by self-conscious increments.

Maisie, Stephanie, and Christine moved along the line with their trays, approaching the steaming bedlam of the serving hatch, where elderly men and confused, exacting women were embroiled in long, hopeless, querying exchanges with the staff behind the counters.

"Does the vegetable soup have meat in it?" one lady enquired.

The fleshy Filipina girl standing by the soup shook her head, her arms folded.

"The last time I was here," a white-haired, stammering

man confided to her, "you did a battered fish. A battered cod. Do you know? A fish in batter."

He was so persistent that she turned and went back into the kitchen to enquire. She returned and folded her arms and shook her head.

"Only what's here."

"What's that?"

"Only what's here," she repeated, finally leaning forward to say it into his ear.

Stephanie had a prawn salad in a plastic dome. Maisie had a sandwich skewered by a toothpick with a regal radish on the top. Christine ordered a hamburger and chips.

"Ten minutes," stated the girl.

"I just can't win today, can I?" said Christine. "All right, I'll have something else. No, I won't, I'll have the burger and chips. I don't mind waiting."

Around the walls of the restaurant was a series of enlarged photographs mounted on huge panels, of grass and wildflowers with a background of brilliant blue sky. The grass was the colour of a billiard table. Each blade was a foot high.

"That's nice," said Christine automatically, glancing up at one as they sat down at their table. "This is the first time I've been up here," she added.

"It's like a ferry," said Maisie.

"What *do* you mean?" said Stephanie, looking around her dismayed, as if she thought she might discover she was in fact on a ferry and might be late to collect the children from school.

"It's like a cross-channel ferry."

"I've never heard *that* before," said Stephanie, placing a prawn delicately in her mouth with her fork.

"Everyone looks like they're going somewhere without actually moving."

"Is it the views?" Christine said, perplexed. "Is it those big windows with all that sky around?"

"Why did you and your husband leave London, Maisie?" Stephanie enquired, as though that might explain her peculiar observation.

Maisie withdrew the toothpick from the centre of her sandwich, which fell over on to its side, spilling out marbled shards of salad. She gathered it up and took a bite out of it.

"We thought it would be nicer somewhere else," she said with her mouth full.

"The question isn't, Why did you leave, Stephanie," Christine advised her. "The question is, Why would you stay?"

"So it wasn't because of your husband's work or anything?" Stephanie persisted. "It was because you actually wanted to leave?"

"He didn't want us to leave," Maisie said. "He thought it was a bad idea."

"He didn't want you to?" Christine said. "Why not?"

"Your food," Maisie said. "There's your food."

The girl from the kitchen was wandering amidst the tables, an expression of resignation on her face.

"Let me get this straight," Christine said when her hamburger had come to rest like a pale, puckered planet before her. "Your husband thought it was a bad idea, with two small children, moving from a city of eight million people to Arlington Park. Why exactly did he think that?"

"Not just here," Maisie said. "Anywhere."

"What, anywhere at all?"

"Anywhere you'd go because you thought it was less."

"Less what?" said Christine, confounded.

"Less anything. Less difficult. He thought that as soon as

we got there we'd forget why we'd left and then we wouldn't know why we were living there."

"Everyone's leaving London now," Christine said, picking up her hamburger with both hands. "It's not just the people. It's all the problems they bring with them. It's the pollution and the crime and the drugs. And terrorism! No one's even thought of that, have they?" She leaned forwards, holding her fingers fastidiously out to either side, and bit. "That's one thing you're safe from here. I mean, why would anyone bother to drop a bomb on Arlington Park? Why would they?"

"I'm more frightened here than I was in London," said Maisie.

Christine stopped chewing in astonishment. "What of?"

Maisie did not reply.

"Are you worried you'll go to seed?" Stephanie said, as though this were a hazard she'd once heard of.

"Let me tell you, there's no bloody excuse for going to seed in Arlington Park!" exclaimed Christine. "For people, it's not second-best to anywhere. They may not have degrees, or doctorates, or fascinating jobs—they may not be the wealthiest people you've ever met, or the most famous and important, but believe me, the people I see here every day are the most diverse, interesting, courageous group of people you'll find anywhere! Take the women I meet at the school gate," she continued, with her mouth full. "You could say they're not important, you could even say they're not great intellectuals. The fact is that they do a bloody good job, and they're all interesting, compassionate people. They all want to help each other and make life easier for each other—they'll pick your child up from school if you're running late, they'll do your shopping if you're ill, and all of them have got children to pick up and houses to run themselves. I mean, how many people do you know in London who would care if you dropped dead in the street?"

At this juncture Stephanie excused herself and took Jasper off to the toilet.

"Are you all right for tonight?" Christine asked Maisie in a low voice, once she'd gone. "Dinner at our house, tonight?"

Maisie looked as though she had either forgotten dinner at Christine's house or wanted to.

"We're, um, looking forward to it," she said.

"It's just that I didn't want to mention it in front of Stephanie. Not that I've got anything against Stephanie. She's a really, really nice person. She's not the world's greatest intellectual—I mean, you're never going to hear anything from Stephanie that you haven't heard a thousand times before. But as a kind, nice person who looks after herself and looks after her kids, you can't beat her."

"No," said Maisie.

Christine picked up a broad, yellow chip with her fingers, dipped it in ketchup, and handed it to Ella.

"I mean, don't you think we all just want to have it both ways? We want our secure homes and our husbands and our lovely holidays, and most of the time we've earned them fair and square, and yet sometimes—"

Stephanie returned with Jasper.

Christine said, "I was just telling Maisie how one of these days I'm going to run off to Lanzarote with a sixth-former."

She dipped another chip in ketchup and placed it whole in her mouth.

"Well, that's a relief," Stephanie said, with flushed cheeks.

"What is?"

"Just a little—you know, a little *scare*," Stephanie whispered.

"What, you thought you were pregnant?"

"Not that it wouldn't have been, you know, *fine* and everything," Stephanie said.

"I wouldn't think it was bloody fine," Christine said. "Did you really think you were pregnant? No wonder you didn't buy that dress."

"Oh, I quite like being pregnant really," Stephanie said wistfully.

"What, actually *being* pregnant?" Christine said.

Stephanie reddened further. "It feels, I don't know— fruitful. Like when you're walking down the street, it's like you've got this big sign above your head saying *I have sex.*"

"Half the teenage girls in Firley have that sign, Stephanie."

"Anyway." Stephanie sat up straight in her chair and crossed her legs. "False alarm."

"We never doubted you and Mark had sex," Christine said. "We never doubted Mark was the biggest stud in Arlington Park. You've got four children already, for Christ's sake. Stephanie's got four boys," she informed Maisie. "Let's just hope there isn't a war," she added morbidly.

Beyond the windows a vast, bruised bank of cloud swept in over the grey prairie of the car park, extinguishing the spears of light that lay everywhere in disordered diagonals like discarded, faulty bolts of lightning. The restaurant darkened. A violent deluge of rain flung itself abruptly down over the defenceless landscape.

"When you think of all the terrible things that are happening in the world," Christine said. "When you think of those earthquake victims in Indonesia. We can't complain really, can we?"

"No," said Stephanie.

"People losing their homes and their livelihoods. All of it destroyed in a matter of seconds before their eyes. We just can't imagine what that's like, can we?"

"Or those people in the lorry," Stephanie said. "I was hearing about that on the radio this morning. That is just my *worst* nightmare—being trapped in a confined space."

"What lorry?"

"You know," Stephanie said. "That lorry. They opened the back of a lorry at Dover and found about fifty people in it, all dead."

"Did they?" Christine wore an expression of distaste. Presently she said, "Actually, I don't mind it so much when it's something people have brought on themselves. I mean, you have to ask yourself, what the hell were they doing in the back of a lorry in the first place?"

"They were asylum seekers," Stephanie said.

"Exactly. I can't feel sorry for them. I mean, I know it's a horrible thing to have happened, but they were breaking the law, weren't they? They brought it on themselves, if you want my opinion. I can't feel sorry for them."

"Some of them were actually *children*," Stephanie said. "I mean, I know I'm just being sentimental, but that was what really got to me."

"To be honest, it doesn't matter to me what they were. They shouldn't have been in that lorry."

"You're so *hard* sometimes, Christine," said Stephanie, with her downward-turning smile. "You're so uncompromising."

"I just think, you know, there comes a point. Like I say, I'd be the first one to come and help if it was something that was outside of your control. If an earthquake razed your house to the ground, you'd have my full sympathy. No, what I can't stand is the guilt we're all made to feel about people who have as much control over their lives as we do. What I can't stand is the complaining. Take that lady at school, that black lady, what's her name?—Cordelia."

"Cornelia," Stephanie said.

"Cornelia. What's her little girl called?"

"Safari," Stephanie said.

"Safari. I mean, what kind of name is that for a child? I'm not being funny, but it'd be like you or I calling our daughter Blackpool Sands, wouldn't it? Anyway, what did this Cornelia do but make a complaint to the school governors about one of the teachers being racist! So now they're having to investigate the complaint and instigate all sorts of official procedures, and basically waste a whole load of time on one single child that they should be spending on educational priorities for all of them. I mean, for Christ's sake. She sends her child to a school where hers is more or less the only black face and then she complains that it's racist!"

Stephanie pouted, and bent down to retrieve Jasper's dummy from where it had fallen to the floor.

Christine said, "I think everyone agrees with me. It's just that they don't want to say so. Don't get me wrong," she added presently. "I've got nothing against Cornelia personally. I think she's a nice lady. God, we're all so politically correct!" she expostulated gloomily, looking out of the windows to where the rain was hurling itself in great careless sheets on to the roof.

"What do you think, Maisie?" Stephanie said.

Maisie looked as though Stephanie had just deposited a live snake in her lap.

"About what?" she said.

"About, you know, who we should feel sorry for."

"I feel sorry for anyone who's got to go out in that," Christine interjected. "That's who I feel sorry for. It's like a bloody biblical visitation. If we don't go now," she informed them, looking at her watch, "we'll have to park half a mile away from the school, and I haven't got a rain cover for the buggy. You'd have thought at least I'd have been able to sort that out by now," she said as they rose from the table. "That shouldn't have been too hard, should it? All this time I spend sorting out the world's problems and getting heated over asylum seekers I could have been finding the rain cover, and making sure Ella has a proper coat, and tidying up the children's room so that Danny doesn't have to get into the same sheets he wet last night, and buying some food for us all to eat this evening. I could just be sorting out my life, couldn't I?"

"Oh, come on," Stephanie said. "You were loving it, trying on all those clothes."

"My problem is that I've forgotten how to have fun," Christine said. "I think we've all forgotten how to just have fun. I get so worked up about asylum seekers and earthquake victims and abducted children and the bloody starving millions that I forget to enjoy myself. That's the tragedy here. I mean, what a waste! What a waste of a good life, not to enjoy it."

She surveyed the broken spectacle of the after-lunch restaurant. The sky was so heavy that the lights had been turned on. Dark-skinned men and women slowly trawled the tables with their big plastic sacks, sweeping rubbish into them.

Maisie, Stephanie, and Christine gathered their belongings and headed for the escalators.

Downstairs the rain fell silently beyond the automatic glass doors, to the acoustics of the perennially splashing fountain.

"Shall we wait and see if it stops?" Stephanie said, sitting on the edge of the fountain with the condescension of a decorative marble nymph.

"I think we're talking forty days and forty nights here,"

Christine said, regarding the vista of the car park through narrowed eyes. "We're talking mating pairs only."

"Jasper, *don't* get out of your chair. No, don't, darling."

Jasper undid his straps and got out of his chair.

"That's silly, Jasper," Stephanie said pettishly, swinging her hair back from her face. "We're going out in the rain. You've got to stay in your chair."

She made to pick Jasper up, but he put his hands on her thighs and braced himself against them. She struggled with him girlishly and he forced her off.

"All right, then," she said in a high voice. "You'll have to get wet. Silly boys get wet, Jasper."

She turned her back on him and bent down to pick up her bags. Behind her he raised his arm, took a swift run-up, and landed a forceful slap on her bottom.

"*Jasper!*"

She straightened up, red in the face, and began petulantly wheeling the empty pushchair towards the automatic doors. Maisie and Christine followed. The doors exhaled them into the startling cold and wind of the car park, where long, grey needles of rain were hailing down on to the asphalt and a kind of smoky emanation of petrol fumes and condensation was hanging in a pall around the lines of cars. The women started to run, Stephanie occasionally turning around to exhort Jasper to keep up with them. Christine reached her car first and once there she opened the boot with a calm that was almost leisurely and proceeded to place her bags in the back while Ella sat in the rain, before unstrapping her and carrying her around to the side.

Christine never liked to panic. It suggested one was taking life in a spirit of entirely inappropriate severity.

She saw Maisie Carrington walking insensible as a cow through the rain, her eyes looking straight ahead, Jasper trotting just in front of her with his eyes screwed shut to keep out the water. A big black four-wheel-drive car, lavishly shiny, ablaze with lights, clouds billowing from its exhaust like smoke from a dragon's nostrils, began to reverse out of its parking space, and Christine saw a look of horror fly into Maisie's face, and saw her lunge forward silently—she did commend her for this, it being an article of panic to shout at children in the path of danger—in order to grab Jasper beneath the arms and lift him out of the way as the car made its black, barge-like progress out into the road.

She watched as Maisie made her way around to the side of the four-wheel-drive, water streaming down her face, with Jasper still in her hands. She held him up at the driver's window. She held him up as Christine had seen on the news people in war zones holding up the bodies of dead children at the passing tanks. Maisie held his face at the tinted glass. She was shouting. Christine could see the woman on the other side of the glass. She could see her white-blond hair, her lipsticked mouth, her big gold earrings, the sunglasses pushed back on her head, the carrier bags on the passenger seat. She could even see her unseasonal tan.

"This is a child!" Maisie was shouting. "This is a child!"

She held the boy up in the rain, shouting. She shouted things Christine couldn't hear. The woman was looking at her with an expression of loathing, with a hatred whose purity had been painstakingly distilled in a refinery of intricate, undisturbed selfishness.

"You stupid fucking bitch!" Maisie Carrington screamed at her, her wet hair plastered over her face, as the woman accelerated out and with a V-sign from her red-taloned fingers roared away.

Christine was surprised. She didn't know what to make of it at all. It wasn't as if the woman had actually *hurt* Jasper.

She probably didn't even *see* him in that great big car. You couldn't go around shouting at people for things that weren't actually their fault. The thing was, she thought as she drove through the rain back to Arlington Park, everyone had their particular bugbears, didn't they? It was one of the things that made people so interesting. Everyone had particular things that got to them, that made them see red.

It was just one of those things about life.

It was Solly Kerr-Leigh who had first thought of having a foreign student in the spare room. She had seen an advertisement in the *Arlington Gazette*. Got a spare room? it read. Want to earn some extra cash?

She had got a spare room, and she did want to earn some extra cash: it was just that she had never regarded the two propositions as being related. Sometimes she sat in the spare room, which had a sash window overlooking the garden and a neatly made double bed whose pillows were always plumped up, and it did seem to Solly like a kind of fund, an investment, in that she expended the same efforts here as she did everywhere else in the house, yet only here did these efforts actually accrue. No one ever came in to squander them. Martin's parents visited twice a year and tactfully left the room as they had found it. Otherwise, it remained for the most part untouched, ringing up its weekly balance of housework.

It had white curtains and a white counterpane, and a beige carpet that was as rich and promising as on the day it had been laid. It had fitted wardrobes on whose rails the coat hangers hung deliriously empty. There was a little antique bedside table with only a vase of dried flowers on it, and a mahogany chest with nothing in the drawers. When Solly sat there, the weight of her family seemed to move away from her, like a great crowded liner decked with lights moving out into a dark ocean. She imagined she was a girl, sitting in her simple girl's room. At other times she felt like a guest in her own house, a person who might be taken care of, though she didn't know by whom. But most of all, in the spare room Solly felt she could see what her intentions had been: it was like a little fold in the densely patterned cloth of life, which by chance had remained unexposed to the relentless glare of her household and hence retained its true colours while all the rest had faded.

And as for money—well, if you had a house to run and a husband and three children and were pregnant with your fourth, it was a question not of getting more but of pawning what you had. It seemed to Solly that her life had a lot of fat: the difficulty lay in finding a place to trim it off, when everything was connected to everything else. That was why it took the advertisement to get her started. It wasn't that she and Martin *needed* money, in the sense of desperation. It was more that everything she, Solly, did, cost it; and once you started to think about it like that, you became sensitive. You saw yourself in a kind of free fall, uncontrolled, expanding and expanding into a great, expectant precariousness. Once, Solly had felt powerful in her expansiveness, but now, pregnant for the fourth time, she felt aerated, overblown, while Martin seemed correspondingly to harden into a lean, vertical masculinity. He went to work and came back again with a kind of rotary, mechanical movement, back and forth, back and forth, round and round and round like the steel arm of Solly's electric mixer, beating her up into a more and more voluminous foam. She felt an immense need to make contact with some kind of restraining surface. She wanted to feel a boundary with the world, before she was diffused entirely into fleshly relatedness. The spare room appeared to her as the place where this boundary could be established. As her point of entry from the lost simplicity of life, so it was also to be her means of return from all this marshy expansiveness towards a new independence. Once she'd installed a television up there, apparently, she could expect to get eighty pounds a week for it.

Martin thought it was a marvellous idea.

"What about the children?" he said doubtfully.

"They won't seem so bad to a foreigner," said Solly. "And I'll enjoy having company the nights you're in Reading."

Tuesdays and Wednesdays, Martin stayed in Reading for work.

"There's no point having it just sitting there, is there?" he said.

"No."

"Eighty pounds a week." He blew out his cheeks and sat back in his chair.

"*If* there's a television. They have to have a television, apparently."

"It might do the children good, having a stranger in the house. It might put them on their best behaviour."

"It might," Solly said.

"They might even learn a foreign language," Martin said.

First there was Betty. She was a Taiwanese girl with a neat, pretty face and a wide white smile, who wore beautiful clothes made of printed silks. One day she came downstairs wearing a pair of black silk trousers with pink roses embroidered on them, little flat embroidered shoes, and a little pink jacket with silk-covered buttons; and Solly didn't know why, but the sight of these things made her eyes fill with tears. They reminded her of something, of childhood, of things that were small and perfect and mysteriously beautiful.

Betty gave Solly's daughter, Dora, a Chinese silk bag with

a long, braided handle. She wrote little letters to the boys, William and Joseph, and left them on their pillows, wrapped around two chocolates in the shape of dragons covered in brightly coloured foil.

"Do you miss your family, Betty?" Solly asked.

"Oh yes, I miss them very much," Betty said. "In Taiwan we are a very close family."

She placed the palms of her hands together with the fingers ardently splayed.

Betty had a French boyfriend who came to pick her up two or three times a week. Solly would open the door and there would be Gustave, standing on the doorstep in the dark with the collar of his coat turned up, dramatically breathing out misty plumes of night air. He looked like an old-fashioned film star, with his collar turned up and his long, delicate nose.

"Ees Betty there?" he would enquire, and Solly would feel not that her life had changed exactly but that it had altered its course, that it had turned a little, away from what was fast and easy and irresistible into a slanting, sideways trajectory where the water was choppier and the winds slightly contradictory. It was more effortful, steering this course, but it yielded more sensation, more movement, more impressions of life. At first Solly wasn't sure what it all added up to. Then she decided that it was like taking a different route to somewhere you went every day. You got to the same place in the end, but saw other things along the way.

On the nights she went out with Gustave, Betty did not return to the house until the next day. If Martin was in Reading, Solly would sit on the sofa alone, feeling slightly implicated in all the life that was being lived elsewhere, as though she had suddenly become the head of an organisation responsible for despatching agents into the field of human experience. Martin returned one Thursday to find Betty sitting at the kitchen table with the children, teaching them to use her laptop computer, and he raised his eyebrows admiringly to Solly over their heads.

"The nights that I am here," Betty said, in her excellent, high-pitched, accented English that was like a fine thread which unspooled continuously from her mouth, "it is perfectly okay for you to leave the children and go out. And please, I will not accept any payment. It is a pleasure for me to spend time with these lovely children. It is okay for you?"

Martin and Solly found themselves facing each other in a restaurant, slightly startled, as though they had hurtled down to their table from a great height.

"Extraordinary," Martin said.

"Isn't it?" said Solly.

"I went upstairs to turn their light out," Martin said, "and there was Betty, sitting on the bed reading them a story."

"Amazing," said Solly.

"And I said, Come on, that's enough, let Betty go downstairs, it's time to go to sleep. And Betty says"—Martin was beside himself with excitement—"Betty says, Oh, *please*, can we just read a few more pages?"

Solly related this tale to several of her friends. She thought she had forgotten some important aspect of it. It always sounded a little as though she and Martin were auditioning Betty for the role of the children's new mother.

She never went into her spare room now that Betty was there, but one afternoon, passing the door, she heard the children in there. Immediately she entered, and found them sprawled on the bed watching television while Betty sat crosslegged on the floor doing her coursework from the language centre. Little foil chocolate wrappers lay discarded everywhere—forty wrappers at least—and the television was spewing out demented rubbish like a box of madness. William had chocolate around his mouth. He was lying on his back with his head hanging over the edge of the bed so that he was watching it upside down. Dora had her legs propped up against the wall and her knickers were showing. Joseph was bouncing on the bed. The bodies of the other two jolted imperviously up and down when he jumped.

Solly was outraged. Suddenly it was all—well, outrageous. Minutes earlier she had been sitting in a chair in the kitchen, her pregnant belly queasily tight, like a great sagging balloon filled to bursting with water. She had heard the silence in the house and guessed that the children had been magnetised by Betty, by her dense, neat form emitting its vigorous waves of attraction. And so she had chosen to believe in something miraculous: to find repose, for a while, with Martin away until Thursday and her flagging body fit to burst, in the concept of intervention. That was the problem, the outrage. She had given in to the temptation of believing something might help.

"In Betty's culture," she explained to her friends, "children are dealt with by means of a non-stop diet of sweets and television. Which is all very well at the time, until someone else has to pick up the pieces."

After six weeks Betty announced that she was returning to Taiwan. Solly was devastated, in a way. She still believed in her religion of Betty—she couldn't conceive of believing in anyone else.

"What about Gustave?" she asked.

Betty nodded. "He is very sad," she said.

In her last week she reprogrammed the Kerr-Leighs' computer and taught them how to set the video recorder. She entered the children's birthdays into Martin's mobile phone, so that it would set off an alarm when the time came.

Shortly after she had gone, Gustave phoned. Qi Shu had left two textbooks at the house which he had promised to collect and return to the language centre.

"Who?" said Solly.

There was a silence.

"Oh, sorry, I forget," Gustave said. "You call her Betty."

"Was that not her name?" Solly asked.

"But of course not," Gustave said sombrely.

Aghast, Solly said, "Why did she ask us to call her Betty?"

"She said people here did not remember her Chinese name," Gustave explained. "It was easier for her to use an English name."

After Betty came Katzmi, a whey-faced, doleful Japanese girl with English so primitive that Solly continually found herself at the edge, at the very limit of her own civilised self, vacillating there as though on the perimeter of a vast darkness. Now that she could no longer communicate, she became aware of how much of her lay shrouded in this inarticulable darkness. Yet she could not navigate it either. It was like a big black prairie she saw from her lit porch. She became a kind of animal, pantomiming enquiries and requests, acting out her own consciousness with bodily heaves and grimaces. Her body, seven months pregnant, spoke for itself, in any case. She was under strain, and Katzmi was too. Blindly, dimly, their natures touched. The contact was like a fine nib guided crazily with fingers encased in concrete. At night she sometimes heard Katzmi crying in her room.

"You?" Solly said the next morning, pointing at Katzmi. "Crying?" She trailed her fingers down her own red-veined cheeks.

Katzmi nodded and looked at her sympathetically.

For the children Katzmi's presence was like the presence of a raw wound in which their worst selves multiplied. It was as though she reminded them that being normal was something they'd only recently heard about and could easily forget. Children needed to be surrounded by confident people, Solly decided. They were like little flames that caught hold of anything unfixed, anything carelessly disposed, and burned it up.

"Eighty pounds a week, don't forget," said Martin.

Gone were the evenings in restaurants; the Kerr-Leighs' spare room was no longer riding high. Solly didn't want to go to restaurants, in any case. She roamed the rooms of her house like a big bear in a small pen. At dinner the children fought and spat out their food, and Dora looked more cross-eyed than usual. Once, Joseph swiped at Dora with his fork and made a little sickle-shaped cut on her cheek that bled. Another time she spilled her Ribena down her front so that it looked like a great bloodstain across her chest, and Solly was too tired and dispirited to do anything about it. Katzmi sat like a graven image in a church, and when Martin was in Reading, Solly found that she inhabited some of Katzmi's impassivity, so that they sat there like two forlorn abbesses in a rioting refectory. William had a gob of glittering mucus on his upper lip that stayed there for two weeks as the repellent testimony to his robustness.

"I'm sorry," Solly said to Katzmi. They were doing the washing up. Katzmi was drying a saucepan with agonising slowness and care. Solly splayed her wet hands penitently across her chest. "I'm SORRY."

Sometimes Katzmi's impenetrability appeared to Solly as a country she had never visited and would never now visit. At other times it seemed to extend a sort of dark invitation to her, like a well into which she yearned to cast her bloated form. Once or twice, when Katzmi was at the language centre, Solly had put her head around the spare room door and was overpowered by its neutrality. There was nothing to show that Katzmi lived there at all, except for a teddy bear placed on the neatly plumped-up pillows, where a mother, or someone imitating one, might have placed it.

One night Katzmi emerged from her room and tried to engage Martin and Solly in conversation. She made futile sounds and gesticulated and laughed pitiably at herself.

The next day someone from the language centre called and said that Katzmi had decided to go and live with another family.

"Is she going back to Japan?" Solly asked.

"No, it's a local family," the woman said.

"A family here? In Arlington Park?"

"They're a local family," the woman said.

Katzmi left. Shortly afterwards, when Solly was eight months pregnant, Paola arrived.

Solly had felt before the way everything altered just before a child was born. It was how she sometimes thought it might be to approach death. Everything grew very slightly remote: the fit of life loosened, as though it were a skin preparing itself to be shed. And although when the baby came it would restart it all with its unstoppable vegetable growth, there was a layer of Solly that was always irretrievably lost. She was depleted, of some aspect of experience, of history: it was torn from her, like the wrapping paper from a present. Generally she believed that this was what she had been born for. She was grateful that she had been able to put herself to such prolific use. And the children gave so much back to you, of course. She was like a sack stuffed with their love and acknowledgement, lumpy on the outside but full, heavy with interior knowledge. It was just that sometimes she tried to think about the past and couldn't. She couldn't locate a continuous sense of herself. It seemed to lie all around her in pieces, like the casings of Dora's Russian doll when all the babies were out.

Martin, on the other hand, didn't seem to have changed at all over the years. He had only weathered a little, like a monument. The more formless and dissipated Solly became, the more astonished she was by his lean, untouched masculinity, his body that had never been plundered, the line that seemed to run unbroken from his toes to the top of his head. He was so—flat. The children were flat too. She realised that Martin was continuous with his child self and she envied him. Life seemed to stand in them all like a standing jet of water in the middle of a fountain. She couldn't imagine what it was like. In the past few years Martin had developed little breasts. You could only see them when he took his shirt off. At night, getting undressed in their room, he would walk around shyly, like a teenaged girl. She thought it must be quite pleasant for him, after all this time, to have developed the breasts of a teenaged girl. It was a sort of consolation prize for all he'd missed out on, though she didn't suppose he saw it like that. If he'd ever envied her her woman's body he probably didn't now. He was loyal to it, that was all. For Martin, her body was like a village that over time had sprawled and grown until it became a bustling centre, cut through with new roads and modern developments, some of them unsightly. It had changed, but it was where he lived.

She was in the garden when Paola arrived, and it might have been the fact that she had half forgotten she was coming, or just the shrill noise of the doorbell piercing the grey folds of the March morning, or the delayed way in which incidents penetrated the great pause of pregnancy and caused her heart to quiver in the jellied depths of her body; whichever it was, it so happened that the moment of Paola's arrival was the moment Solly was besieged, out of the blue, by a crisis of the flesh.

She was out there with Joseph: the other children were at

school. He was riding his plastic tricycle. Solly, dressed in tracksuit bottoms, was standing on the wet rectangle of lawn in one of those null states she often entered in the presence of the children, when she forgot that she existed, or at least forgot to act as though she did. Joseph's tricycle wouldn't go. He was shunting it an inch at a time over the lumpy grass. Solly stared at the brown fence and the brown trunk of the tree and the brown earth of the flowerbeds. In the deadening grey light the yellow plastic of Joseph's tricycle possessed an almost intolerable reality. It seemed vaguely to Solly to be the colour of her life, of midweek mornings spent at home with children. Time extended around her like a grey ocean, moving imperceptibly in its depths. She could not distinguish her own body: it was part of the grey ocean, on which only the shred of her soul floated, swaying this way and that.

Then she noticed, in the far corner of the garden beneath the tree, a little clump of primroses. She walked slowly across the grass and stood over them. They were so delicate, so pretty—she towered over them like some dumb, shaggy creature that has just issued from its cave, examining the beautiful intricacy of life. Their petals were beaded with rain. She looked at them, dimly remembering the line of a song.

The flowers all wet with rain.

What was that song? What was it? She sang the line to herself.

The flowers all wet with rain.
The flowers all wet with rain.

Out of a deep cavern of memory it came. It was a song by Van Morrison—someone she knew used to play it on a guitar. Then, like a little fork of lightning, her recollection lit its own instantaneous path down the twisted ways into the cavern of memory. She remembered a boy, a boyfriend she had for a while who played that song on his guitar. She was eighteen or nineteen—she remembered wearing jeans so threadbare her slender knees showed through, sitting cross-legged on the floor. She sat cross-legged on a rug on the floor, twisting in her fingers a string of beads she wore around her neck. She remembered a lamplit room, and the music, and the taut, ravenous feeling of her young body. How strange that she should have forgotten it! How strange that it should have been there all along, this memory, alive and intact but buried, hidden, like the child in her belly was hidden!

It was then, just as Solly brought forth this naked recollection, expelled it into the light, that Paola rang the doorbell; and the sound flew like an arrow across the garden and pierced its flesh and a jet of hot sensation came flooding out. Solly stood as it passed over her, the overpowering memory of youth, the release of her eighteen-year-old self, all the imprisoned reality of Van Morrison and her minstrel boyfriend and flowers that trembled with beads of rain. It was so beautiful! It was so beautiful and yet so lost, so utterly lost and unavailing!

The doorbell rang again.

"Mummy!" Joseph shouted crossly, pointing towards the house.

With shaking legs, Solly went lumbering inside and down the passage and opened the front door. A woman stood there with a large suitcase.

"Solly Curly?" she said.

"Kerr-*Leigh*," Solly automatically amended.

It had required a certain bravado, all those years before, to insist that her name be hyphenated with Martin's rather than replaced by it. That was what she thought marriage should be: the state of hyphenation. Yet most of the people they knew pronounced it as the woman had just done, as one word with the emphasis on the first syllable. That syllable was Martin's: it seemed a particularly insidious form of discrimination.

"Paola Rocco," the woman said in a firm, businesslike tone. She rolled the *r* expertly.

"Oh!" said Solly.

Paola extended a slim brown hand across the threshold and Solly took it. She was still in her dream of Van Morrison, and the feeling of Paola's hand took her by surprise. It was as though her, Solly's, flesh, the thick hide of her accustomed self, had been peeled back and a softer, more receptive surface revealed. It felt like Paola's hand had spoken to her. The sensation of a warm brown hand, a stranger's hand, passed into Solly as if through an open vein. The guttering image of the girl in the threadbare jeans flared into life again.

"Did you forget me?" Paola then said, with a little crooked smile and a penetrating sideways glance.

"Absolutely not," Solly said emphatically, standing back to let Paola in.

When Paola pulled her suitcase into the hall, Solly was surprised to remember that she had to press her enormous body right against the wall if Paola was to get it past.

"She's Italian," she said to Martin on the telephone.

Martin was in Reading.

"Right-o," he said, as though preparing for the Italians was one of the many ordinary things he could accomplish in a day.

"It's just that for some reason I thought she would be Spanish. Did you think that?"

"To be honest," Martin said, "I forgot she was coming."

Solly felt more than usually chagrined by this remark. Whenever there was a baby coming, Martin started forgetting things. She felt that he did it to lower her expectations of him.

"She's very stylish," she said.

"Is she?"

"Very."

"Well, she won't last long in our house, then," Martin said.

Solly was outraged. "Why do you say that?"

"All I'm saying," Martin said, "is that it's not the sort of place you could imagine a stylish person would want to spend much time."

"What a thing to say about your own family!"

"It's true," said Martin stubbornly. "Look, I'm not saying it's your fault. It goes with the territory, that's all. Children and style don't mix. There's all their stuff, for a start. How can you be stylish when you're always sitting down on pieces of Lego, or stepping in some half-eaten thing they've left on the floor, or having to watch videos about weird creatures with television sets in their stomachs? And then you pull up next to some girl in a sports car at the traffic lights and realise that you've still got one of their jingly tapes playing—"

Solly was silent.

"The other day," Martin continued, "I opened my brief-case in a meeting and pulled out one of Dora's pink plastic ponies—you know, the one with the long, sparkly blue hair. That was not particularly stylish. You're the same," he stated when Solly still did not speak. "You're always saying that there's no point in wearing nice clothes because they just get ruined. You say you don't have time to wash your hair or put on make-up. It's not anyone's fault. It's just the way it is. That's all I'm saying."

On her first evening Paola asked if she could take a bath. A while later, Solly became aware of a smell—a beautiful, exotic smell—stealing into the kitchen and intertwining itself with the brutal aromas of the children's supper. She went out and stood at the bottom of the stairs. The smell filled the hall: it seemed to stand in an airy column of lavender and pink. Solly breathed it in, mesmerised. It was the smell of flowers, of a garden at dusk. It was the smell of flowers all wet with rain. The children joined her at the bottom of the stairs and like her lifted their faces upwards.

"What's that?" said William.

"It's perfume," said Dora.

"It's bath oil," said Solly.

Alarmed, William turned on his heel and returned to the kitchen.

When she descended, Paola asked:

"What is the name Solly?"

She was wearing white jeans and a white sweater, a uniform Solly looked at in alarmed, darting little glances. No one in the Kerr-Leigh household had *ever* worn white: it was inappropriate for the local conditions, which required clothing suitable for manual labour. Solly could not have been more surprised if Paola had appeared naked.

"It's Solange, really," she said. "That's a French name."

She was frying sausages for the children. Their little fat impertinent forms hissed and spat at her from the pan.

"Solange." Unlike Solly, Paola pronounced it correctly. "Your mother was French?"

"No, she's English. I suppose she just liked it."

"It was a little—what—daydream?" Paola twirled her hand fancifully in the air.

Solly saw William approach Dora where she lay on the carpet watching television with her thumb in her mouth and kick her in the head.

"William!" she shrieked, moving swiftly towards him from the stove with the frying pan full of sausages still in her hand. Smoke and grease billowed up into her face. "I saw that! *And* you were wearing your shoes!"

Dora wailed, her hand to her head, her thumb still in her

131

mouth and her eyes never leaving the screen. William stood there sullenly. Solly felt that she hated him. She noticed that his eyes were too close together. In fact, his whole face looked as though at some point it had been squeezed hard on either side. She returned to the stove, where Paola was delicately picking lint off her sweater.

"You were saying—about your mother," she said.

"Oh yes." Solly felt flustered. "She did love France. She'd have liked to live there."

Paola shrugged. "Why didn't she?"

"I suppose no one would let her," Solly said, a little daringly.

"You as well? You wouldn't let her?"

"She could go now. There's nothing to stop her now, you know."

"Maybe it's too late," Paola said. "You have to save up some life for that. Maybe she spent it all."

Solly considered this while she served the children their supper. She considered it as she dragged them up the stairs and stripped the clothes from their strong, writhing bodies. She thought about it as she waded, exhausted, a kind of red light showing around the edge of her vision, through the devastations of their rooms. She threw the covers on top of them, snapped off the lights, closed the door on their screams, and trod heavily back downstairs, gripping the banister and wondering what—if anything—remained to her of the fund of life she had been given.

"I will make a light vegetarian dinner," Paola said when Solly returned to the kitchen. "I have all the ingredients. I would be pleased if you would share it with me."

She had stacked the children's plates in a neat pile beside the sink. The candles were lit. The television had been turned off. There was music playing, unidentifiably soft.

"Are you sure?" Solly said, feeling that her world had been twitched to the side, like a curtain that is obscuring the view, and not particularly minding the feeling.

"Of course," Paola responded, with proprietorial severity.

Solly collapsed into a chair.

In one month's time she would have another baby; she thought that perhaps she had changed her mind and would not be needing it now. Suddenly she saw her life as a breeding ground, a community under a rock. This baby had occurred almost by itself: it seemed to her to have arisen out of an abject mulch of flesh, out of bodies so long confined together that they spawned other bodies. There was a lack of light, a lack of higher purpose to it all. How could she have forgotten to find out what else there was? How could she have stayed there, under her rock, down in the mulch, and forgotten to take a look outside and see what was going on? All at once she didn't know what she'd been thinking of.

"Where in Italy do you come from, Paola?" she asked blearily.

Paola was chopping something very finely with a knife.

"Bologna," she said.

"Oh." Solly yawned. "Like the sauce."

Paola tilted her head sceptically to one side, as though to an English foul committed at football, and continued chopping.

"I hope the children won't bother you," Solly added.

"They are not mine," Paola replied.

"You're meant to like them more if they're yours."

This was the type of thing you were permitted to say in Arlington Park at the end of a long day's domestic slavery, but Paola appeared to take it seriously.

"You don't like them?" she said. "They seem quite normal to me."

Solly laughed, but tears surged painfully to her eyes.

"I'm glad they do," she said, and in a way she was quite glad.

She was surprised to discover that Paola was thirty-four.

"What have you been doing all this time?" she wanted to ask, but instead she said, "What brought you to England?"

"There was a man," Paola said. "When the man left, I decided to stay."

"An Italian man?"

Barely perceptibly, Paola nodded.

"He had a job here. He is an"—she paused—"aeronautical engineer. After a year he had to go home."

Solly was seething with questions. It was strange: in Paola's presence she felt herself to be a failure, yet a part of her believed that a woman of thirty-four with no husband or children was the greatest failure of all. It was a kind of unstoppable need for resolution that grew from her like ivy over the prospect of freedom and tried to strangle it. She couldn't bear the idea of loose threads, of open spaces, of stories without endings. Did Paola not want to get married? Did she not want children, and a house of her own? She sat there in her white sweater, delicately eating. Solly, a sack stuffed with children, a woman who had spent and spent her life until there was none left, sat opposite her, impatient for more.

"My husband goes away for work on Tuesdays and Wednesdays," Solly said.

Slowly Paola nodded.

"Then on those days we can eat together like this," she said.

When Paola was at the language centre and the children were at school, Solly went into the spare room. For a while she stood, alert, as though listening. She heard the sounds of a bird singing in the tree outside and cars passing along the road. She heard the sound of Paola's clock on the bedside table, ticking slow, Italian seconds. The room was full of a new, pillowy scent. Presently she opened the wardrobe door. There was the white sweater on a hanger. Other things hung there too: a pair of black trousers, a tiny jacket with embroidery on the collar, a beautiful ruffled shirt. She put her fingers to the fine cloth. She took out a pair of high-heeled leather boots with narrow toes and stood them next to her own swollen feet. Then she went to the mahogany chest of drawers and looked at all the bottles and jars that stood on it. She found the bath oil, in a glass bottle with a stopper. She looked in Paola's pink satin washbag and found make-up in heavy little black enamelled cases and a foil packet of contraceptive pills. She opened one of the drawers and took out lace garments, things with buttons and ribbons, a garter belt, and a long, fine, gossamer-like pair of stockings. There was a small black leather case hidden amongst the underwear and she opened it and saw a pair of pearl earrings lying in a white satin bed.

She felt a terrible pain at the sight of these things. It seemed both an ally of the pain she had been caused by the primroses and a negation of it. What were her threadbare jeans and her string of beads compared with this? They were the abortion, the pitiful remnant of her feminity. She felt she had nothing—nothing! She forced herself to look in the mirror that hung above the mahogany chest, and the sight of her face brought tears to her red-rimmed eyes. It was blotchy, lined, pixillated with stress. Her hair stood in a sort of brown frizz around it. Was it real, this terrible feeling of injustice? Was it rational and real, or was she mistaken, was there some explanation for it, something that could make it all equal and right?

At the back of the drawer she found a photograph of a

child, a little boy of two or three: a nephew, she supposed, or perhaps a godson. He had thick, dark, curly hair. A kind of yearning rose automatically in her breast. She felt like a machine, like an animal—she was automatic, voracious, unstoppable. She would have sucked the little boy right out of the frame if she could. Oh, to have self-control! To keep a child in a frame at the back of your drawer, next to a pair of pearl earrings!

She returned to the kitchen and sat in her chair. An intense feeling of shame descended on her. In her belly the baby squirmed powerfully. She clutched at it with her hands. No one could ever understand the feeling of a human body struggling inside you. It defied understanding. If you thought about it, you would go mad. If you thought about it, you would feel you were all alone in the world, and that even the baby wanted you gone.

In the evening, when Martin returned, Solly immediately went and lay down on the sofa in the sitting room. She stayed there until she had heard the children be fed, bathed, and taken away upstairs. She felt that if she had to spend even one more minute with them she would explode. She heard Martin bellowing on the top landing, and the sounds of multitudinous footsteps running this way and that. Really, Martin was wonderful. He was what you called a hands-on father. The trouble was, he was never here.

"Any—ah—thoughts about dinner?" he said at one point, creeping into the sitting room and looking at her over the back of the sofa.

"No," she said.

"Right." He furrowed his brow and went away again.

Later she heard the sound of the front door. It was Paola. She listened to the sound of Martin and Paola talking in the kitchen. Martin would say something, and after a long pause

Paola would say something much shorter. Presently she heard the soft sound of Paola's footsteps going up the stairs and the little thud of the spare-room door closing.

"She seems all right," Martin said when they were in bed.

"She's nice," Solly said.

"A bit—you know—mysterious and all that," Martin ventured.

Solly wondered what "all that" might be, but was too tired to ask.

"How old do you think she is?" Martin said.

"She's thirty-four."

"Really?" He seemed surprised. "Then she's only two years younger than you."

"And you."

"I suppose so," Martin said. "I'd have thought she was younger than that," he added, somewhat professorially, as though working out women's ages was something for which he had a certain renown.

"That was what she said."

"Did she? Oh."

Martin turned out the light. Solly lay on her back with the great dome of her belly gilded by yellow light from the street-lamp outside. The thought of the coming night filled her with dread. Now that the baby was almost here she could not find non-being even in sleep. All night she was held in a kind of ante-room of unconsciousness, a place of movement and noises and yellow light.

"Do you think she likes, you know—girls?" Martin said next to her in the darkness.

Solly did not answer. After a while she wasn't even sure he'd said it. In the strange, whirling, light-cluttered realm of her body she felt only an immense confusion. She felt she contained everything, all good and evil, every possibility, everything in the world all jumbled together, shaken up like the sea by a storm so that nothing was clear and separate; it was all opaque, nauseating, full of litter and rubbish. She burned to expel from her this great, mounting force of debris, to clarify herself. In this state she did not feel hyphenated with Martin. All night, in her skimming, whirling sleep, she felt merged with him, unshielded, indistinct. She had no protection from him. It was the worst kind of terror really, to live in a body and yet feel it offered you no protection. It became difficult even to distinguish dreams from reality. Everywhere things merged and were jumbled all together, bad and good.

What separated you, Solly dimly thought, was your moral sense. That was all you really had. That was the only way you could tell things apart. Once you'd lost that, you'd lost everything.

It transpired that Paola had a job. Three afternoons a week she gave advice at a law centre down in the city. It was just a little hobby, she said. She didn't know enough about English law to get a real job. That was why she was here trying to improve her language, to get a qualification.

"What sort of people do you—advise?" Solly asked.

"People with problems," Paola said severely. "Poor people."

In the kitchen cupboards, where Solly had cleared a space for Paola to put her things, there was now a little collection of fascinating items. There were jars of herbs and packets of lentils and dried beans, and a wooden box filled with sachets of something called a *tisane*. When Paola was out Solly would unscrew the jars and smell what was inside. She would gaze at the fragrant sachets in their box, all neatly arranged. Paola was a vegetarian. It seemed, somehow, to emphasise her distance from the crude life of the body. Opening Paola's cupboard, Solly was overcome by the same sensory feeling of femininity she had experienced amidst the contents of Paola's underwear drawer. It gave her an innocent, unsullied feeling of sex. Solly's cupboards were full of giant supermarket value-packs and bottles of Martin's Worcestershire sauce. In the past Solly had felt proud of these things, practical and proud, but now they seemed monstrous to her in a way. Why had she required such bulk, so much heaviness? What was she afraid of?

She had gone outside with a pair of scissors and cut the primroses, and arranged them in a glass on the kitchen table. By the end of the day they had wilted.

"In Bologna I had my own law practice," Paola said.

"Did you?" Solly was amazed. "What happened?"

"Nothing." Paola shrugged. "I gave it up. I couldn't see the future there. I lived only in one dimension."

Solly was silent. Did Paola believe that a life with the Kerr-Leighs was a life of more than one dimension?

"I prefer my little hobby. It has more reality."

"But you must have had friends, and family, and—all sorts of things!" Solly blurted out.

They were sitting at the kitchen table, around the wilted primroses. The children were in bed and Martin was in Reading. Solly had opened a bottle of wine. In a surfeit of emotion she sloshed some more of it into Paola's glass.

"For me those things were not reality," Paola said. "They had become a kind of—"

She put a slim brown hand in front of her eyes.

"A blindfold," Solly said, surprising herself.

"*Esattamente*," Paola said. "A blindfold."

"Did you never think of getting married?" Solly said. She was a little ashamed of her own vulgarity, but she couldn't help it, eight months pregnant and overblown as she was.

Paola laughed, staring down at her wineglass, around

which she had arranged her fingers in a kind of web on the tablecloth.

"I was married," she said. "For four years I lived with my husband."

Mortified, Solly said no more. Presently Paola got up.

"Just a minute," she said. "I am coming back."

She returned a few minutes later and placed a glass bottle with a stopper on the table in front of Solly.

"I got you this," she said. "For the bath. It is my own favourite. I saw it in a shop on the way home."

In the night Solly flipped open her eyes. A great sense of reality had summoned her out of her kaleidoscopic sleep. She lay, drinking in the hard surfaces of the room, the unleavened darkness. Her whole being seemed to be pressing against this reality. She wanted to cast herself into it, but it was depthless and flat. It was like wanting to cast yourself from a diving board into a pool empty of water.

Was the photograph in the drawer a photograph of Paola's own child? She believed, with an insane, hormonal intensity, that it was. It was this realisation that had woken her up. The child must have died! Her distended stomach heaved at the thought. Her heart pounded in her chest. Tears sped profusely out of the corners of her eyes and ran down through her hair on to the pillowcase. She lived at one moment in the burning core of this knowledge and the next in the fearful apprehension of herself as the harbour for it. Somehow she had been found as the harbour for this terrible occurrence! A woman with a dead child had found her, lost in the grey folds of Arlington Park, had found her and come to lodge in her brimming nest, had embedded the void of herself right here, like a clot next to Solly's heart! She couldn't bear it—it was too much, too much!

Outside, it began to rain. It rained hard, hard and suddenly. A thunderous noise began to beat at the windows in the dark, a deafening, joyous, uncontrollable sound like the sound of applause. Solly clung on. She clung on, as though to the deck of a ship in a storm. The rain beat at the windows and she clung on, to the solid matter of her life, to her flawed possession of it. It seemed the windows might break and the storm sweep her from the deck; she wanted to rouse the children from their beds and lash them to her under the covers, to find Martin and bind herself to him as though to the mast. Oh, it was terrifying, this journey of life, this turbulent passage through days and nights, never stopping, never knowing what it meant, only that you must cling, cling and never let go!

In the morning, in the jaded light, the grey rain still falling steadily at the windows, Solly rose and looked at herself in the long mirror. She seemed sharply in focus. She seemed full of new information, as though a page had been turned in her soul. She felt becalmed, solid, ordinary. She took the children to school and returned with Joseph, who moved quietly around the kitchen all morning, rudimentary, absorbed, as if demonstrating the simplicity of existence. Solly sat in her chair. The issue of Paola had receded, like the sea at low tide: it lay still, a blue line on the horizon. Solly felt cured of a kind of restlessness. She felt able to distinguish herself. She sat in her chair identifying herself, as the chair identified itself, as the table did.

But by lunchtime the wind had picked up in her. Joseph cried, and spilled things, and pounded at the back door, wanting to get out; and when Solly carried him upstairs to his bed he kicked her with his thrashing feet, so that a feeling of physical panic, of excess, drove the air from her lungs. She looked at her watch and realised that in another hour she would have to go and get the children home again. She didn't know how she would do it. She didn't know where she would find, in a single hour, the fortitude to get through what lay ahead. Passing the door to the spare room she stopped and laid her hand on the handle. She abjured herself not to enter: she absolutely forbade it. It would signify that she had returned to a condition of weakness, for it was an addiction in its way. Desperately she wanted not to subside again into that weakness. She thought of the girl in the threadbare jeans, and the image made something stand up in her, something that enabled her to remove her hand and proceed down the stairs. On the third or fourth stair she stopped. It was the idea of weakness, the idea of it as a steady state. It made her angry. It made her wonder what there was for her in the life she had made for herself. It made her wonder what the point was of being strong. She went back up the stairs and went in. This time she found something unsatisfying, something unavailing in Paola's things, for they were exactly the same as before: there was nothing new, except a receipt from a shop Solly found on her bedside table. She studied it for a while, before realising it was the receipt for the bath oil Paola had bought her. It was disappointing, that she herself was starting to show up in the mysteries of the spare room. It suggested they were not mysteries after all. Suddenly she felt sickened by her own prurience. She went to her and Martin's room and put on make-up in front of the mirror, regarding her own reflection with a sinking feeling of comfort, as though it were a reliable boyfriend she had returned to after a hopeless infatuation.

At half past four, the first seed of pain planted itself at the base of her spine and slowly branched, fire-like, all around her uterus. She leaned against the kitchen counter while at the other end of the room the children and the television revolved in a grey, indistinct mêlée of noisy contradiction. Paola returned at six o'clock to find Solly on her hands and knees on the floor while grey smoke issued from the frying pan on top of the stove.

"It has started?" she said discreetly, kneeling down beside her and placing a hand lightly on her back.

Solly nodded. Something in Paola's manner made her want both to laugh and to cry. It was her distant femininity again, her unsullied distance from this crude business of reproduction.

"Shall I phone your husband?"

"He knows," Solly said. "He's stuck in traffic."

Paola snatched the frying pan from the stove with a look of determination, as though it were a barking dog she were facing down.

"My mother's meant to be coming," Solly added. "Only she doesn't seem to be in."

"I will begin with this," Paola said. "For the children, no?"

When Solly next looked, the children seemed to be sitting at the table eating. Paola was playing a game with them involving three overturned cups and speaking to them in Italian. They observed her politely. The scene looked miniature and somehow idyllic, as though Solly were watching a film about an Italian family who had overcome various trials, or were about to embark on them. When she looked again they had gone. She looked at the clock—half an hour had passed. All that time she had been on her hands and knees on the kitchen floor while a few feet away the children ate their supper. How funny it was! Paola returned.

"Your husband phoned," she said. "He is still late."

Slowly Solly got to her feet. Somehow, another half an hour had passed.

"I must put the children to bed," she said.

Paola laughed.

"They are already asleep," she said.

"Oh!"

"Shall I phone the hospital?"

"Not yet," Solly said. "They don't like you to come in early."

Paola shrugged. "As you want."

"Really, they don't. They try to send you home again."

Paola had opened her cupboard and was searching amidst the packets and jars.

"Sit down," she said. "I will bring you a herbal remedy."

Solly wanted to remain standing. A feeling of terrible constraint choked her throat. Why should she have to submit to this stranger, now of all times? Why, in her hour of greatest need, should she be brought to heel by the eternal requirement that she be polite? Paola set a bowl of steaming water on the table. Solly felt that if she had to breathe in that steam she would suffocate.

"Please," Paola said tersely, pulling out a chair.

Solly sat down. She put her head over the bowl and breathed in the most consoling fragrance imaginable. It was like a projection of her inner state, like something she had invented herself.

"It helps, no?" Paola said.

"Oh!" said Solly, delirious with release.

"My mother gave this to me before my son was born."

Solly lifted her dripping face.

"Where is your son?" she said.

"He is at home," Paola said. "In Italy."

A great bewildering wave of knowledge passed over Solly.

"Why is he there?" she said.

"He lives with his father," Paola said. "That is not so strange," she added, looking Solly in the eyes. "You think it is strange, but really it is not. He is all right. He is with his father. He is alive. He is happy that he is alive."

Sitting there, Solly felt suddenly as though she were growing smaller. She was shrinking, diminishing, while Paola seemed large, as large as a tree, as large as a house. Beside her Solly felt small, like a child. Tears ran incontinently down her cheeks and dripped into the steaming water. She was a child and Paola was a mother: large, large as a tree, in whose shade Solly felt happy to be alive.

The baby was a girl. It was lucky, Solly thought—another boy might have sunk her. But instead, like a little podium or plinth, the baby gave her a new, higher view of the world. When she was with her, Solly remembered that she had turned against Martin and the children a little: it seemed to her to be a sort of advance, a development. She would not come down again from her plinth. She would live at that new angle to them—she was determined to. And now that the baby was born and the world's garbage, its mixed-up good and evil, had receded from her veins, she felt rather knowl-edgeable and grand. All the things there were to lose she had lost giving birth to the other three. So the fourth seemed more in the way of a credit: she loved it more and cared about it less. Her head was clear, and when she closed her eyes she saw mountains and valleys and great cities, cities full of peo-ple; and she felt a part of it, really, of all that monumental life, that grandeur. One day, passing two women in the street, she heard one of them say to the other, "Apparently all you have to do is remember to lift your mouth a little at the corners." So she tried to do that too, and found that it helped.

The spare room was under threat once Paola had left. Should they get another student? Or should they extend into it, like a great glacier moving along a valley floor and driving itself with a kind of stately violence into every cavity? Martin suggested he might find a use for it as an office. William said he was sick of sharing with Joseph and wanted a bedroom of his own. Solly stood firm. As she said to her friends, she thought of putting Dora in with the boys and renting her room out too. She might even get something for the other half of her bed, the nights Martin was in Reading.

She had a postcard from Betty in Taiwan, and a letter from Paola, who had gone back to Bologna, as she put it, for a season. She sent a piece of Italian lace for the baby, but Solly kept it for herself. She bought more bottles of the bath oil, too. These were her riches. It was a sideline, and everyone had to have one of those. One was in a sense—an Arlington Park sense—living off the fat of the land. In fact, several of her friends had started letting their spare rooms out too. But it was Solly who had thought of it first.

The rain had stopped. The park stood wet in the new afternoon light, as if it had just been born.

A fresh wind was blowing, stirring the bare branches of trees, lifting old leaves and bits of litter from the grass. The sun tossed in the clouds. Light fled across the sodden grass, electric, pursued by shadows. The wind ruffled the surface of the puddles and the sun unfurled along the paths and lit their muddy creases. Tangled clumps of bushes quivered, drying, in their matted greenery. Here and there jackdaws alighted in the deserted spaces and hopped speculatively over the grass. A magpie stood impudently on a path. Now that the rain had stopped, the sound of traffic from the road that circumscribed the park could be heard; steadily it refilled the emptied air.

All day the park had lain empty, forgotten in the rain, but now people were starting to arrive. They were issuing from their cars and from their houses, from streets and side-streets, and coming purposefully down the paths. They came with their dogs and pushchairs and kites and walking sticks. They filled the paths, and as more came they started to disperse, moving out over the wet, virgin grass, seeking their own regions, so that the jackdaws were forced to spread their ragged wings and yield up their lonely territories. The magpies in their black and white and navy uniforms leapt smartly up into the trees.

It was three o'clock and the children were not yet out of school. Women pushed babies in prams along the paths. Toddlers in padded jackets rode their tricycles while their mothers walked slowly behind. An elderly couple in soft shoes went hesitantly forward into the fresh wind and lingered near the benches. A young man in an anorak flew his kite, his legs astride on the grass, his arms braced against the powerfully tugging strings as if he were holding on to the world itself. The wind filled out the cheeks of the kite and it zigzagged crazily from side to side; it struggled to escape up into the sky while the man struggled to hold on to it.

The wind blew and the trees moved their bare branches and the people moved, and the sun spilled brilliant patches of light on the grass. The women pushed their prams along the paths and the clouds sailed past overhead. The old couple sat down on a bench and looked left and right. More people were coming: people in tracksuits and white shoes, running side by side. Two lean, grey-bearded men ran past dressed in black. A girl in a tight vest and headphones ran past. A man in shorts bounded by on long, fantastically muscled legs. A fat lady pattered along behind, her delicate feet barely leaving the ground. A woman with hair cut in steel-grey waves marched in step with her husband: they flung out their elbows, conversing in indignant tones. A young woman on rollerblades propelled a pram along the path and the couple moved aside, still conversing.

On the grass the man struggled valiantly with his kite. A tall, drooping girl with a melancholic face loped past him, gasping. The man in shorts came round again and the old man on the bench looked at his watch.

The mothers were taking their children to the swings.

148

They walked slowly along the far edge of the park, in abstracted pilgrimage behind the tricycles. Against the blowing, tossing sky their dark forms moved steadily with a kind of processional grandeur. The wind lifted their hair and the sun raked them with waves of electric light. In the distance the playground looked miniature. The tiny shapes of children in red and yellow and blue went back and forth on the swings. The see-saw went up and down. Children climbed the ladder and went down the slide. Slowly the procession moved towards the clockwork mechanism of the playground.

The man in shorts came round again. The old man consulted his watch.

"Fifty-five seconds," he said to his wife.

Suddenly, from amidst the bushes, a great dog appeared on the path. It stood proudly silhouetted in its clipped black fur, its tail erect. A woman came behind it and flung a stick out over the grass, and the dog sprang away after it. From every side of the park more dogs came: little cantering dogs, big golden dogs with fountains of hair, messy spaniels with muddy, matted coats, tiny prancing dogs, dogs that sniffed the ground and dogs that galloped wildly over the grass. They ran round in circles and figures of eight, chasing, skidding, lifting their legs against the tree trunks, diving after sticks and rolling on their backs. Round and round they ran, full of abundant, senseless life, making crazy patterns on the wet grass. People came after them, holding leads and sticks and balls, calling. They came in jackets and scarves, and they walked in straight lines that the dogs scribbled all over. Their voices filled the rinsed air.

"Angus! Angus, come here!"

"Daisy!"

"Bella, here, girl! Bella! Bella, heel!"

"Fritz! Fritz!"

"Dai-*see*!"

In the playground, the women did not call.

They pushed their children back and forth. They moved self-consciously, red-cheeked, the wind whipping their hair. They seemed confusedly disconsolate. It was as if they couldn't decide what they were. They felt stiff and clumsy amidst the swings and the see-saw, yet their feelings were new and raw, like the feelings they supposed their children to have. Pushing their children back and forth they seemed to be remaking the world, building it again to exclude themselves, hammering it closed with the rise and fall of the see-saw. What would become of them? Where would they go, with the world closed to them? What would they do with their bodies that felt so stiff and clumsy, now that the future had rehoused itself in children clad in red and yellow and blue? Little piles of dried leaves lay everywhere, like piles of shorn hair. A fence stood around the playground to keep the dogs out, the mad charging dogs with their streaming tails. Oh, to be an animal! To be a mad kinetic creature tumbling forward through life, running, rolling, sniffing, charging over the grass streaming fountains of hair! The wind lifted the piles of leaves and whirled them around. The children went back and forth.

A little boy fell over into the wood chippings around the swings and stood up bellowing, bits of wood clinging to his coat, his face smeared with dirt and mucus.

"Oh dear," his mother said, kneeling heavily in the wood chippings. "Oh dear, oh dear."

She rose with the boy in her arms, and wood chippings stuck all over her trousers. She patted him and brushed off his clothes.

"What shall we do now?" she said. "Shall we go down the slide?"

The swings went back and forth like the pendulums of little clocks.

It was half past three and the older children were coming out of school. In their uniforms they trailed after their mothers across the park, eating apples and chocolate bars. They ambled along the paths with their flapping coats hanging down their backs and their arms free. They moved in great uniformed knots. They walked along unconsciously. Some of them shoved and chased each other. A few rode bicycles or scooters. They were carefree, unaware, yet somehow stilted in their uniforms, marked out. A boy kicked a stick towards his sister and she picked up a big handful of dried leaves, red-faced, and tried to throw them back. The handful of leaves exploded impotently and fluttered over her hair, over her shoulders. The boys shoved each other and ran around the benches.

Two mothers walked ahead of them, talking. They wore smartly buttoned coats. Their hair was cut short and firmly styled. Their arms were full of schoolbags. Sometimes they stood, talking, and waited for the children to catch up. Now and then a runner overtook them in white shoes, moving swiftly out over the grass. Though there was no need to, the women in their coats moved aside a little to let the running people past. Their children blocked the path in sprawling, ambling groups, and the runners had to overtake them anyway on the grass, but still the women moved aside, talking, their heads erect, their eyes scanning the horizon. They did it as a form of gesture. They were like politicians: they understood the ways of the world but they had become inactive in it. Their physical life was a kind of shorthand. They moved aside to indicate their own awareness, and their powerful knowledge of life, at whose centre was the realisation that nothing could be fundamentally changed.

"Leave it, Freddie," one of them called to her son, who had flung himself on another boy on the grass and was tearing up the green blades and throwing them in his face. "I said, *leave* it alone."

The boys rolled over so that now the other one was on top. In turn he ripped up handfuls of grass and crushed them in his victim's face. The woman tutted.

"Why waste my breath?" she said.

The other one rolled her eyes. "Sometimes you think you might as well not be here, don't you?"

They kept their faces slightly turned away from each other as they talked, their eyes scanning the horizon.

"Dan's away in Paris all week."

"Is he? It's all right for some."

"He's filming again."

"Is he?"

"They were there for about six weeks earlier in the year, but they've had to go back because they forgot to film the Eiffel Tower."

The other woman snorted. "That was clever."

"It's mad, isn't it? I'm like, you know, just let *me* organise this. Just stand back and let me do it. You stay at home with the kids, and I'll sort out Paris."

"You feel like you could, don't you? They act like it's so difficult, but half the time you're thinking, you know, I could do that."

"I'll do Paris, the tower, everything, and I'll do it in half the time."

A runner passed and they moved aside a little.

"Richard's always going on these conferences where nobody seems to even know what they're meant to be talking about. I say to him, you know, what do you actually *do*? What do you actually *achieve*? I think they go just to stay in the hotel and get pissed in the bar."

"Well, why not, I suppose."

"I suppose. It's a bit mad, though. Even Richard admits it's a bit mad."

"Freddie, get off the grass! I said get off the grass! You're getting wet!"

"Sometimes you think the world's gone mad, don't you?"

"Excuse me—*Freddie*!"

The wind blew and the kites zigzagged overhead and a plastic bag went bowling across the grass in the sun. The woman on rollerblades pushed her pram along the path. The baby waved its little grasping hands in the air. Effortfully the woman drove it with her wheeled feet, wobbling over ridges in the tarmac. The kites dodged and dived above her. Dogs tore across the path. The baby waved its tiny fists in the sun. People ran past in their white shoes, overtaking. They ran as if they were bearing important news. One after another they ran past the wobbling woman towards the horizon, like solitary messengers bearing away the information of every passing minute.

In the children's playground the swings went back and forth. In their bright padded coats the children staggered from the slide to the see-saw, or sat on the little wooden animals, their cheeks red in the wind. The mothers stood in their fenced enclosure and watched people moving across the park. The people moved and everything around them moved too, the clouds hurtling across the sky, the tossing sun, the grass bending this way and that in the wind, the branches and the bushes, the kites and balls, the dogs and the springing birds, the cars passing along the distant road. The whole mechanism of the world, running on, running like a machine: time poured into it like a blank river, and set off all these infinitesimal movements!

It was painful, in a way; for them, it was a form of agony to watch it. Standing on their wood chippings in the playground, the women were as though snared in the mechanism. They were caught between the blank river and the churning wheels. Trapped as they were, every movement caused them pain. The diving kites hurt them. The people in their white shoes seemed to be trampling them underfoot. The dogs frightened them and made their hearts thump in their startled chests. It was only the swings going back and forth that they could tolerate.

The mothers of the schoolchildren no longer had to stand in the fenced enclosure. They stayed far away from it, in their smart coats, on the other side of the park. Whenever they saw it, saw new children on the swings, saw new women standing there self-consciously, it caused them to feel a strange sense of bereavement. They were seeing something they knew but had lost. It was a feeling with which they were familiar. It was this that had given them their powerful understanding of life. They knew that you lost the good along with the bad, both equally. They weren't interested any more in things you could lose, in time or love or the feeling of a baby in your arms. They were interested in things that stayed with you for ever: houses, possibly husbands. And themselves, of course. What they wanted to avoid was destruction. Like politicians, they were interested in survival.

"Oh, Freddie, *look* at you! You're *soaking*. Well, you'll just have to stay like that. No, we're not going home. You'll have to stay wet. What did you think was going to happen if you rolled around on the grass? I'm sorry, but it's not my problem. No, I don't care if you're cold. You'll have to put up with it. You should listen in future when I tell you not to do something."

The women sighed, and moved their eyes circumspectly around the park.

"They've got to learn, haven't they?" Freddie's mother said.

Her friend nodded. "You're making a rod for your own back otherwise."

"They've got to know what the consequences are."

"It's like everything. You can't protect them for ever. They've got to become independent. They've got to listen. They've got to know that if they don't listen they're putting themselves in danger. You tell them not to run out in front of cars and they've got to listen. You tell them not to go off with strangers and they've got to listen."

They stood in the wind and the sun, arms folded, eyes moving.

"Isn't it awful, about that little girl?"

"Yes! What was she called?"

"Betsy Miller. *She* was taken from a park, you know."

"Do they know what's happened to her?"

The woman shook her head, her eyes on the horizon. "*That's* why they've got to listen."

Now the older children were coming into the park: groups of pubescent girls with long ponytails, tall thin boys with their school ties loosened around their necks, sixth-formers talking on their mobile phones. Their bodies seemed to be struggling against their clothes. It was cold, but most of them carried their coats and sweaters and wore their shirts unbuttoned at the neck and hanging out at the waist. They were like creatures made of a substance that clothes would not adhere to. The girls had bare, hairless legs beneath their school skirts. They shrieked and tossed their hair and talked excitedly as they walked along. They shrieked as though everything tickled them, as if the whole world were a ticklish place that beset their writhing, sensitive forms. The sixth-formers slouched and moved their lips at their phones. Some of the boys walked alone, their satchels strapped across their chests, their hands in their pockets. They plodded across the park looking at their shoes.

The shrieking girls flapped and settled like birds on the benches. Some sat on the arms, some precariously on the high back. The old man looked at his watch. After a while, he rose, helping his wife to her feet, and they walked slowly off down the path. The kite made a dive near the bench and the girls shrieked and looked at each other and shrieked again.

A willowy girl walked slowly across the grass amidst the chasing dogs, talking into her phone; and her absorption seemed to drive itself steadily onwards like the prow of a boat through yielding water, so that the dogs and the people fanned out behind her like ripples, dispersing, vanishing.

Two sixth-formers slouched past the mothers in their smart coats. They flicked their manes of hair. They murmured in each other's ears. Their skirts were short and their long, bare, insolent legs were smooth and brown. Automatically the women looked at their watches.

"Well, I suppose we'd better be getting home," one of them said.

"Yes, time to get back," said the other. "Freddie! Come on, we're going! *Freddie!*"

In the children's playground the women were buttoning coats, brushing down trousers, wiping noses. They strapped their children into their pushchairs, and one after another they let themselves out of the gate: out into the park, out into streets where everything moved, where time set everything whirring and churning and grinding again and you felt the agony of the turning wheels.

After they'd gone, boys in their school uniforms hopped over the fence and sat on the swings, and walked up and down the see-saw so that it thumped on the wood chippings. The shrieking girls lit off from the benches and moved in a chattering flock across the park.

The wind died a little; the men packed up their kites.

The lowering sun receded behind the clouds. The trees were still. A flat, grey light enveloped the park. The jackdaws came down from the branches on big, quivering black wings and hopped over the grass. They cawed to one another, opening their sharp, terrible beaks. The traffic rumbled on the road. Here and there people ran silently on the paths. A child's glove lay forgotten on the ground.

Quietly, the park filled with its own inhuman atmosphere. It renewed itself in the grey light. It fell into a kind of trance, an old stillness. Cold air rose from the earth. The bushes darkened. The paths lay in shadow. The trees grew indistinct.

All around the city the lights were coming on.

At a quarter to four, Juliet started to prepare the library for the Literary Club.

Arlington Park High School for Girls was a Victorian building that stood along the park in its own grounds, behind high stone walls. It had a faint look of a hospital or hospice, with its circular lawn and flower beds hedged round with municipal tarmac. All day, middle-aged women strode purposefully here and there, clutching armloads of paperwork and files. Bells rang; the grounds filled and then emptied again. At lunchtime the rich odour of reheated food suffused the building and hung in a meat-smelling shape around the doors.

In the entrance hall there was usually an atmosphere of restrained hubbub, of scheduled human congress occurring mindful of the clock, like that of a station platform. The rubber soles of the girls' shoes squeaked on the stone floor as they came and went, and their little shrieks of laughter echoed around the domed ceiling. The portraits of past headmistresses, with their dates inscribed below, observed the modest commotion from the walls. They were colossal women, grey and solid as granite. They were mountains of experience, and they came in all the different shapes that mountains come in. There was one Juliet always liked to look at, Mrs. Walker-

Jay, whose dates averred that she had spent thirty years as the captain of this redoubtable ship. She had grey hair cut short and a bosom of rock, and her small blue eyes looked down on the hubbub as though time were passing not there in the milling hall but in the glacial blue of her unmoving eyes, which saw nothing, nothing whatever, to surprise them.

It took Juliet at least fifteen minutes to rearrange the library for the Literary Club. Though it was after school hours there was always some sixth-former at a table in a corner who looked as though she'd been there for a year, slumped over in an irremediable swamp of paper and chemistry textbooks. Juliet tried to persuade them all to leave so that she wouldn't feel self-conscious if the discussion grew heated. There was a study room assigned for the purpose, she told them one after another, and each time they would sigh and slam shut their books and heave themselves resentfully to their feet. It was always the scientists who were the worst. They had a sort of maleness about them, an aura of election. Once or twice they had asked why the Literary Club couldn't move to the study room instead. Juliet informed them that exclusive use of the library on the last Friday of the month was and always had been a perquisite of the Literary Club. If they wanted to stay here, they'd have to join. She gloried, a little, in this part of the fifteen minutes. She felt she was in a sense on the front line, defending art from the barbarian forces of rationality.

She pulled out all the tables and moved the chairs into a circle. Then, on a tray, she brought in her controversial supplies of coffee and biscuits. The headmistress had pointed out to her that consumption of food and drink in the library was forbidden, but by the slenderest of margins Juliet had prevailed. She explained that she wanted the Literary Club to have a relaxed, social atmosphere. Unlike her forebear, the present headmistress did seem to find this quite surprising.

She seemed to wonder what a relaxed, social atmosphere had to do with anything that occurred on the school premises and did not, in however tangential a way, have a positive bearing on examination results. In this respect, Juliet felt, she was a much smaller mountain than any of her predecessors, who would surely have taken a more rounded view of life. It was all anybody thought of now, flogging these girls for all the grades they could get out of them. The better the results, the more pupils, and revenue, the school attracted.

And what was it all for? What was the point of it? In what sense did the girls, even the scientists, profit from their hard work and their grades? Sooner or later they would meet a man and it would all be stolen from them. That girl with her chemistry textbooks would meet a man, and little by little he would murder her.

At the Literary Club, Juliet tried to stave off this inevitability, in whatever limited way she could. She tried to acquaint them with the nature of the beast. They were meant to select the book for the next month's discussion by committee, but unrepentantly Juliet steered them towards works that represented the truth, as she saw it, of female experience. She intended to keep things as contemporary as she could, and to prioritise women writers; but how could she resist *Madame Bovary*? How could she fail to direct them towards *Anna Karenina*, towards a woman dead on the railway tracks, put there by men? Then, sometimes, she capitulated and let them choose for themselves. Often they chose something that had been adapted into a film. The discussion always took an odd turn when that happened. The girls compared the book to the film, appearing to believe that the second had preceded the first. They referred to the characters using the names of the actors who had played them. Juliet would drink her coffee and stare out of the window, and try to relish the fact that at that very moment Benedict was walking home with the children and putting his key into the door of an empty house.

A girl with a long rope of hair down her back and an armful of chemistry textbooks slammed into the library and looked around blankly at the new arrangement of tables and chairs, the circle of coffee cups. Her shirt was untucked, more by accident than design, Juliet imagined. The headmistress, Mrs. Shaw, was a stickler for shirts being tucked in. She walked around the school making little downward tucking motions with her hands every time she saw one out. She looked as if she were doing a square dance. It was exactly that marginal, fixated type of control that convinced Juliet that the centre, the core of life, was being neglected. Who would teach these girls? Who would tell them the truth? Not Mrs. Shaw, doing her square dance for the punters. Besides, the school uniform was not of the sort with which it was advisable, or even possible, to take liberties: a regulation tartan kilt, a shirt, a dark-green blazer. Some of the girls wore ballet slippers, louchely trodden down at the heels. Most of them wore at least some jewellery. A few wore perfume. Juliet would smell it when they came to her desk at the end of a class to hand in their exercise books. Did they know why they wore it? Did they know why they put jewellery on themselves, and perfume? Or was it blind instinct, blind, a native need to display themselves, to attract?

"I'm afraid it's the Literary Club in here now," she said to the blank-faced girl.

"Oh." The girl surveyed the chairs, the coffee cups.

"You can join us if you like," Juliet said. "It doesn't matter if you haven't read the book."

The girl said nothing.

"We're doing *Wuthering Heights*," Juliet said. "They've just made a new film of it."

With her chemistry books clutched to her chest she appeared to be thinking.

"What time do you finish?" she said.

"Sometimes we run over," said Juliet, "but we're usually all done by quarter past five."

She was about to add that she was sure she could find someone to give the girl a lift home afterwards if that meant she wouldn't be collected. The girl moved towards the door with her armful of textbooks.

"Right," she said. "I'll come back at five-fifteen, then."

Juliet heard the others in the corridor outside.

"Come in!" she called.

In they came, farouche in their ballet slippers. One after another they looked at Juliet and gasped. A few of them merely widened their eyes. One of them made a sort of grimace, as though the sight of her hurt. Then, one after another, they went and sat down in their chairs. Immediately they began to lean across and murmur in each other's ears.

"Thank you!" said Juliet above the noise, her hand self-consciously at the bare nape of her neck. "That's quite enough, thank you."

The other teachers had responded to the disappearance of Juliet's hair in funny, anomalous ways. It was as if this dramatic act had caused them to come out of their little lairs and burrows, their little private tunnels of life. Suddenly she saw how different they all were. Nikolai, the enormous Greek-Cypriot maths teacher, had clasped her in his giant arms and embraced her, bellowing, "A new life! A new start!" over and over in her ear. The women in the office had touched their own cropped, styled heads. Was it a rite of passage, this cutting off of hair? Juliet had never thought about it before. She met the classics teacher, Mrs. Perkins, in the hall, and Mrs. Perkins had blushed and sped up, nodding her head up and down. "Much more practical!" she whispered happily as she went by. As for the headmistress, she approached Juliet at the end of the day, after eyeing her from afar down various corridors. Such encounters were not, Juliet felt, Mrs. Shaw's forte. She lacked the wit for them. She lacked the ability to see a thing and know it for what it was. In vain she strove for the majestic style of Mrs. Walker-Jay.

"I see you've had the chop," she said deeply, making the tucking motion, only this time around her neck.

It didn't sound right. Wasn't the chop what men had, when their wives decided they couldn't stand any more children?

"I feel like a new woman," Juliet said. In a way it was true. "I don't know what took me so long. It's the best thing I've ever done."

Mrs. Shaw's own hair was a wispy little perm, silver with blond highlights.

"Is it?" she said. She seemed troubled. "It's lovely on a young girl, though, don't you think?" she continued unexpectedly. "I like to see long hair down a young girl's back."

Juliet supposed she'd at least get a laugh out of Benedict later with that one.

Another knot of girls drifted in, trailing their copies of *Wuthering Heights*, sixth-formers in black eyeliner flicking back their fringes, shuffling in their ballet slippers, hunching their shoulders and walking from their hips. There was a girl with her hair in a single bunch on the side of her head. There was an enormous girl and her tiny best friend. All of them gasped at the sight of Juliet, shaven-headed like a nun. It began to irritate her. Did their lives lack excitement? Had they never seen someone have a haircut before? It was unnerving, to have so much of their attention; to be the object of their depthless gazes, the subject on their pink, delicate lips. All day, from class to class, it had been so. It made her realise how little of their attention she usually had. It made her realise how immersed they generally were in themselves, in their fresh new bodies, in their vain little heads. They were so vain, so conceited! They went through life never looking at anyone, never thinking of anyone but themselves! In the grounds Juliet often saw their mothers, smart, competitive women who nonetheless shrank a little, visibly withered, when Hermione or Emily or Laura came slinking out like a self-satisfied little cat and handed over her schoolbag like a duchess. Even some of the sixth-formers were still collected by their mothers: they sat waiting outside the gates in their big, expensive cars with the engines running, applying lipstick to their wrinkled mouths in the rear-view mirror.

Oh, it was vexing, vexing, this trap of sex! Never, never did she feel in life the sense of recognition, the companionship, the great warm fact of solidarity that she found between the covers of a book! Sometimes she could get near it, that warm spot, here in the library on a Friday afternoon: she could crank them up, these girls, get them speaking her language. But it was an effort, a great performance, a show she put on just to make them act for an hour as if she and they did speak it, the same language. She wondered whether the books she loved consoled her precisely because they were the manifestations of her own isolation. They were like little lights in a wilderness, a moor: from a distance they seemed clustered together, multitudinous, but close up you saw that miles and miles of empty blackness separated them.

The girls were murmuring again.

Juliet opened her copy of *Wuthering Heights* where she'd marked the page.

" 'I've dreamt in my life dreams that have stayed with me ever after, and changed my ideas,' " she read in a clear, carrying voice. " 'They've gone through and through me, like wine through water, and altered the colour of my mind.' "

She put the book down. They were looking at her, all of them, like a field of flowers.

"Who says that?" she said. "Do you remember?"

Murmuring, they conferred.

"Catherine Linton," one of them said.

Juliet sat back in her chair and folded her arms and crinkled her brow to denote perplexity.

"What do you think she meant by it?" she said. "They 'changed her ideas.' They 'altered the colour' of her mind. What do you think she means?"

She remembered the cockroach. The cockroach had altered the colour of her mind. It had stained her with its brown, nauseating tint. She had cut off her hair and still it was there, its legs stirring in the roots. She scratched her head and felt the little amputated tufts, the absence.

A girl called Tiffany put up her hand.

"Well, you know when you have dreams?" she said, in a little breathless voice, showing the intricate metalwork on her teeth. "And sometimes you get, you know, confused? And you're not sure whether what happened in the dream really happened?"

"She means that she has visions," interposed a clever, rather overweight girl called Harriet Fox. "She's saying that her dreams reveal things to her that alter her perception of ordinary life."

Juliet wondered if Harriet Fox ever had visions. She supposed there was no reason why not.

"I never dream," said someone. "Never."

"Everybody dreams," Harriet said. "You just don't remember them."

"I don't! I swear!"

"When I was little I used to sleepwalk," someone else said. "My parents used to have to lock all the doors to keep me in. Once, in the middle of the night, I got out and went to the next-door neighbours' house and got into their bed."

Everybody laughed. There were hoots and squeaks and then a great outbreak of murmuring. They did so love to talk about themselves. She supposed it was because they had come so recently to consciousness. They were what was happening in the world: they were the latest, the news.

She decided to give up on dreams.

"What do you think the book's about?" she called out.

Immediately there was silence.

"It's about love," said a girl Juliet didn't really know, a new girl. Her name was Rosa. She was pale and thin and freckled, with protuberant teeth.

"Is it?" Juliet said, pantomiming surprise. "Who loves whom?"

"Heathcliff loves Cathy," said Rosa. "And Cathy loves Heathcliff. But she marries Edgar Linton."

"Why would anyone love Heathcliff?" Juliet scowled. "He's horrible, isn't he?"

"He's sexy," said one of the sixth-formers, Sara Pierce. She looked around at them all unrepentantly. "In the film he's really sexy."

"I preferred the other one," said someone else. "What's his name?—Edgar. He's really nice."

There was a flurry of protestations and avowals concerning the two actors. Juliet looked out the window. The sky was grey. The light was ebbing from it, ebbing, standing back to let the darkness come.

"Heathcliff's a bastard, isn't he?" she said over the noise. "He hangs Isabella's dog and throws a knife at her. He turns Hareton into a delinquent. He goes around threatening to kill everyone."

"Bastards are sexy," Sara Pierce unerringly declared.

"What's sexy about them?"

Sara gave an insolent little shrug.

"What's sexy about bastards?" Juliet asked again. She hoped Mrs. Shaw wasn't anywhere close. She imagined her outside the door, listening, doing her tucking motions at speed.

"They make you think you can't get them," said Sara.

"And that's sexy, is it?"

Sara shrugged again. "Yeah."

"Why does Heathcliff do it, anyway?" Juliet asked. "Why does he do all these horrible things?"

"He's angry," Harriet said.

"Why's he angry?"

"Because when he was a child they didn't treat him properly."

"That's right. And why didn't they?"

"Because he was different."

"Exactly," Juliet said. "We don't like it when people are different, do we? We like everybody to be just the same."

There was murmuring.

"Take this class," Juliet said. "Take all of you. You're all white. You're all pretty well off, or you wouldn't be here. You're all the same, really, aren't you?"

"You're white," Sara Pierce observed.

"They wouldn't employ me if I wasn't," Juliet told her.

It was true; but all the same, it was excessive. The girls looked confused. More than that, they looked embarrassed. They all stared down into their laps, or fiddled with their hair. She imagined them going home, telling their bored, avid parents. Mrs. Randall says we're all the same. Mrs. Randall says we're all white. Mrs. Randall says you have to be white, or you won't get a job. She thought of Mrs. Walker-Jay, down in the hall with her dates like the dates on a tombstone. She saw

167

her icy, penetrating eyes. She hadn't meant to go down this road. She hadn't meant to go that way at all!

"What I'm trying to say," she said, "is that to understand a man like Heathcliff, you've got to understand what it's like to be different."

"Like black?" Tiffany said.

"Exactly," Juliet said.

"Or disabled," said Harriet.

"Exactly!"

"Some people get bullied for being different," said Rosa.

"*Exactly*. Heathcliff got bullied for being different. They called him a Gypsy."

"In the film he's white," said her curse, Sara Pierce.

"Well, in the *book*"—Juliet held it up—"he's dark-skinned. More to the point, he's an orphan, a street child. Mr. Earnshaw finds him in Liverpool, on the streets, and brings him home."

There was more murmuring. In a moment she would call the interval and make coffee. They always liked that. It lifted them, and made them come the next time.

"What other ways are there of being different? What does being different actually mean?"

"It means not being the same as everyone else."

"Does it? Is that all it means?"

There was silence.

"Do you think it might mean," said Juliet, "not doing what's expected of you?"

She looked around at them all. When had she not done exactly what was expected of her? In the sixth form, before her exams, her father had promised to give her a hundred pounds if she got straight As. For him it was just a curious form of gambling, really, but it egged her on. A hundred pounds! It had seemed enough to buy freedom itself. She had imagined freeing herself from her parents. She had imagined herself freed, of human relationships themselves.

She had got her straight As, but somehow the cheque had never materialised. She felt sure that if she had lost the wager her father would have wasted no time in referring to the hundred pounds he was sadly unable to give her. But now that she had her As—well, what more did she want? Was she greedy?

"Take Emily Brontë," she said. "Take the Brontë sisters."

She sensed a little uprush of resistance from the circle of girls. There was the slightest rolling of kohl-lined eyes. Was Mrs. Randall off again? Was she going to lecture them again, about how awful it was a hundred years ago, two hundred years ago—anyway, long before any of them, including her, were born—to be a woman?

"There they sat, in that cold parsonage, up on that rainy, windswept hill. It was the smallest, coldest, bleakest place imaginable. The graveyard stood right outside—they were surrounded by death! Their mother had died, and two of their sisters. Their father was a cold, puritanical man. Once," she told them, "a family friend gave the girls a present of some boots, made of pretty-coloured leather. Their father took them and threw them all in the fire."

The girls found that, at least, alarming.

"Why did he do that?" asked Sara Pierce.

"He thought they would make the girls vain," Juliet said.

There was murmuring.

"That was, like, so vicious?" said Tiffany.

"God, I'd go *mad* if my dad did that!"

She recalled reading somewhere that Patrick Brontë had furthermore ripped to shreds a dress of his wife's, some years before. It was a valuable dress, from before her marriage. It was the only lovely thing she possessed. She had kept it locked in a chest upstairs. He had taken the key and cut it to pieces with a pair of scissors. Oh, he was a murderer, all right.

"Who'd have expected those girls," she said, "to write three of the finest novels in the English language?"

He'd taken the key and cut it to pieces with a pair of scissors. She'd always, somehow, identified herself with one or another of the sisters, with Emily or Charlotte. Now, though, she found that it was with the mother that her sympathies lay. Their mother, whose dress was ripped to shreds, who did not write one of the finest novels in the English language. Instead, she had died, murdered—there was no harm in calling a spade a spade—by her husband. It was left to the daughters to avenge her, to break free. It was left to the daughters to make their mark on the indifferent world.

She thought of the scissors tearing through the cloth. The hairdresser's scissors had been cold on the back of her neck. They had snipped and snapped all round her, round her ears and eyes, round her throat.

"*Wuthering Heights* is not a book about love," she said to them. "It's a book about revenge."

It was the sixth-formers who had the coffee, really. The younger ones just had the biscuits. Juliet asked them about the film, which she hadn't seen, and let them chatter on. She handed them their cups. She watched as they luxuriated a little, stretched like little cats in the steam that curled around their faces. They liked it when she served them. In serving them, she saw, she was reminding them of their mothers.

"Thank you," said Sara Pierce, closing her eyes for an instant, smiling a satisfied little smile.

"Thank you," said Harriet Fox, a little startled, a little severe.

Of their mothers, who over the years had filled them in

with countless acts, like countless dabs of paint applied to a portrait. Their mothers had coloured them, shaded them, rounded them out. Each of them, each woman, had felt the sense of her own artistry as she dabbed away with her brush. Each of them had felt herself to be an artist, creating this girl, this daughter. Over the years, steadily, painstakingly, each of those mothers had transferred her soul, had lifted it from her breast, had transferred it little by little in dabs of paint. Now they waited in cars with the engines running, empty, voided, applying lipstick in the rear-view mirror to their wrinkled mouths.

Was that what Juliet would be, one day? Empty, all poured out into Katherine, into Benedict and Barnaby? Dead, yet living? It was a quarter to five. The library was filling with purple light. It was the edge, the very edge of evening. It was the time when one thing became another: a boundary was crossed, a modulation occurred. A feeling gripped you, gripped you in your soul and hauled you over. As a student this was the time she used to love, this time of dusk, with its deep, involving modulations. She would sit in the university library and watch it happen, the passage of time, the change of one thing into another; and she would feel reconfigured, carried over into the next thing, a part of it all. This library, the school library, was similar but smaller, miniature somehow, like a library in a doll's house. It made her feel that she had grown, or it had shrunk, she wasn't sure which. It was like a representation of her distant past. It was, in a way, a little sad: sad in the way Katherine's outgrown clothes were sad, or Barnaby's discarded toys. She looked at the books on their little shelves and they seemed to urge her back on herself, to tell her to get out, get out and live while she could.

Sara Pierce was looking at her with black-rimmed eyes over her coffee cup.

"Why did you cut it, then?" she said.

She had pulled her shirt-cuffs over her hands and wrapped the hands around the cup. She was perched on the edge of one chair and her feet were on another. Her knees were pulled up to her chin. It was a posture they liked, these sixth-formers. It was suggestive of a sort of grand reluctance to make contact with the brutal surfaces of the world. Juliet had probably sat like that herself at one time. But she didn't any more.

"Why not?" she said cheerfully, looking at Sara Pierce's feet in their ballet slippers. Sara Pierce was the highest practitioner of the art of the ballet slipper. She had scuffed them and trodden them down until she could not really be said to be wearing shoes at all.

Sara Pierce sipped. "You must have had a reason," she said.

"I was bored of it," Juliet said.

Sara raised her eyebrows sceptically and sipped again. "What, you just suddenly got bored? After all this time?"

Put like that, it did seem a little irrational.

"That's what happens when you're my age," Juliet said. "You suddenly get bored."

Sara looked sceptical again. It seemed she was trying to decide whether she should care if that was what you did or not.

"You realise you're waiting for something," Juliet said, "that's never going to happen. Half the time you don't even know what it is. You're waiting for the next stage. Then in the end you realise that there isn't a next stage. This is all there is."

"So you start having things done to your hair," Sara said, so scornfully that she appeared, in fact, to be well acquainted with this phenomenon. "Or you get plastic surgery. And you start obsessing about the house so that no one's allowed to do anything in case they mess it up. You're like, you know, why do they have to eat? It just makes a mess. Why do they have to change their clothes? Why don't they just wear a kind of plastic suit? Why do they have to come home at all? Why don't they just go and stay in a hotel?"

Juliet gave her a businesslike smile.

"Well," she said, "let's hope you don't end up like that."

"I won't!" Sara spat. "No way. I'm not even going to *have* children. I'm going to live on my own. And I'm never, ever getting married. Marriage is just another word for *hate*."

Well, there you are, Juliet thought.

After they'd gone she put all the tables back and all the chairs, and she took the cups out on her tray. She'd managed to get them going in the second half. She'd got them thinking, about the fair-skinned, lucky Lintons and the angry Heathcliff. She'd got them thinking about revenge. One day they would rise up, the outcasts, the unjustly treated, and smite it down, smite it all down where it stood. She hoped these girls knew which side they were on. She hoped they'd be careful.

She went down the stairs, down into the hall, past Mrs. Walker-Jay. She called goodnight to a crop-haired woman left in the office. She went out into the darkened, empty grounds. It was just past five o'clock: the sky was violet and black, bruised, swimming with clouds. A last faint gauze of light hung over everything. The grounds stood petrified in their stillness. She recalled that they were going to the Lanhams', she and Benedict. She wondered what it would be like. She thought of Christine, and what she would say. How *are* you?

It was strange: it didn't really mean much to her, this school, this place, this suburb with its streets and shops and park, these people she knew. Yet she was filled suddenly with a sense of possibility. All she needed was the chance of her Friday afternoons, to step aside for a moment, to take a single step away and look out, look up. Then she saw beauty: she saw the world not filtered through her veil of anger but as it was. Could she not tear down this veil of anger? Could she not bend them a little, these rules, this rod of marriage? Might that not be her single achievement, her masterpiece? To say to Benedict, I cannot go on as we are. We have to change things, just a little.

You had to love someone, to say that. You had to be prepared to give, in order to ask for something in return.

She passed through the gates and out into the street. The park lay before her in the deepening dusk. She could see a few huddled figures hurrying on the paths. The park seemed to be sinking into a dark sleep. It seemed to be folding in on itself. Then suddenly Juliet saw, rising from the dark folds, rising from the trees, a pair of swans. They were flying side by side, throats outstretched, beneath the descending night. Their bodies were a pale, unearthly white; together they flew in a kind of ecstasy, lifting themselves from the shadows with their slow, labouring wings. Juliet watched them. She watched their glimmering forms fly through the dark. Side by side they flew, beautiful and alive, exulting.

At six o'clock, when the last bruised light of afternoon had ebbed away and blackness stood at the windows, Dom Carrington opened his front door.

The door had not been opened all afternoon. The hours that had passed behind it, and the scenes that had taken place there, had elapsed so slowly and with so little expectation of interruption or rescue that Dom Carrington might have been making his entrance, miraculously and inexplicably, through a slab of granite. No one had come in and no one had gone out, since Maisie Carrington had returned to the house with her two children at half past three; and when the door opened—as though of its own accord, her husband being in possession of a key—Maisie experienced a vertiginous sense of event, of sound and change and movement, and of a strange uprushing of time, as though the whole compressed day had suddenly been uncorked and allowed to come loudly exploding out.

In the grey, homogenous spaces of such a day—a bottled weekday that stood in its ranks of identical fives, for whose contents repetition could give you a sort of taste, and equally, or consequently, a distinct aversion—Maisie could enter a rarefied state in which she was continuously aware of the fact of her own existence. This fact was either trivial or overwhelming: either way it enveloped her and held her suspended, like a foetus in its fluids, within itself. She could spend a whole day—a whole set of days—thus ensnared, without knowing how she had been caught or when she might be released. Like a leaf borne along one minute by a rushing river and the next snagged on the tines of a fallen branch, or misled to whirl aimlessly in a marginal little pool, she remained static amidst the tumult, the continuing onrush of things close by. It struck her as quite possible, in this state, that the same random forces that had put her there might forget to retrieve her; that the day might never end and the front door never open, discharging her husband from the world through whose viscera he had been steadily making his way since nine o'clock that morning. Sometimes, when he appeared, Maisie believed that not one minute had been added to the personal aggregate of her life. At others she seemed to have lived a century since she saw him last, or retreated one: for the first half-hour or so they derived from different eras, whose manners and mores were so mutually unfamiliar that a special clarity of diction seemed to be required for communication between them to become possible. Dom would explain to her the principles of his employment at the solicitors' firm of Salter, Dixon & Wray. She, in turn, would describe his children to him, as though he had never met them before, or as though they were something of which he might eventually be persuaded to make a considered purchase. They were like people in an advertisement, or a play: this was something Maisie had said on occasion, to break the tension. Dom did not seem to want to be in a play—or he didn't want her to say that that was what he was in, anyway. Increasingly she thought that, after all, he did want to be in a play. He looked slightly desolate when the tension was broken, as though it were something she had dropped that he considered privately to be important. Sometimes, when he walked through the door, he looked for a second like he thought he had walked into the wrong house.

He looked like that now: he moved his head around furtively, casting little darting glances at everything. He said:

"What's been happening here?"

The overhead lights were on all around the ground floor. Their hard orange brilliance was reflected in the black uncurtained windows. The rooms—kitchen, sitting room, a room at the front, the cluttered hall where Dom stood enquiringly— had the yellowed appearance of a network of well-lit underground tunnels.

Maisie said, "What do you mean, what's been happening? Nothing's been happening."

The direction of the light made the sitting room look as though it were listing to one side. Big, sagging bookshelves went in uneven stripes across one wall. The empty black mouth of the fireplace stood open in a frozen protest. In front of it an Indian rug lay twisted in an attitude of torment. Discarded toys made patterns over the floor like the patterns of land masses on a globe, halting where they met the obstacle of the sprawling sofa indented with craters where people had sat and eventually got up again. Maisie felt rather than saw the reality of the kitchen, whose full extent was shielded by the half-shut door. It receded from her in a long, soiled, debris-strewn segment.

"Where are the girls?" Dom said. He said it as he might have turned the key in the ignition a second time, having failed to start the engine with the first.

"They're upstairs."

"Oh. Everything all right?"

"Everything's fine."

"They're just—what—playing on their own?"

"I don't know," said Maisie. "I don't know exactly what they're doing."

Despite the fact that Maisie suffered, she did pity her husband in the moments of his homecoming. When he opened the door, her implication in the domestic life of the household, and his innocence of it, were each at their furthest extent: it was in those minutes that 32 Roderick Road, steeped in her presence, gave off its strongest atmosphere of sordid confinement, like an old shoe. She felt sorry for him as the first rancid wave hit his senses; she didn't doubt that it occurred to him to wonder whether the same door that had just manifested him might make him disappear again. She imagined his nightly progress along the dark pavements, past rows of shops, beneath streetlights, through the damp, mottled air, along numberless avenues where numberless people lived, as he journeyed towards this warm den of compromise; as he unearthed it again and again, night after night, from its fundamental anonymity. Why did he bother? Why didn't he just keep walking? Dom ducked his head and made for the stairs, passing her as she emerged from the core of the house like a hermit crab from its shell to stand at the doorway of the sitting room. Their eyes met.

"I'll just go up and say hello," he said; he meant, to "the girls," which was the collective name by which the two distinct solar systems—Clara and Elsie—that perennially revolved, star-spangled, in the centre of the black universe of Roderick Road were known to those responsible for taking care of them.

Earlier in the afternoon Maisie had thrown Elsie's lunchbox at the kitchen wall, where it burst like a firework and sent up a great fountain of wrappers and crumbs and sandwich crusts that pattered slowly down on the worktops. Elsie and Clara watched her do this with a certain confused admiration, until she shouted at them, "You're ruining my life! You're ruining my life!"—which dispelled their confusion but illuminated their small white faces dramatically with fear, so that they had clung together like children in a fairy tale before a fulminating ogre. Maisie did not recall her own mother coming out with accusations of this sort: rather, her parents had organised their resentments into scheduled episodes of authorised violence, of a dispassionate, patronising kind. Maisie had frequently been chastised with a wooden spatula whose special duties did not excuse it from the usual work of scraping the sides of the mixing bowl, manoeuvres Maisie would regard with anxiety; she had been told that she was rude, or lazy, or naughty, or spoilt, and even that final charge was levelled without a quiver from the regime, a sign that there was anyone to blame for it but herself.

There were times, in the hours she spent with Clara and Elsie, when she believed herself to be compensating them for these small, incessant brutalities that they had neither witnessed nor, mostly, knew about, and for the unyielding atmosphere in which they had occurred, the years of her childhood that unfurled behind her like a bolt of thick, unpatterned cloth. At other times they themselves appeared to her as people who had come into the world to constrain and criticise her, to record her comings and goings from the concept of normal behaviour, as though they were small, reincarnated versions of her parents. When this happened, her soul rose up against the injustice of it: she saw herself as imprisoned for life—violent feelings poured from her in a righteous torrent, feelings that came as though from some geological past, like lava. These feelings—hot, illuminated, solidifying greyly in seconds where they happened to come to rest—spoke to her momentarily and thrillingly of her own essence. They were like great, bright discharges of power, which unfortunately could not make their way through the world in some theoretical, unbodied state. They sought a more permanent record of themselves. They sought an object—Elsie's lunchbox—on which to make the mark of catastrophe.

Maisie had told her children about the spatula, partly to make them feel sorry for her, and partly to provide them with a category in which to place their memories of her own delinquent outbursts. They listened with the same half-admiring expression they had worn in the kitchen this afternoon, but they seemed distinctly troubled too: she saw the realisation pass across their faces that if that had happened to Maisie, there was no reason why it couldn't also happen to them. Maisie did not find this a particularly satisfactory response. It seemed both to disregard her feelings and to accuse her of something, which was more or less the spirit in which the original punishment had been administered.

Now Dom was downstairs again: he said something to her as he passed through the sitting room on his way to the kitchen, where he took off his suit jacket and hung it on the back of a chair, unbuttoned his cuffs, rolled up his sleeves, and turned to the sink, like a nurse arriving at the beginning of her shift. She followed him and stood in the doorway. The kitchen was the dingiest room in the house. Everything in it—the walls, the ceiling, the cupboards and doors and window-frames—was thickly and uniformly painted the same colour, as though something terrible had happened there, something that had resulted in the walls and cupboards being indelibly stained so that someone had decided to paint them rather than clean them. Elsewhere in 32 Roderick Road the Carringtons' possessions had leavened the sterile atmosphere of the house, but in the kitchen they could make no impression. It was here that Maisie felt most divorced from her own motives, saw her husband and children most as the strangers they occasionally were. It was here she felt most often that they were in a play, and that it was not a play she liked.

The kitchen was like a person with whom she had tried to get on and failed: barely tried, so impatient was she to settle into her enmity with it. The Carringtons had never met the people from whom they rented the house: they had been away, for years apparently, so that to Maisie their lives had taken on a cast of failure whose roots appeared to lie here, in Roderick Road. She felt it might have been to escape the kitchen, or what they had done in it, that they concealed themselves. The room, the house, even Arlington Park itself, increasingly wore for her the lineaments of a lived past into which future possibilities were unable to intrude; of a fundamental sadness that was the unalterable relic of experience. She was so accustomed to feel the presence in herself of a power of renewal that she had been slow to sense that it was no longer there; that she now existed on a kind of loop or circuit that took her round the same places and brought her back again and again to the same things. It was not defiance but inability that explained her failure to impose herself on the kitchen: an appetite for cleanliness and order, for things to be cleared away so that they could be begun again, was simply no longer a desire she visited on her circuit. Instead, she closed the door, as though on an invalid who sickened and worsened behind it, steeped in his own germs; and that was how things remained until her husband, the nurse, came home, hung his jacket on a chair, and silently commenced his shift.

"Guess where I went today," she said to his back.

He stood at the sink, his hands plunged in a ferment of water from the taps. A white drift of foam bloomed and expanded in the bowl, as though magically issuing from his fingertips. She could see his reflection in the black window in front of him. He looked creased with electric light, like a drawing of himself that had been crumpled up. She saw that he had disentangled the wreckage of plates and saucepans and cutlery in the sink and stacked everything into soiled, categorised piles on the sideboard.

"Where?"

"Merrywood."

She saw him smile in the window.

"Did you? What were you doing there?"

"I went with Christine Lanham, and the lovely Stephanie Sykes."

She wasn't sure he'd heard her: he was making a noise with the plates. The water beat down into the sink. He moved up and down the sideboard like a member of an orchestra playing a xylophone, generating noise with gestures that articulated themselves mutely through the back of his shirt.

Sometimes Maisie was awed and intimidated by the classical way her husband's shirt clothed his shoulders, by his slim waist and the strainless fall of his dark-blue trousers around his hips. He looked to her like a statue: he had a lot of what she thought of as finish. He particularly looked like this in his suits, although naked his pale, fine, muscled body had it too. Most people of their age looked in their own bodies like they were carrying bags, or parcels, or sometimes even heavy suitcases, but her husband looked carefree, like a child. She saw his white neck and his fine, light-brown hair. She saw his face in the window, his wide, slanting eyes and mouth, his pointed nose and chin. His eyes were green. He was as beautiful as a girl, or a cat: she did not always think this, but when she did, he seemed to have nothing to do with her. Next to him she felt swarthy and burdened. Sometimes he looked shifty, seedy even, when he said or did the wrong thing and the mistake was smeared over his transparent surfaces. Also, when he was angry with Maisie, he got restless and guilty and petulant and spoke in a high-pitched voice, more like a hamster's than a cat's.

"They went into all the shops and tried on clothes," she said. "Then we had lunch in this restaurant that was like purgatory. It was on the top floor and it had big photographs of green fields on the walls, and windows all around so that you could see all the roads and the motorway."

"It sounds nice," he said impenetrably.

"There were all these people there. It was like lost property, but for people. I didn't know why they were there. They looked like someone had forgotten to come and get them."

Dom said, casually, "They were there for the same reason you were there, weren't they?"

"I don't know why I was there. I had a fight with a woman in the car park."

"Did you?" In the window he was not smiling. "What did you have a fight about?"

"It was about her car. She had this stupid car. It was like a giant black stag beetle. She was this stupid little woman with dyed blond hair and gold earrings and she sat up there about ten feet above my head behind her tinted windows, driving this car like it was a Sherman tank."

"What did you have a fight about?" he said, a little more indulgently.

A bubble of indignation rose into Maisie's throat and lodged itself there. "She tried to run over Jasper."

"Who's Jasper?"

"My boyfriend," Maisie said in a strangled voice. After a while she said, "He's Stephanie's son."

"And he's your boyfriend?"

"He's three. I was joking."

"Why did she try to run over Jasper?"

"How should I know? She wasn't looking where she was

going. She was sitting there having an orgasm with her seat vibrating and her foot on the pedal, feeling four litres of fuel injection from her big black—"

"All right, all right. That's enough."

"If you hit a child," she persisted, "with one of those cars, then you're more likely to kill them, and you're more likely to hit them because you can't see them, not to mention the mushroom cloud of carbon monoxide you're spewing out getting your lazy, ignorant little arse to Merrywood just so you can indulge your other source of sexual gratification, which is fucking shopping—"

"Did you say that to her?"

"I said it, but she had the window shut."

Her husband looked as though he wished to know whether human civilisation always took this form.

"She said some things too. I could see her mouth moving behind the glass. She looked like she'd sat on the gearstick."

"And what did Stephanie make of it?"

"She didn't particularly seem to mind that this Nazi was about to reverse over her son."

Dom had finished washing up and was now energetically drying the plates with a tea towel, which he flourished like a maitre d'.

"No," he said. "I can't see her getting hysterical."

"She'd get pretty fucking hysterical if someone stole her hairdryer," Maisie observed. "She'd get pretty damned jumpy if her husband's salary didn't come rolling in like a Pacific breaker every month, or if people stopped thinking she looked like Felicity Kendall."

Dom opened the cupboard and lifted the plates into it in a white celestial stack.

He said, "It's just that she always seems very calm."

A couple of months earlier, Maisie had gone away for two

full weeks to stay with her sister Georgina in Edinburgh, leaving Dom to take care of the children. It had pleased her, in a malevolent way, to imagine him assuming her existence in Roderick Road: it was part of a private strategy with which she hoped to meet the bleak necessity, the onerous task, of implanting him with the uncomfortable knowledge that she could not endure the life they were making for themselves. It was a first move, a pre-emptive strike: all the time she was away, the thought that she might return to find that Dom had packed up the house and handed back the keys, declaring that he hadn't known, that she, they, couldn't possibly stay in Arlington Park, that thought was like a torch of hope she carried in her breast. In the event, he had taken an earnest, faintly condescending pleasure in it, as though she had asked him to learn some obscure language in her absence; for it had been her idea to leave London for this green, ruminative, inchoate suburb, and if he acted—not just then but increasingly—as though he were going along with her, as though it were not just his intention but his life's sad purpose to master the pointless hobby of her, then whose fault was it but her own?

Georgina had pneumonia, and children the same age as Maisie's. She seemed to find it curious that Maisie, in a fever of emergency, had abandoned her responsibilities in order to assume a more or less identical set elsewhere: it hinted at an unstable level of dissatisfaction. It was true that Maisie believed that if she herself had got pneumonia she would die, of despair if nothing else. She was in a sense rushing to her own bedside, much as she sometimes cared for her child self through her children. Georgina took antibiotics; her husband looked after their son and daughter. There was nothing really for Maisie to do except talk, conversations punctuated by the phrase "But are you *happy*?" which her sister pronounced with striking, corrective regularity from the depths of her pillows, so that by the end of her stay an impression had been formed of Maisie herself as sick, enfeebled, and demonstrably astray. She wandered around Edinburgh, with its meat-smell, its hard light, its cold and invigoratingly arrogant buildings. When she returned to Roderick Road, Dom was in possession of the map of her unhappiness: he knew its tracks and paths, its features, knowledge he now called on every time she attributed some special perniciousness to the school gate, or the supermarket, or the park; he could refute her, in the very lair of her discontent.

She said, "Is calm what men call housewives they find sexually attractive?"

"Stephanie's not so bad," he said. "That's all I'm saying."

"I hate her," Maisie said, just for something pointlessly violent to say. Clara appeared in the doorway as she said it.

"Who do you hate? Daddy, who does Mummy hate?"

"She's the patron saint of this stupid place."

Dom raised his narrow eyebrows.

"I thought Christine Lanham was the patron saint. Or that other one. Dewdrop."

"Dinky. I don't think so. No, people just like Dinky because she's rich. Actually, they do envy her in a way, because her husband died."

"They wouldn't envy her that. No one would ever invite them to dinner if their husbands died."

Maisie was pleased by this idea.

"Dinky doesn't get a lot of dinner, it's true," she reflected. "She gets a lot of coffee. You could power a turbine from the caffeine in her bloodstream." She added, "The thing about Stephanie is that if you stuck a pin into her she'd say she was really enjoying it."

"I think she's just very content with what she has," Dom observed. "And do you know what? There's nothing actually wrong with that."

Do you know what had lately become, Maisie didn't know from where, one of Dom's catchphrases, and was a sign that they were in a play. She wrenched open one of the kitchen cupboards and dramatically removed a bottle of wine and two glasses from it.

"Do you want some?"

"I won't," Dom said. He said it in the way she imagined he might have declined to join in acts of group thuggery as a schoolboy. "Aren't we going out later?"

Maisie shrugged. "I don't know," she said, though she knew perfectly well and had arranged a babysitter.

"We're going to the Lanhams," Dom informed himself. "I'd better start getting the children ready for bed."

"I'll do it," Maisie said, nevertheless pouring herself a large glass of wine and entrenching herself with it at the kitchen table. "The top of Mount Kilimanjaro's melted," she added. She held up the newspaper for him to see. There was an aerial picture of the brown, cloacal mountain-top, faintly streaked with the white of glaciers that were retreating like time from a middle-aged life.

"When are we supposed to be there?"

"I don't know," she said.

She read the paper, which said that the mountain-top hadn't been visible for eleven thousand years. It was that kind of fact, she thought, that discredited even the most heartfelt demonstration of concern for the situation. When she looked up she saw that Dom was still standing there, silently regarding her with a combative eye.

"What's wrong?" he said.

"Nothing."

"Something's wrong."

"I'm absolutely fine."

"Then why won't you tell me when we're supposed to be there?"

She had an impulse to lift her shirt and reveal to him her soft, mounded stomach and her mottled breasts, but she realised that this would upset him. Instead, she said what she was supposed to say, for had they ever been expected for dinner at a time other than eight o'clock? It was her next line in the play, though she had fought to keep it down. "Eight o'clock."

"Right." Dom ducked his head. "Did you realise it's seven-fifteen?"

She rose, wondering why he didn't put the children to bed himself if he cared so much what the time was. She guessed the answer was that he had taken her at her word: she had said she would do it. He probably thought there was some important, sentimental reason why, a reason that might even have been himself, tired at the end of his week's work: if this were so, it struck her as sad that he had to fabricate her generosity towards him out of so little material, or make a point of honour out of something that didn't really exist. The fact was that she wanted to put the children to bed in order to atone for the incident of the lunchbox, and also, less reflectively, to conceal this incident from her husband lest one of the children chose the bedtime hour to reveal it. By tomorrow it would have passed from their view; until then, she could stifle them.

She ascended the stairs heavily, and something in their tread and extent, their borders and spindles beaded with dried splashes of thick cream-coloured paint, the blue ribbed carpet that travelled up them like a penitentiary road, caused her to believe that she would always be walking up these stairs and that this moment would endure for ever: the splashes of paint were like pieces of frozen time, the line of the carpet passed like a rod through the centre of her life, skewering her manifold selves. She thought she might never move on from it: it was like a cave she had come upon, a habitable, convenient cave on a too-long journey. It seemed possible that she could just live here, here on the turn of the stairs. They would step over her as they came and went. She would sit there and think of all the stairs she had climbed over the years, and feel that by stopping she had at least acted decisively and conclusively in one area of her life.

She wondered whether she had always been like this: she couldn't remember. Had she always confronted each minute in this way, half-heartedly squaring up to it with the idea of backing down always somewhere in her thoughts? She wasn't sure. There was nothing in their situation in Arlington Park she could say she hadn't chosen, except to actually live it, yet she didn't think that she had ever been so close to the possibility of cowardice. When she thought of her life before— of her twenties, and London, and work, and the house near Goldborne Road—she saw herself always animated by a nameless dissatisfaction: it had filled her out, like the wind fills out a sail, and propelled her along while she did her best to steer a course. She didn't know exactly where she was going, just that it was necessary to remain in motion while avoiding outright disaster.

And this wind, this variable force of discontent, had carried her to places whose specific and localised nature troubled her even as she was driven to accept them. The problem was that when it blew, it came from everywhere, from great vacant, generalised spaces; yet it could only send her to what was fixed and narrow, to what already existed. Always, it transformed amorphous impulses into material facts. Her need to love became her relationship with Dom; her need for significance became her research job at a small television production company in Shepherd's Bush; her need for an object became a three-bedroom house in Goldborne Road; her need to express herself became her two daughters, Clara and Elsie. But this same noisy wind of possibility blew through it all, blew and blew, so that she felt they were wrongly positioned, that they had put themselves where they were exposed to strain, constantly fretted on every flank and in every crevice; she wanted a sheltered place where her shiftless need for change and movement couldn't get her. That was what she had thought, anyway. Now that they were here, in Arlington Park, a new and pacific understanding had descended on her, had enveloped her like an unstirred, unending silence. She saw that they had lost what made them live: that the difficulty and necessity of managing that force grew in proportion to how strongly you felt it. And it was, after all, a necessity, perhaps the only necessity, in that without it she appeared to be para-lysed. She was like a boat in a harbour where the tide has gone out, lying helplessly on her side in the mud with the neutered fin of her rudder drying in the still air.

There was a pile of clothes on the stairs in front of her, all tangled up where the children had left them. It seemed they had stepped out of them where they stood: the sleeves and knotted tights and crumpled skirts still bore the imprint of their bodies, like discarded skins. She bent down to pick them up, and when she closed her fingers around them she saw a kind of writhing black movement in the pile, and she flung it away from her with a loud shriek and galloped up the stairs to the landing.

"My God!" she cried. "It's a snake!"

Clara and Elsie had issued from their bedroom and stood quavering before her. They were both naked. They stared at her from their white bodies.

"There's a snake!"

"Where?" said Clara interestedly, bending to look around Maisie as though it might be sitting in a friendly coil behind her, waiting to be introduced.

190

"Down there! In the clothes!"

Her heart was pounding idiotically against her sternum. The landing reeled around her in undulating walls of electric light. She watched as Clara went past her and began making her way sturdily down the stairs.

"Don't!" Maisie said faintly, though it sounded ridiculous, as it was clear to them all by now that there was unlikely to be a snake on the landing. Clara continued her progress down the stairs.

"Is this the snake?" she said. She looked disappointed.

In her hand she held a pair of Maisie's tights. One of the legs was strangely swollen. There was a knot tied high in the thigh.

"We made it," said Elsie beside her. "That's our snake. We stuffed our knickers down it."

"Oh," said Maisie.

"Did you really think it was a snake?" said Clara, pleased.

"We took all the ones from the drawer," said Elsie. "Then we put it down the stairs to frighten you."

Clara came back up the stairs.

"I thought there might have been a real snake as well," she said despondently.

Maisie walked ahead of them into their room, whose profound disorder had a sort of grace, like that of a patch of dense forest: a certain natural beauty that arises out of things moving and falling and being left undisturbed where they lie. She felt entombed, unprotestingly, in the untidiness of the house: it was draped over her like a shroud with no openings for her arms and legs, so that when she walked around it or reached out to touch it she felt a kind of dragging following movement, and a sense of amputated numbness. Little plastic figures—of horses with gaudy pink fountains of hair, of girls with encephalitic heads, of miniature train drivers and men in hard hats, of jungle animals and red Indians and tiny women with plaits and gingham aprons—lay everywhere on the floor on their sides, as though some strange conceptual explosion had flung them there. A large rough-skinned lizard with the fork of its pink plastic tongue exposed was propped victoriously on the prone body of a Barbie doll. A plastic head almost the size of a child's head, streaming blond synthetic hair from little puncture marks in its rigid, flesh-coloured casing, lay severed in the middle of Elsie's bed, staring at the ceiling with its blue, fronded, wide-awake eyes.

"My God," Maisie said, sitting down beside it and stroking its cold, silky hair.

Beneath her feet, beneath her buttocks, were little pebbly crunching mounds of resistance that gave like dried leaves under her weight. There were balls of tissue paper and the empty lids of felt-tip pens, hair slides, and plastic combs and pencil sharpeners, marbles and rulers and crayons and the little rubber carcasses of burst balloons; there was a rocking horse draped like a tramp in layers of contradictory garments, through which his head protruded with despondent dignity; there was a multicoloured landslide of Lego that spilled out over the tracks of a toy train. There was a big disorderly heap of books on the top of which a small magnifying glass rested. There were clothes, new and old, clean and dirty, that had escaped their allotted places and were joined all together in riotous celebration.

"Here, Mummy."

Elsie stood before her, proffering a crushed slip of ruled paper. Maisie looked at it. There was a faintly drawn, smudged picture of a rainbow and next to it, in large spidery writing, the words "I love you Mummy love Elsie." The paper was torn and there were three telephone numbers written across it in an adult's handwriting. She took it from Elsie's trembling

hand. It was a dangerous place to live in, a family: it was as tu-
multuous as the open sea beneath a treacherous sky, the shift-
ing allegiances, the flurries of cruelty and virtue, the great
battering waves of mood and mortality, the endless alterna-
tion of storm and calm. A downpour would come or a re-
prieving ray of light, and in the end you didn't know what
the difference was, what it all meant, what it added up to,
when set against the necessity for just surviving and getting
through.

Maisie said, "You haven't got any clothes on."

"I know."

"You've got a babysitter coming tonight."

Elsie's round eyes were level with her own. She saw the
troubling significance of her remark register itself in them, as
though they were two round, still pools into whose dark wa-
ters she had poked a stick.

"I don't want a babysitter to come."

"Well, she's coming."

"Who is it?"

"Katie."

"Katie." Elsie thought. Then she nodded unhappily. "I
like Katie," she admitted.

"I'd much rather stay here with you," Maisie said, because
in a way it was true.

"Are you going?" Elsie said. She thought and then she
said, "*Where* are you going?" with a little smile, as though forgetting to say "where" was something she'd done last year,
when she was three.

"We're going to a dinner party."

"Oh." She thought again. "Are you going to like it?"

"I like you," Maisie said, picking up her small, dense,
fleshy body and plunging her face into her neck. "You're the
only thing I like."

Elsie was speaking into her hair. She could feel her mouth moving, like something small that lived there, just above her ear.

"What?"

"I said, what about Clara?"

"Clara too. You and Clara."

"And Daddy."

"Daddy too."

"And Katie."

In the bathroom Maisie looked in the mirror. I am thirty-eight, she thought. I am Maisie at thirty-eight. This did not seem to be the same thing as saying, this is Clara at six, this is Elsie at four, which she did far more often. She did not know whether anyone had ever crystallised her like that, had stopped her in time and commemorated her. It seemed just then a terrible thing not to know: to have to guess at, and to conclude from something unclaimed in her face, something unauthored and anonymous, that the answer was no. She could have been anything she wanted to be: that was the spirit in which she might have taken her parents' limited and discriminatory love, rather than being left by it to wonder what she actually was.

She saw her parents infrequently now, sporadic occasions on every one of which, nevertheless, they succeeded in repeating with crushing and meaningful regularity their mantra, the manifesto of their post-service years. It was that if an adult still blamed her parents, the problem was not theirs but hers. This nugget of self-absolution was intended to have special significance for Maisie, and it did, in that it proved that her resentments had their basis in fact—facts that her parents were eager to send to oblivion now that the regime of their household had drawn to its ambiguous conclusion and they were free of their children. They didn't want to be put on trial for things that had happened long ago: they wanted to wallow in their guilty retirement, from which distant perspective the years of child-rearing seemed to sit on a mountain-top of accomplishment. They had climbed that mountain, and they expected to be congratulated for it, and to be allowed to congratulate themselves. They said it had been wonderful, but if you criticised them for something they spoke of the hardships of the terrain, and of the particular, stubborn obstacles their children—Maisie more than the others—had placed in their path. If those children, as adults, still blamed their parents, then evidently they knew nothing about life.

Maisie did blame them; she didn't see why she shouldn't. The older she got, and the closer to the sources and perils of life she became, the more incriminated they seemed to her. She blamed them not only for the parts of herself they had damaged but for damage, wreckage, wherever she saw it: she blamed them for the brown, blighted fields that stood around Merrywood, for the roaring roads that scythed through delicate places, for the pylons and the petrol stations, the ugly overpasses and office buildings, for the shops and supermarkets that stood redly in their fresh sites, as though they were stained with blood. Wherever she saw greed and carelessness and monstrous self-will she blamed them, for it all seemed to come out of a common fund of selfishness, of heedlessness before the fact of beauty.

She even blamed them for the melting snows of Mount Kilimanjaro.

"Can I wear this one?" said Clara. She was talking about a nightdress.

"Whatever," said Maisie.

Her face: it was like a garden in winter, bare, cut back,

monotonous. Once she'd got used to looking at it, it didn't seem so bad: it answered her second enquiry with the same polite silence it had answered her first, so that she began to get the idea of it. She remembered more often now to wear make-up and it had proportionately less impact. She couldn't remember the last time a man had looked at her as anything other than part of a boxed set that included his wife.

"Are you sure?" Clara said.

"Of course I'm sure. It doesn't matter."

"But it's clean," Clara said.

She tried to locate the statute which Clara seemed in fear of violating, but couldn't. Had she ever told them they couldn't wear clean clothes? Had she given them the impression, as Clara's face seemed to indicate, that if they wore clean nightdresses without asking her she would do something unpredictable?

She said, "What's wrong with a clean nightdress?"

Clara appeared reasonably unable to answer this question. She gave a quick little smile and pulled the nightdress over her head. When her face came through the hole she twisted her head about brightly, like a periscope. Then she thundered off to her room. The next time Maisie looked, Dom was standing at the bathroom door.

"I'm getting ready," she said.

He looked at his watch. She realised that he was still in a play.

"I'll read them a story, then, shall I?"

"It's not, you know, roadworks. I'm not diverting traffic here. I'm just putting on some eyeliner."

"I wish I could wear eyeliner," he said obscurely. He crossed the landing to Clara and Elsie's room.

"You could change out of your suit," she said. "We'd all feel much safer."

She brushed her hair and put on different clothes. When she went into the girls' room, Elsie lifted her rosebud face and said, "You look beautiful, Mummy," and Maisie felt strangulated, almost overcome by the fear of falsity and death, of dying without the truth having been unearthed and allowed to prevail; without justice having been done to her obscured and muffled soul. She wanted to feel cold, wet rain on her face and soft grass under her feet, and to hear sounds that were not the sounds of cars passing on the other side of the windows along Roderick Road.

"You do," Dom said formally, bobbing his head, "look lovely."

She sailed down the stairs like a galleon, like a great ship of war, past the snake that lay stuffed beside the skirting board and reminded her of her own roiling, delirious volatility, past the tangled pile of dead clothes, and into the hall, where she was arrested by the sight of Dom's briefcase leaning, collapsed, against the wall. It was a scuffed brown leather satchel with brass clasps. It had belonged to his grandfather, a lawyer and amateur poet, back in the warm, liberal vaults of his family history. Nothing survived from Maisie's ancestry: her family past was like a meadow on which her parents had built the monolithic modern structure of their marriage. But Dom had lots of things: furniture, pictures, a first edition of Rudyard Kipling's *Just So Stories*—things which suggested he had arisen not out of particular wealth or significance but out of layers of love, of care. The first evening they had spent together, Maisie was waiting for him in the dusk outside Covent Garden tube station, bent over tying her shoelace, and that briefcase had manifested itself before her eyes. He had flung it down on the pavement next to her as if it were the sign of himself, and when she stood up he had clasped her in a great hug in the warm violet light of that summer evening.

Oh, how she had loved him! How she had loved him! It was a torrent of love, of rightness and recognition: his beauty and rightness, the unspoilt feeling of him, his beautiful slanting eyes—he was like something that had come down from the highest mountain-top of her being. And it was so hard to tolerate the intrusion of time, which emptied itself into them like a sewer into a running river, which cast its litter and lumber, its detritus, upon them; it was so hard to go on from what had been sufficient, from that moment in the dusk, from what was beautiful, without destroying it! She touched his briefcase with her fingers and tears surged to her eyes, as though he were dead or absent when he was merely in the room above, reading to their daughters in his socks. How could she feel this grief, this melancholy, when that was how things were? She wondered whether, if they had never set foot on the path that had led them here, to Roderick Road, they might have survived in that evening, that moment in the purple light of Covent Garden; whether they could have lived in it, like strange flowers in a hothouse. They could just have gone on and on, and perhaps even had Clara—she wouldn't have spoiled the symmetry of things really, the line. But Elsie! What about Elsie? She couldn't live without Elsie—Elsie was her root, her past self! And then living with two children in the churn of London, the great rotating machine, flogging themselves across the city and back in order to work, always living their lives neck-deep in people and cars and chaos, in the thick vortex of multitudinous screaming wants . . .

The problem was that they had gone too far: at least if they had stayed in London she would be able sometimes to return to Covent Garden on a summer's evening and remember. As it was, they were like a deported family with no access to the things that had brought them together: they were un-historied, displaced. The Dom who had come down from the mountain-top now worked at a small solicitors' firm in Arlington Park, and he did so at her urging. As for her, she did three slumberous days a week at a local post-production company that got a lot of wildlife documentaries, in which the world was made to seem as though no one had ever lived in it but the lions and the penguins, and which presumably gave unwonted succour to people who found it easier to believe that the earth was vigorous and miraculous than that their own depthless, costly existences were wrecking the place. The people she worked for would put the snow back on Mount Kilimanjaro for the duration of a shoot. They wouldn't think there was anything strange about it at all.

And what had she done it for? For what? Because she too wanted to spend, she too wanted to destroy! Her ancestry was in her, after all: she'd wanted to cash in luck and love and see what she got for them—she'd wanted to trade them in, for something easy, for the ride! She had this idea that life in a place like Arlington Park would reveal her to herself, would show her who she really was; when in fact it had merely told her that she was only what she strove to be, what she had the guts and the good sense to go after. She had thought that if she could just put something away from herself, force it off like a fallen beam she was pinned under, then she would feel free: a lot of people thought that, though her husband wasn't one of them. He wouldn't have moved an inch if she hadn't borne him along with her. She thought of him as something very valuable, in a glass case: a case she had shattered, so that he went everywhere unsheathed, unprotected, and having lost his context, it was hard to know what qualities to ascribe to him. She feared she had damaged him, so that she could no longer love him; that was why she wept beside his briefcase.

Her parents owned a villa in a new development in Portugal, a snorting four-wheel-drive Volvo, and a house in a

Leicestershire village whose grounds were so saturated with weed killer that no birds sang in the trees. They didn't think they were destructive: they thought they were admirable, and that the only reason they might be criticised was because people envied them. It was another tenet of the manifesto. Even the taxman envied them—that was why he took their money. They were delighted with Maisie's move to Arlington Park and they feared it: the two notions stood opposite each other, on two precipices divided by the gorge of failure. They liked the idea of Dom and Maisie being devolved away from the centre, the hub, to a place where nothing was likely to happen to them of which Maisie's parents might be forced to be jealous. They wanted them kept down, but they certainly didn't want them to go under. With their canny, assessing eye they saw the possibility that life in Arlington Park might provoke all kinds of disorder: anomalous things that were hard to explain, hard to find a place for. There was the house, for a start. Although it was charming in a cottagey, bohemian kind of way, Maisie's parents did not mistake it for a place where people ought actually to live. And why had they come to Arlington Park at all, if not to provide their children with a garden? Then: it was certainly a shame that Dom had taken a cut in salary and given up his partnership—but did Maisie really need to work, with the children still so small? Arlington Park itself was rather nice, though: quiet and green and prosperous and, as her father noted, full of good, expensive cars.

She wiped her eyes and went into the kitchen, as she did several times each day, in order to walk once around it and then go out again. She always expected to find something, there at the furthest point of the house: it was like the end of a pier, where seagulls might wheel and waves fling themselves at the harbour wall, and you waited for some clear thought to come to you over the open sea. She saw her reflection in the black window full of glare and gave herself, her life's companion, a strange, encouraging salute. The light adhered bleakly, slickly, to the folds of her face and clothes and then lost itself in a background of fathomless darkness, so that she seemed to be illuminated in the frame of the window out of a lowering, incipient nothingness. It was like a portrait of death; like a picture an artist might paint of himself in an access of terror and despair and self-knowledge. She felt she could have supported this nothingness, could have borne it and swallowed its dark information, if only there was something else, something elsewhere: if there was snow on Mount Kilimanjaro, for instance, she could have claimed her portion of insignificance and gone quietly in the knowledge that a righteous world of nature, of truth, survived her own incompetence.

But she was not insignificant: nobody was any more. And to fail at life when there was nothing beyond your living of it, no intransigent reality to revolve on and on in its mysterious justice! When flowers bloomed crazily in mid-winter and lakes dried up and icebergs melted, when forests died and living creatures were poisoned, made chemically hermaphrodite, when the whole well of life was poisoned, tainted, stained—

The doorbell rang. Katie, the babysitter, stood on the doorstep, her mobile phone clutched to her ear. She gave a little wave to Maisie with her ringed hand as she advanced herself over the threshold.

"Are you?" she said.

She was dressed as though for a summer's evening on a beach. Her legs were bare and she wore turquoise flip-flops with thick rubber platform soles. She wore a short pink pleated skirt and a pink vest with the word *Babycakes* written in pink sequins across its straining chest. Between the skirt and the vest her midriff disclosed itself, plump, white, and unblemished.

"*Do* you?" she said.

An aura of scented hot air gusted from Katie's trenchantly

straightened blond hair. It had the starchy smell of ironed clothes. It was dizzying, Maisie thought, to estimate the amount of time Katie spent with her hairdryer. Her hair hung in a weirdly synthetic curtain, out of which her face looked with a kind of suspicious inquisitiveness. Maisie imagined her going over it again and again with the hot shrieking instrument, as though she were painstakingly grafting sterility on to the world, or administering some generalised punishment for waywardness.

"Will you?" she said. "Have you? *Are* you?"

Maisie stood with her arms folded and looked up the stairs. She could hear Dom moving around their bedroom and the rattling sound of drawers being opened and closed. Beside her Katie seemed to be moving towards a conclusion.

"All right, then," she said. "All right, then. Okay, then. All right. All right." She kept her head stationary throughout this string of affirmatives, as though mindful of her hair. "All right, then. Bye. Bye. Bye."

She held the phone away from her, looked at it as though to see if it was going to tell her anything else, and switched it off with an emphatic pink enamelled finger.

"Hi," said Maisie. "How are you?"

This question appeared to precipitate Katie instantly into dark thoughts.

"I'm not too bad," she said bitterly. "I suppose I've been worse."

She hitched her little sausage-like handbag further up under her hairless armpit.

"Did you walk here?"

"My boyfriend dropped me," she said. She laughed mirthlessly. "He dropped me at the end of the road. He won't drive down here because it's too narrow. He says he can't turn round."

Maisie shrugged and said, "At least it wasn't raining."

"Horrible, isn't it?" said Katie mysteriously. "I hate this weather. It gets me down. I like sun."

"I think everyone likes sun."

She wanted to tell Katie that when she held her hairdryer near her head she was transmitting radiation directly into her brain. Katie made a little moue with her small pale mouth, as though she doubted anyone liked the sun as much as she did, or had any right to.

"We're going to Gran Canaria next month," she said, adding a *d* to "Gran" and pronouncing "Canaria" heavily, like "malaria."

"That's nice," said Maisie.

"It should be. My boyfriend's dad owns a bar and some holiday flats out there."

Destroyers! Maisie thought. *Wreckers!*

"It's the third time we've gone out," Katie said. "I'm really looking forward to it."

Maisie said, melancholically, "It's nice to have something to look forward to."

"It's the food I can't stomach," Katie said. "I don't really like Spanish food. And the people are quite chippy. I mean, it's not like it's the best place in the world. It's not like they've got white beaches or anything. In some places the sand is actually black. They get a lot of sun, but the beaches aren't anything much. Not like in the Caribbean. In the Caribbean the beaches are actually white. I'd really like to go there. My boyfriend doesn't want to, though. He says he wouldn't like the people."

"What people?"

"The natives. You know, the people who live there. He just thinks he wouldn't like them."

Katie deposited her white form on the sofa and placed her

hair behind her shoulders. One day she would die, would leave this place with her piece of it, her bloodied chunk, gripped in her painted clasp. She met Maisie's eyes meaningfully with her small, round, blue look.

"What I say is, you can't let other people hold you back," she said.

Maisie heard her husband's tread on the stairs; she felt him coming towards her, as though out of the core of some unseen fire or furnace, where he was remade for her, manufactured again and again out of his absences. She felt an almost unbearable sense of his reality, of his life and of the task, her task, of keeping these representations of him together, making them continuous. That was love, that work of deciphering and interpolating and testifying: to bear witness to something in its entirety, that was love. He bounded down the stairs, ready to be himself again, ready for anything. Up for it, as Katie's boyfriend apparently wasn't.

"I'll be one minute," Maisie said.

She passed him in the doorway. He was wearing a dark-blue shirt and black trousers. He looked as stealthy as a panther. His slanting eyes followed her. He smelled clean and good. He did not look at his watch; she got away, up the stairs, and behind her she heard him say in the echoing spaces of the sitting room, "How's it going, Katie?" and she heard Katie's diminishing "Not so bad, I suppose."

She went into the cluttered darkness of Clara and Elsie's room. She looked at the twisted forms of her sleeping children. The headlights of a car passing along the road outside swept the walls with a firm, yellow shaft of light. The sound of the engine rose and died away again. Maisie stood in the centre of the room; the intrusion passed right through her, like wind through the boughs of a tree. She looked at her children in their tangled sleep and she felt that she had deceived them, that she had stolen them from their rightful homes and carried them off with her on her getaway, her flight from authority. And yet there was nothing in the world she wanted for them, nothing in the whole world except for them to live, like two stolen bars of gold in a carpet bag, within her possession. There was nothing in the world they needed, only for her to believe they belonged to her. And it was this belief, so necessary, that had marked her, as one way or another it marked everybody. It made you manifest, visible. It took away your anonymity, perhaps for ever; and wherever you went, there you stood, between yourself and the world.

She thought she might discuss this matter with Stephanie Sykes.

Outside, in the dark, blowing street, Dom said to her:

"What were you doing at Merrywood, anyway?"

"I wish you'd been there," she said. "Everything would have been all right if you'd been there."

He didn't speak. He walked along next to her in his coat with his hands in the pockets. She looked into the lit-up windows of the houses that gave directly on to Roderick Road. She saw a man sitting in a reclining chair reading a newspaper. She saw an empty dining room, with chairs like erect ghosts around the table. She saw a woman lying on a sofa covered by a blanket, staring up at the ceiling. She saw a heavily furnished sitting room empty of life but for a little hairy dog, who jumped to his four sturdy feet and lifted his muzzle proudly when she looked in. She saw a woman holding a baby on her hip, vanishing through a doorway.

"Will it be all right?" Dom said. "At the Lanhams'?"

"I guess it will be okay," she said. "We don't have to worry. They have to worry."

They walked along silently.

Dom said, "Just don't get angry with everyone."

Maisie thought.

"I *am* angry with everyone. I worry that if I don't get angry I'll die. So maybe I should just die. Maybe you want me to die."

There was a pause before Dom said, annoyed, "I don't want you to die."

The sky overhead was big and black and billowy and heavily draped with sagging clouds; and there were no stars, just the beady red and white lights of aircraft moving in and out of the horizon, stitching their paths over the billowing purple and black; and the wind bore the sound of them to their ears, and the steady distant roar of the ring road came in great looping waves and reports. There was the smell of cooking from the houses, and of the pavement still damp in the darkness from the day's rain, and of diesel from the road ahead, and a green, veiled smell from the park beyond that. Through a gap in the houses Maisie caught a glimpse of a little perspective that opened out, with barely perceptible drama, down the gentle slope on the other side of Roderick Road. It showed another row of houses, and another, and another, until just the roofs of the last line were visible, bristling with aerials and satellite dishes. She looked at the sky and then she looked at her shoes, at the ground they were making, the little gains they made together, one after the other in their merry servitude.

She said, "What did you do today?"

Dom said, "I attended a seminar on the correct procedure for the prosecution of parking fines."

She took his arm in its heavy coat. She put her hand with his in the pocket and he grasped her fingers. They walked together along the dark, deserted tunnel of the street, towards the junction where it swept around the corner to the main road.

She said, "I went to the park this afternoon and everybody's dog was called Maisie. I swear there were about four of them. Everywhere I went I could hear people calling, Maisie! Maisie!"

She laughed out loud and the sound rang up and down the street.

"Mai-sie! Come on, Maisie! Come here, Maisie! Come here! Good girl!"

Christine was stuffing the chicken breasts when her mother rang.

"What did you decide? The chicken or the fish?"

Viv had given her a recipe for salmon glazed with Rose's lime marmalade.

"I'm doing the chicken," Christine said. "It's just easier, isn't it?"

Viv was silent in Newton Abbot.

"To be honest, Mum, I can't be bothered with fish. I feel with chicken that I know where I am. I just thought, you know, why not make life easy? Why make things more difficult than they actually have to be? Do you know what I'm saying?"

"The fish was easy," said Viv.

"I just couldn't be bothered."

"It was easy, Christine. And with chicken you can never be sure. You could send them all home with salmonella poisoning. You'll wish you'd bothered then. Larry always used to say a chicken was a filthy bird." Down the phone Christine heard her mother take a drink of something. "After he worked on the chicken farm that summer he wouldn't touch it. He said the cages were so crowded most of the birds never once stood on their own legs. They just sat there in their own leavings pecking each other's eyes out."

"That sounds like our house on a Saturday morning," said Christine.

"It's no laughing matter," said Viv. "Make sure you keep your surfaces clean with chicken. Don't touch the cooked meat with any implement you've used for the raw."

"Get you," said Christine, holding the phone under her chin and tearing the cling film off another Styrofoam package of chicken breasts. "You and your technical jargon."

"If you'd done the fish I wouldn't be worrying," said Viv. "Then there's all that scandal about the black market in meat. People getting meat off the back of a lorry and then changing the sell-by dates. You think you're eating fresh produce when in fact it's half-rotten. A lot of restaurants buy their meat that way, apparently. The Asians are the worst. That would affect you more than it does me. I can't stand their food." In Newton Abbot, Viv took another drink. "Apparently they cover up the taste of the meat with the sauces so you can't tell."

"Oh, I like a good Indian," said Christine.

"That's what your father used to say," said Viv. "He used to say the only good Indian was a prawn biryani."

With a knife Christine slit open a chicken breast and forced the herb butter into the jellied flesh with her fingers. It was hard to get the butter to stay in. It kept coming away on her fingers. She prised open the slit and wiped her fingers all over the veined insides. Liquid ran out and coated the gobs of butter and made them slippery.

"You've put me off these now," she said.

"Where did you get them?" her mother asked.

"The supermarket. They were on three for two."

Viv tutted. "They inject them with fluid to make them look bigger, you know. That's what they say. At least with a

209

fish you know it's clean. Though now they're saying the fish are full of rubbish from the water, aren't they? Make sure you wash your hands after you've touched them, that's all."

Christine had given up trying to stuff the breasts and was hurling them one after another into the roasting dish. She tipped the herb butter in on top of them and then tore off a sheet of foil and smothered the whole dish with it. With both hands she crushed the bloodied Styrofoam trays and cling film all together and dropped them into the bin.

"Are you out tonight?" she asked her mother.

"No."

"I thought tonight was your bridge night."

"I didn't fancy it," said Viv.

"Didn't you? Why not?"

"They're all so old," said Viv dramatically. "Yet they seem like they haven't lived."

Christine rolled her eyes and emptied the remains of the herb butter into the bin on top of the Styrofoam trays. There was only a strip of foil left in the box, so she threw that in too.

"So what are you doing?" she said.

"I'm sitting on the floor," Viv replied, "drinking a very nice bottle of Rioja."

"How long have you been doing that?"

"Since five. I went to see the new Tesco's with Angela and she dropped me back here about half four. They've built a new Tesco's superstore on the ring road and of course Angela wanted to see it. I wasn't bothered one way or the other, really. It's not what you'd call exactly exciting, is it? Then she said did I want to spend the evening with her and Bill instead, but no thank you very much, I thought, not another evening with those two. Bill talking golf all night and Angela still offering you cups of tea at ten o'clock when you're gasping for a drink. No, I thought, I'd prefer my own company."

"You said you enjoyed bridge last week."

"It was the novelty. The novelty's worn off now, though the others don't seem to think so. They all seem to think they're having the time of their lives."

There was a pause. Down the phone Christine heard a click and then a long exhalation of breath.

"Are you smoking?" she said.

"Just the odd one or two."

"Christ alive."

"That's another reason not to go to the bridge club. You're not allowed to smoke. They make you go outside, like a dog. It's funny, really, when you think about it. There they are, all prim and proper, all obsessed with good health and living a longer life, and what have they got to live for? What are they doing with all this life they've got? Playing bridge to pass the time!" Viv took another drag. "Larry would have seen the funny side of that."

Christine was rooting out plastic bags of salad from the fridge and tossing them on to the table. Then she took out a bottle of ready-made salad dressing and a half-full bottle of white wine, slammed the fridge closed with her hip, and, with the phone still wedged beneath her chin, pulled the cork from the wine bottle with her teeth.

"Look, Mum," she said, tipping the wine into a glass, "I know it's not easy being on your own. He's only been dead six months. Just give it a bit of time."

"People always tell me that," said Viv. "I say, what do I want to give it time for? I don't have much time to give. Your father took most of it."

Joe appeared in the doorway and looked at Christine with a chagrined expression. He tapped his watch meaningfully with his finger. After a while he went away again.

"He had his boat and his golf and his Friday night at the

pub. What did I have? He'd never let me on the boat, for a start. I was never allowed anywhere near it. What did he think I was going to do, sink it? The trouble was, Larry was selfish. In his case it came from being an only child. They never learn to share, only children. That's why I didn't stop at Stephen. I wanted to, but I couldn't do it. I thought, I can't let this go on into the next generation. I can't just perpetuate this disease. I was never a family person, though. No one ever taught me how to be. I never knew what on earth to do with you and Stephen on a rainy afternoon. Everyone else always seemed to be making fairy cakes. But I just thought, if I want fairy cakes I'll go and buy them."

One by one Christine tore open the bags of salad and emptied them into a big bowl. Then she made a crinkled ball of the bags with her fists and dropped it into the bin. She took a long swallow of wine.

"I know what you mean," she said.

"It wasn't like it is for you now. You just put yours in front of the video and you don't hear from them for the rest of the afternoon."

"That's right," said Christine.

"We were expected to actually do things with children. And then the food you had to make! We couldn't just open a box of fish fingers like you do and call it a day. Then when Larry came home he'd want *his* meal. I sometimes felt like I was manning the buffet car of a British Rail train, serving separate sittings. But in those days it was expected of you."

There was another click, and an exhalation.

"What about Stephen?" said Christine. "Have you seen his house yet?"

"It's not as nice as yours," said Viv indifferently. "They've got no taste, him and Samantha. They've only been there a fortnight and they've got it all tricked out like a whore's par-

lour. It's all gold fittings and swag curtains and these great sofas with fringes. I said to them, look, you two, this isn't it at
all. It's all minimalism these days. It's all floorboards and
white walls. You want to ask Christine's Joe, I said. He'll tell
you. He's an architect, he knows about style."

"I'll bet they thanked you for that."

"They've got televisions in all the rooms," said Viv. "It's
like a Holiday Inn."

"You'll enjoy seeing the children, though," said Christine.

"I've been seeing more of them than I planned," said Viv
ominously. "Last week he and Samantha invited me round
and then announced that they were leaving me with all three
and going out!"

"That was nice."

"Then he phones up and says would I like to have Oliver
two days a week because Samantha's decided to go back to
work. I said, why are you asking me? You've got money, why
don't you pay someone to do it? He acts all hurt and says, but
I thought you'd *want* to do it, Mum. So I say, why would I
want to do that? *You* don't want to do it, and you're his parents."

"And that went down well, did it?" said Christine, empty-
ing a bag of potatoes into a bowl and slamming it into the mi-
crowave.

"I always imagined that families were loving things," Viv
said disconsolately.

Christine looked at the kitchen window, with its black
squares of oblivion.

"You could be forgiven for imagining that."

"I grew up in a home, you see."

"I know you did, Mum."

"I used to look at families and think they were like a tree
of love. All these connected people rooted to the ground."

"That's a lovely thing to think."

"And I was just this little scrap, you see, this little piece of rubbish being blown around in the wind. That's how you feel, growing up in an institution."

"Your childhood wasn't easy, Mum."

"Only now I look back and I feel that I've been robbed. I feel I have even less than I started with. All I see is selfishness and greed, Christine. I feel them sucking the life out of me."

With the phone in the crook of her neck Christine tore a black plastic bin liner from a roll and shook it open. Then she went around the table sweeping newspapers and magazines and empty drinks cartons and Ella's felt-tip pens into it. She knotted the top of the bin liner and then shoved it behind the armchair in the corner. She looked at her watch. It was nearly eight o'clock.

"I didn't tell you," said Viv. "I drove past it the other day."

"Past what?"

"The place where I grew up."

"What were you doing all the way out there?"

"I made the journey specially. I don't know why, but I wanted to see it again. They've turned it into a hotel."

"Have they?"

"And I thought, what if I went in and booked a room? I sat in the car, all the time thinking I was about to get out and go in. I wanted to find my old room, you see. I wanted to find my room just as it was and get into my bed."

Christine put back her head for an instant so that the phone nearly fell off her shoulder and fixed her eyes on the ceiling.

"I thought that if only I could get into my bed everything would be all right again. It was the strangest feeling, Christine."

"That *is* strange, Mum," she said, going out into the hall. She found a vase of flowers that was standing on a shelf and carried it unsteadily with one hand back into the kitchen, so that some of the water slopped over on to the floor. She deposited it heavily in the centre of the table and gave the blooms a shake. "What do you think made you feel that?"

"I don't know. I only know it was what I felt. It felt like that was my rightful place. It felt like home."

"That was a strange thing to feel, wasn't it?"

"Then I came back and phoned up *Yachting Weekly* and put in an advertisement for Larry's boat."

"You didn't!"

"And a week or so later a gentleman came to the house, offered the full price, and towed it away. I tell you, Stephen was spitting with rage. He'd been biding his time, you see. He was so angry he wouldn't talk to me. Samantha told me they were all very disappointed. We hadn't liked to bring it up, she said, out of respect for Larry. Get that, out of respect for Larry. We didn't think you'd be getting rid of his things so soon, she said. I said to her, I've done you a favour, girl. That boat made me a widow before I had a grey hair in my head. I'm selling the golf clubs next."

"Good for you, Mum."

Christine wrenched open a drawer, took out two handfuls of cutlery, and walked around the table dealing them out.

"It's all one way in a family, Christine. It's all selfishness and greed. Don't let it happen to you."

"No, I won't, Mum. Do you think we need napkins? Or is that just too boring and middle class?"

"Follow your instincts, love. I'm no expert."

"Well, in for a penny," said Christine, walking around the table again with the napkins.

"Won't they be coming in a minute? Shouldn't you be

215

getting ready? Have you decided what you're going to wear?"

"I bought a new top today," said Christine. "I might put that on, see if anyone notices."

"You make them take notice!" Viv injuncted drunkenly.

"I'll do my best, Mum."

"Christine?"

"What, Mum?"

"Make sure the chicken's cooked right through, won't you? All these people coming. You've got your reputation to consider."

Upstairs, Joe was shaving and Ella was sitting on the bathroom floor in her pyjamas, with her thumb in her mouth and Robbie under her arm.

"Didn't you put her to bed?" exclaimed Christine. "I've been downstairs all this time thinking that at least you'd have put them both to bed."

"You were on the phone!" Joe said, indignant.

Christine folded her arms and looked at him. He was wearing a clean, well-ironed blue shirt and a pair of clean beige canvas trousers. His damp dark hair was slicked back from his face. He looked like the people she sometimes saw through the windows of what she thought of as trendy offices, people who were incomprehensible to her. The room was wet with condensation from the shower. It smelled of toothpaste and deodorant.

"Haven't you been having yourself a nice little beauty session?" she said.

Joe made perfect paths down his white cheeks with the razor.

"I put Danny down," he said. "I put him down half an hour ago, while you were on the phone."

"Well, couldn't you have done Ella while you were at it?

plate?"

"I didn't see why I should," said Joe, sticking his chin out pugilistically and running the razor over it.

"What do you mean, you didn't see why you should?"

"I didn't see why I should be up here doing all the work while you're on the phone."

"I just happened to be doing all the food as well, for your information. I just happened to be knocking up bloody dinner for eight, while you're up here beautifying yourself."

"I don't understand why you can't tell them to call back later," said Joe. "I mean, we've got people coming for dinner, and the phone rings twenty minutes before they're due to arrive, and you settle in for a nice long chat."

"While you're up here shaving and hoping that dinner for eight people will just appear by magic on the table, is that it?"

"Why can't you just say, look, it'd be lovely to talk to you but I'm busy now and I'll call you in the morning? Instead, it's half an hour. I hear the phone ring, and I think, right, that's another half an hour gone."

"I was talking to Mum," said Christine.

"Oh well, that really couldn't wait, could it? That was a real emergency. It's been at least ten hours since you last talked to her."

"She was a bit down, that's all."

"Whenever I hear you talking to your mother," Joe said, observing himself in the mirror, "I always know that it's her because the conversation's so one-sided. There are these big gaps and then you say something like *oh dear*, or *don't worry*, or *I'm sure it'll be all right in the end*. And then there's another big gap while she talks about herself again. They're completely one-sided conversations. She never asks about you. She just goes on and on about herself."

"She can talk about herself if she wants," said Christine.

"What's so bloody wrong with talking about yourself? At least she keeps in touch. You have to ring your mother to remind her when it's your birthday. At least Mum is an open, vulnerable person. At least she's not another selfish, self-satisfied old lady who sits there being disapproving because I have a glass of wine when I'm pregnant."

"She's completely selfish. She's the most selfish person I've ever met."

Christine was outraged. "How can you say that?"

"Look at what she was like with your dad. Completely selfish. Always on at him to get rid of his boat and stop going to the pub and stop enjoying himself. She couldn't stand to see him enjoying himself without her. She wanted all his attention. You're not like that."

"I can't be bothered to be," said Christine.

"That's not what you used to say," said Joe, with a wounded expression. "You used to say you thought it was important that we both had separate lives."

"That was before I realised that separate lives meant you going off surfing for the weekend while I look after the children."

"You had that weekend in Barcelona," Joe observed.

"You're right," said Christine. "I did. I should never have come back, that was my mistake."

She picked up Ella, carried her to her bedroom, dropped her on the bed, then switched off the light and closed the door.

"Mum had a difficult childhood," she said, returning to the bathroom.

"That's what you always say."

"Well, it's true."

"You can't blame everything on your childhood. I don't go around blaming everything on my childhood. What would be the point? It's over and done with. There's nothing you can do about it. You might just as well get on with your life."

Wet towels lay all over the bathroom floor. One by one Christine picked them up and dropped them into the laundry basket. Then she sat down on the edge of the bath and watched Joe put in his cufflinks.

"Do you know what she did?" she said.

"What?"

"She went back to look at the home she was in. She drove all the way to Cornwall to look at it. Apparently they've turned it into a hotel."

Joe washed out his shaving brush and put the soap and razor back in the bathroom cabinet. He was always tidy, at least when it came to his own things.

"I think that must have been quite upsetting," Christine reflected. "To go back to the place where you felt so much misery and see people there just enjoying themselves."

"She would have preferred it full of unwanted children, would she?"

"She nearly booked herself into her old room," Christine said.

Joe laughed. "That would have been good," he said. "She'd really have had the last laugh then, sitting there ordering room service. Why didn't she do it?"

"She just didn't."

"I expect she was worried she might have a good time."

"Just lay off!" said Christine. "I'm sick of you. Just leave her alone."

Joe slapped aftershave on to his glowing cheeks.

"That's me done," he said.

"Get you," said Christine morosely.

He looked at her. "Are you staying like that?"

"Why, don't I look nice?"

219

"It's just I thought you might, you know, get changed. Put on some make-up."

Christine opened her eyes wide. "You don't think I look nice as I am?"

"Your shirt's got something all down the front."

Christine examined it. "That's all right," she said. "That's just butter. And a bit of garlic. From stuffing the chicken. Just, you know, from getting dinner ready for eight people downstairs while you were up here shaving."

"You've made your point," said Joe.

"Have I? Are you sure?"

Joe sidled towards the door.

"You really piss me off sometimes," she said after him, as he went out.

Christine took off her shirt in front of the mirror. She put her hands under her breasts and pushed them upwards. Then she looked at herself smoulderingly from the side.

"Christ," she said.

She tore open her make-up bag and tipped everything out. With her fingers she rubbed foundation all over her face. Then she scrabbled about for her compact case of eyeshadows. There were four different shades in it, like little bruises. She used them all, starting with the darkest and working all the way up to her eyebrows. She went round her eyes with a pencil and then, leaning into the mirror, applied two coats of mascara. With a brush she rouged her cheeks and then rouged them again, because she still looked a bit white and worried. Then she unscrewed her jar of powder and plunged in the same brush, in her haste spilling half of it over the worktop. Powdered, her face looked frozen, suspended, like a face in a painting. She regarded it with narrowed eyes. She made a moue with her mouth and a little fan of wrinkles sprang up around her lips. If she grimaced the other way, two

220

transverse wrinkles would appear down her cheeks. She took a lipstick and drew a big red mouth on herself. Then she blotted some of it off with tissue paper and smouldered again in the mirror.

In the bedroom she removed the rest of her clothes and opened the wardrobe, where the long mirror fixed to the inside of the door showed her reflection full length. She'd had enough of herself today, after the changing rooms at Merrywood. What she wouldn't give to have the body she'd had ten years earlier. She hadn't appreciated it at the time. When she met Joe she'd had a nice little figure, big chest, slender hips, white skin like elastic. The funny thing was, all she could think about in those days was social status. She was mesmerised by the sense of a hierarchy. It seemed to stand there, like a big mountain she couldn't lose sight of but everyone else ignored. It stood there, the question of who she was and what she was worth. Everywhere she turned, it gave out its challenge to her, the great big hard fact of itself. She didn't know exactly what it meant or even what it was. She just knew she was at the foot of it.

That changed the minute she met Joe. Suddenly she was closer: suddenly there was detail, texture, sensation—the texture of his cotton shirts and sheets, the food he ate, the wine he drank, the sounds that came out of his mouth, the things he lived with and for and touched every day. When she was with him she had to think with the front of her brain. She didn't think with her body. It all happened at the front of her brain. Entering his house for the first time all those years ago, and seeing his pictures, his antique furniture, his architecture books, the rugs, the chess set, the dried flowers in a bowl, the front of her brain had burned with pressure. It was like being held upside down, the desire to laugh meeting the total certainty that she was wrong, that she was ignorant; it felt like a vein in the centre of her forehead was about to burst. A man buying antique furniture! A man living by himself, not ignominiously but well: for Christine, it was uncharted territory. When they made love, she did it not with her body but with the front of her brain. He was like a patch of sunlight she had to keep herself in. The dread, the terror of falling into shadow, of going back to where she'd been before: she pretended she was easy, that this was just another passage of life, but she was not. She lived in terror of her expulsion from the light. She lived in the front of her brain until it hurt. Somehow, her life had become contingent on this one chance, this opportunity of Joe: it was some flaw in her upbringing, in her parents, perhaps in her own personality too, that she found it so difficult to better herself and yet so ardently desired to. Expelled from Joe, she saw quite clearly a life like her parents' life, a semi in Newton Abbot that was waiting—minatory, patient—to claim her. She saw that another chance might never come her way. She thought and thought her way through it. She adhered to Joe with the front of her brain until it seemed as though she was awake even when she was sleeping next to him.

It was a shame really, she thought now, regarding her heavy thighs in the mirror, her mottled mound of stomach. After all, she'd had a nice little figure. Somewhere inside her it was still there, straining to come out. When she thought of men it did a little dance. It strutted, it moved its slender hips. She thought of a young man, broad-chested, eager. There was a boy she saw sometimes who lived across the road, with brown eyes like chocolates. She thought of him. She could teach him a thing or two. She'd do it with her body, not like the girls he probably knew, self-conscious girls who did it with the front of their brains. She'd ravish him in her brass bed, amidst her antique furniture, and he'd be grateful for it. Or perhaps she'd go across the road, to whatever pitiful room he lived in, and stand there fearless, powerful, blind. It'd be a bit much, doing it in her and Joe's bed. She would go to his room, bringing with her her aura of the mountain.

Downstairs the doorbell rang. She pulled the new top from its bag and tore off the labels. She remembered the tarty one, the one Stephanie liked. Should she have bought that instead? The new top, the purple top, was ample and respectable. She'd bought it with the front of her brain; she couldn't stop herself. She thought of the men who were coming, married men, and they seemed to her like children, hard work and only indirectly rewarding. She poured her efforts and energy into them and it seemed to go into the masonry, into the foundations. It seemed to ensure not satisfaction but continuance, the future continuation of everything that could never be brought to a resolution. It seemed to ensure that she would never, herself, receive any attention. Why was it always her, cementing the masonry, the foundations? When would she be free of it, this feeling that all life was work, this strange, compelling sense that without her the sky would fall in on Arlington Park, its avenues darken, its households revert to some oblique and savage condition? She could not imagine not being here, that was the thing: her hold on existence was manifested solely in these streets and these houses, and the people in them. None of them, not even Joe, understood what it was to be so proximate to oblivion. They were hallmarked, like silver: they saw the world as categorised, not chaotic. But she, Christine, was only one generation removed from abandonment: she, the offspring of a scrap, a piece of litter blowing in the wind, felt always the presence of the enormous darkness from which she had come.

She put on a brown skirt with the purple top. It wasn't an outfit for seducing the boy over the road, but at least it was slimming. She thought that perhaps she would end like her mother, sitting alone on the floor in a room somewhere, drinking a bottle of wine, a misshapen fruit dropped off the tree of love. She could hear voices downstairs, men's voices booming and a woman's laugh. She turned to leave the room, but then she stopped, and looking over her shoulder at herself in the mirror, she lifted her skirt and thrust her bottom towards the glass.

The English race," said Joe Lanham to the men, "is dying out."

He leaned across and offered the wine around. Benedict Randall and Dom Carrington were sitting side by side on the sofa. Dave Spooner was perched on the footstool by the fireplace. Joe, seigneurial, was in his favourite chair, an original Georgian chesterfield he had once quietly removed from a manor house the firm were refurbishing into flats before the reclamation people took it. They were in the upstairs sitting room. It was one of the features of the Lanhams' house, the upstairs sitting room. It went all the way across the building, with windows on each side. The Lanhams' was a Georgian house, tall and narrow. The kitchen was on the ground floor and went all across the building too. It often happened, on evenings such as this, that the women congregated on one floor and the men on another.

"What do you mean?" Dave said. "Do you mean morris dancing and all that?"

The Spooners—Dave and Maggie—were among the Lanhams' oldest friends. They appeared in the Lanhams' wedding photographs. Dave always went along on Joe's Wednesday nights at the pub. You knew where you were with the Spooners. They were part of the bedrock: they were solid.

"I mean the race itself," said Joe. "The Anglo-Saxon race."

"And is that a bad thing, for you?" said Benedict. He was slumped into the corner of the sofa with his legs crossed at the knee and again at the ankle. He held his glass by the stem and swirled the wine around in it, and plunged his nose into it before drinking.

"It's a Wine Society wine," Joe told him. "I find they're usually pretty good."

Dave held his glass up to the light appreciatively.

"Excellent," he said.

"I'm asking whether it's a tragedy, in your view," reiterated Benedict. "The end of the English."

"I think it's sad," said Joe.

"In what way sad?"

"Sad that we won't exist."

"What's your evidence that we won't?"

"I don't need evidence," said Joe. "I see it with my own eyes."

Benedict swirled the wine around in his glass again. Precipitately, he tipped his head back and drank, draining the glass to the bottom.

"Do you?" he said, wiping his mouth with the back of his hand. He looked around at them. "We all seem pretty English here to me."

Dom cleared his throat and leaned towards Dave Spooner.

"What do you do, Dave?"

"I make labels," Dave said.

Dom was sitting on the edge of the sofa with his knees jutting out and his elbows digging into them, as if he were playing strategic chess. He nodded once, acknowledging Dave's move.

"Labels?" he said. "Do you mean, as in clothes?"

"Labels," Dave repeated. "They come on an adhesive strip. We make them blank, and then you print on them whatever you want."

"It's one of those funny things, isn't it?" Joe said. "We all use them, but we never stop to think about where they actually come from."

"Well, yours probably come from China," Dave said. "If you're talking about general administrative labelling, like what you'd use in the office. We sell to a smaller, high-quality market. Home businesses, a few art galleries. Even the National Trust. You'd be surprised."

Silence fell.

"And how long have you been doing that for?" Dom said.

Dave considered. "About six years."

"Right." Dom nodded.

Joe leapt out of his chesterfield.

"Let's put some music on," he said. "Liven things up a bit."

"I can't stand those morris dancers," Dave said to the other two. "All that skipping about shaking bells. And those shoes they wear with the buckles, and the white frilly trousers. Skipping about like a pack of ponces." He shuddered. "It sends a shiver down my spine."

Downstairs Christine was admiring Maggie Spooner's exquisite mohair shawl.

"Look at you," she said, fingering the soft grey wool. "Look at you, all soft and gorgeous and womanly."

Maggie was pregnant. She looked like she had a cushion stuffed down her front, Christine thought. Her stomach was big, but she was as thin as a stick everywhere else. She had a kind of pride about her, with her lithe, pregnant body and her exquisite mohair and her face that looked recast somehow, flushed, bronzed. She looked like a woman in the wilderness, a pioneer woman or an Amazon, who might spend the day running through the jungle hunting with her spear before squatting down in a grove of banana leaves and giving birth. It wasn't an idea you would normally associate with Maggie Spooner. Only she looked so powerful all of a sudden, so—iconic.

Wasn't it amazing, Christine thought. Wasn't it incredible how the spring of life just bubbled up, rose up in these thousands of houses, amidst all this solidity: in the midst of everything that was so fixed and hard, the spring of life bubbled up eternally, giving and giving. She imagined Maggie running barefoot with her spear across Arlington Park. She seemed to be alone in some definitive way in her lithe, pregnant body. Her face was the bronzed face of a warrior woman. Having drunk from the spring of life she had shed her association with men, had left Dave mending his motorbike in the back garden and run out with her spear.

Christine drank deeply from her glass. It had to be admitted that the two children Maggie already had were among the least attractive Christine had encountered. But still—she was ploughing her patch of life, wasn't she? She was getting everything out of it she could, and Christine saw nothing wrong in that. And to see her now, tonight, as she was, all bronzed and warlike—well, you could see she was really living. What did it matter what the future held, what it all added up to in the end? What did it matter if the child in Maggie's belly was another tow-headed dwarf in the style of her younger son, Harry? The point was, you had to live in the moment. What was the good of getting and getting if you couldn't look back and say there, there I was really living! A lot of the people Christine knew were obsessed with money. What was the point of that? It was experience that made you rich: it was life itself, bubbling up through the floorboards. When she thought of this house she shared with Joe! It was a casket, a coffer of riches, memories piled high in every room, every corner full of the sense of life growing, accruing, amassing interest.

No, give her Maggie any day. Give her Maggie over people who were prettier or more intelligent, people who were wealthier, more important, more exciting. Give her Maggie every time, over people who questioned everything and complained and were never satisfied. They were the ones she couldn't stand, the ones who criticised and complained. What did they ever do for anybody? What difference had they ever made?

"Look at you," she said to Maggie, touching the single pearl Maggie wore on a silver chain around her neck. "That's nice as well, isn't it? Sort of understated. Elegant but understated."

"Oh, that," Maggie said. "Dave gave me that for our anniversary."

"Of course he did," said Christine, satisfied. "Isn't he a nice bloke? Just, you know, gives you a gorgeous necklace for your anniversary. Isn't he lovely? You don't get famous for doing that, do you? You don't get social status, or people thinking you're important for giving your wife a necklace on your anniversary. Do you?"

Maggie looked at her, perplexed, out of her bronzed Amazonian face. Her eyes were round and blue. They were like two little blue flowers blowing thoughtless in a meadow.

"I don't know," Christine sighed, tipping more wine into her glass. Maggie's glass was still full. It rested on the table beside her like a misted goblet of light. "You have to wonder sometimes, don't you?"

She looked at Maisie and Juliet Randall, who were standing talking by the kitchen units. Why had they separated themselves? Why didn't they come and sit down at the table, where the wine was flowing freely and Christine had lit a scented candle; where she was trying to build up a warm core of female association, a little warm fire out of the fact of them all being women, in it together while the men sat upstairs? Instead, Maisie and Juliet stood by the kitchen units, as far away as they could get. They stood there conversing like people at a convention, not touching, not warm, not clinging together on this raft of life as it went over the black waves of oblivion. Christine didn't know why she'd invited them. Give her Maggie every time. She scrutinised Maisie's attire and decided that she'd evidently smartened herself up a bit. She was striking-looking, in a way. She was entirely in black, a black shirt that was quite smart and a black pair of trousers. It was all right, but Christine never liked it when people wore all black. It just seemed like such a negative statement. It was like saying you'd given up hope. At least she was wearing mascara, which helped.

And Juliet had finally cut off that terrible hair! She'd had it since she was a schoolgirl, when Christine first knew her. Juliet was the year above. She'd gone about with that hair down to her waist as though it was against her religion to cut it. She was all clever and superior in those days. She'd seemed full of information, programmed, like a rocket being prepared for a long journey into space. It had surprised Christine no end to find her all these years later, come to earth in Arlington Park. She'd bumped into her on the High Street a month ago with two small children, carrying her shopping. She didn't know why, but she'd expected Juliet to be miles away, out there in space, in a different orbit altogether. She'd often thought of her since school, thought of her twinkling in a distant constellation, a university professor maybe, or a writer—a person, anyway, who gave Christine in Arlington Park a sense of perspective, of the reach of the universe, of its strange but necessary dimensions. It was this sense of order that allowed life in Arlington Park to be what it was. You had to have the professors and the politicians, the clever and the rich; and equally, she supposed, you had to have the starving millions, God help them. You had to have the top and the bottom for the middle to become possible. So it did not please her to find Juliet here, carrying her shopping in plastic bags. But then again, why not? Why not have her here, enriching the soil, ploughing her information back into it—what harm could that do? Perhaps one of those girls she taught would shoot out into space one day and burn there like a star. Then they'd be able to say that Arlington Park had given the world a prime minister or a best-selling author, a person of note, someone to fix this place more firmly still at its core, to fortify its connections with life at every level. Wouldn't that be nice?

Upstairs the men had music on so that she couldn't hear the timbre of their conversation. She didn't fancy the look of any of them really, except Dave Spooner. Juliet's husband was all bandy legs and no neck, and Dom Carrington was a little too refined for her tastes: he looked at you with those eyes as if it really mattered what you said next, and then was silent for a minute after you'd said it, which Christine found disconcerting. Also, he had a little perfect look about him which contradicted Christine's sense of what the opposite sex should be. What was a man if not a rough thing you rubbed up against that gave you all your smoothness? A man should be a rough, splintered thing, solid, imperfect, abrasive, and thick-skinned, like a tree-trunk with a rough bark. You needed to feel yourself purified by your contact with a man. You needed to come up against him and feel the attrition of conflict that sent you back smoother, polished, rubbed clean. But Dom was like marble. With a man like marble, like glass, where was the friction? Where was the sticking point that relieved you of the questing sense of irritation, the itch, the crawling, questing need for some roughness to find a purchase on? Dom would make you feel like a rhinoceros trying to relieve its itch against the stalk of a daisy.

No, tonight it was Dave she liked, simple Dave, his hands greasy with motorbike oil fastening a pearl on a silver chain around your neck. You just didn't want to get stuck talking to him, that was all.

"I've had one of those days today," she said to Maggie, suddenly bleary. "You know, those days when you don't stop."

Maggie nodded sympathetically with her face like an Amazon's bronze shield.

"It's all been coffee here and lunch there and tearing around to drop off one child and pick up another and solving the world's problems in between, and then suddenly I'm stuffing chicken breasts for eight. Do you know what I mean?"

"It's just so busy sometimes, isn't it?" said Maggie.

"And then you think, you know, I could just have stayed here. I could have put Ella down for a nap, sat in a chair, and read a magazine. What would have been so wrong with that?"

"I've been doing yoga," said Maggie. "I find that really helps."

"Yoga." Christine stared into the revolving depths of her wineglass. "Why not? Why not fit in a bit of yoga while you're at it? Why not make space for a bit of transcendental meditation while you're planning the day?"

"You've just got to make the space," agreed Maggie.

Christine gazed at Juliet with her bobbed hair, at Maisie frowning and nodding, her arms folded defensively across her chest.

"The thing is," she said, "we're all so different, aren't we? You've just got to steer your own course. That's all you can do really, is steer your own course through it and not think too much."

"That's right," said Maggie.

"Because it's hard sometimes, seeing all these differences as positive. Sometimes you can look at it all and think, you know, what's it all about? Where's the logic behind it?"

"That's right," said Maggie.

"You can start to see the world as a terrible place."

"That's right."

Christine emptied the remains of the bottle into her glass.

"Speaking of which," she said. "Has there been any news about that girl? The one who went missing in the park."

Maggie winced and closed her eyes. "They found her," she said.

"Did they?"

Maggie opened her eyes again and there were the blue meadow flowers.

"They found her in a field a few miles away from where she was taken. She was dead."

"Was she?" Christine considered it, her glass at her lips, and then swiftly downed the contents. "Oh well."

"You say you're a teacher," said Joe.

Benedict nodded. He looked surprised.

"Where do you teach?"

"Hartford View."

"Blimey." Joe whistled and sat back in his chesterfield. "That was a bit of bad luck. Couldn't they have found a job for you up here?"

"I quite like it," said Benedict.

"There are plenty of good schools up here," Joe said. "There's even that private one, you know, the College. You'd probably get paid more, going private."

Benedict appeared to consider it.

"Probably," he said.

"What I can't stand about schools," said Joe, leaning forward, "is all the political correctness. You know what I mean. You can't call a blackboard a blackboard."

"They're whiteboards now," said Benedict.

"Exactly!" bellowed Joe, laughing.

"No, I mean they're actually white. We don't use blackboards any more. We use interactive whiteboards."

Joe was nodding enthusiastically.

"And if a teacher lays a hand on a pupil they're either a racist or a paedophile, aren't they? And the whole class has to be held back because Aqbul can't understand English. It's just ridiculous, isn't it?"

"I know a chap whose son goes to Hartford View," said Dave. "He says to look at some of them coming out at the end of the day would shrivel your balls to peanuts. He says they're like animals, some of them. These sixth-formers, great big black guys six feet tall, you know, with their trousers halfway down their arses. He says it's a nightmare."

"And if you laid a hand on them you'd get called a racist, right?" said Joe. "Even though you're half their size."

"Most likely you'd get your head kicked in first," Dave observed.

"You're braver than me," Joe said to Benedict. "You wouldn't catch me walking past it, let alone going to work in it."

"It's not so bad," said Benedict. "Most of the students are perfectly nice."

"Nice!" repeated Joe, shaking his head and laughing. "That's a new one—nice!"

Benedict sat with his nose lifted slightly into the air, as though waiting for order to be restored. Joe crossed his legs and looked at him, red-faced, with his hand over his mouth to suppress further outbursts of mirth.

"The thing is," Benedict continued, "you're all they've got."

"How do you mean?"

"For a lot of them, school is the only organized thing in their day."

"And whose fault is that?" Joe demanded.

Benedict looked surprised again.

"Among other things, it's the parents' fault."

"My point exactly!" said Joe, slicing a broad finger through the air.

"But the parents aren't really the issue," said Benedict, gently rapping the arm of the sofa. "What you've got are these children."

"Some of them six feet tall," Joe said to Dave.

"And you've got to do what you can for them."

"I know what I'd do for them," said Joe. "I'd make them speak bloody English. I'd say, you want to come to our schools, then you've got to speak our language. By force if necessary."

Benedict laughed loudly.

"I would," Joe said. "I'm not joking. Where do you think Christine is with this food?"

"She probably got lost on her way to the cooker," said Dave.

"Got sidetracked by a bottle of wine, you mean," said Joe. "She's been going since about six. We'll have to keep her airborne somehow. We don't want her crash-landing before we've had a chance to eat something."

"How long have you lived here?" Dave asked Dom.

"About six months."

"Oh, not long, then. Where were you before?"

"London."

"Well, you're well out of that, at least."

"Maisie doesn't always think so," said Dom, ducking his head. "But yes, I suppose we are."

"Doesn't think she's better off here?" said Joe. "You've got to be kidding me."

"She'll get used to it."

"You couldn't pay me to live in London," said Joe. "Bloody terrorist capital of the world. There they all are, hob-nobbing in Bayswater, free as birds, and getting their teeth done on the National Health Service while they're at it."

He got up and went to put on more music. His eye alighted on something on a shelf and he lifted it carefully down and took it over to show the others.

"Look at this," he said. "I found it the other day in a junk shop in Weston-super-Mare. It was just sitting there in a box of old rubbish. I cleaned it up and it works like a charm. It's a collector's item, original eighteenth century."

It was a pair of painted figurines beside a painted palm tree, carved in wood and mounted on a wooden plinth. The standing figure was a man in military uniform with an intricately carved moustache, holding a sword in his clasped hands. The other was a dark-skinned man in a loincloth, kneeling with his head bent forwards over a carved tree stump and his wrists delicately bound behind his back.

"Watch this," said Joe.

He turned the key in the side and wound up the mechanism. In little jerks the soldier's tiny sword ascended until it was held above his head. Then it came down on the back of the dark-skinned man's neck. There was a hesitation and a little click, and then the man's head came off and fell into a basket. Joe laughed uproariously.

"Isn't that terrific?" he said. "Look, the head's attached to the shoulders by a piece of string that comes out of his arse. You just pull it and it pops back up again."

He pulled the piece of string and the little head rose out of the basket and made its ghostly way back up to the severed neck. Then he wound the key and showed them how it worked again.

Christine didn't see how she was supposed to know if the chicken was done. She'd given it a good innings—it was as roasted as the contents of a charter flight home from Tenerife. She stabbed one of the parcels of flesh and tried to peer in-side.

"Oh, I don't know," she said, slamming it back into the oven for another precautionary blast.

"Tell me how I can help," said Maggie, manifesting herself before Christine's eyes. She had even shed the mohair shawl in preparation. That was what you got from people like Maggie: real support.

"Aren't you nice?" said Christine.

She went to the bottom of the stairs and bawled her husband's name. Then she returned to contemplate the salad, which seemed to have deflated to half the level it was before.

"This looks a bit tired," she said to Maggie. "What do you think?"

Maggie peered fastidiously into the bowl. Above their heads came the sound of footsteps, as the men mobilised themselves to descend.

"I'd have been quite happy to leave them up there," said Christine. "I don't fancy them tonight. I feel like they're no bloody use to anybody."

"Have you got any cucumber?" Maggie said. "Any spring onions, or chives? I'll go and look in the fridge and see what I can find," she concluded when Christine didn't reply.

Christine was mutinous. Couldn't Joe have helped, instead of spending most of the evening out in his workshop and the rest up in the bathroom with his face six inches from the mirror? He hadn't even put the children to bed! And now here she was, worrying about salmonella poisoning and the fact that her salad looked like a compost heap, and the funny way Maisie Carrington stared at her, and the way Juliet seemed sort of superior and above it all, and her top, that Stephanie said made her look like the bloody Archbishop of Canterbury. It just wasn't on! She bet Dom didn't make Maisie cook dinner for eight while he stared at himself in the mirror; even old bandy legs probably lent a hand when Juliet was tired. Yet there was Joe sitting upstairs like the lord of the manor, drinking wine, while Christine was fighting it out down here alone!

"You're useless, you are," she hissed in his ear when he came strolling through the doorway, glass in hand.

He looked around absently, as though wondering who had said it.

"You heard me," she said, turning on her heel.

Was this what they meant when they talked about sexual inequality? Was this it, the front, the hump, the line of battle? She'd never seen her father so much as boil an egg, but then her mother had never mowed the lawn or mended the kitchen cupboards either. It had never seemed worth the bother to Christine, trying to sort it out when it was all so much of a muchness; but now she wondered whether that wasn't exactly what kept you in your place, this acceptance of things, so that you were forever going round and round in a circle and never getting anywhere. If you accepted things, where were you meant to go when it got unacceptable? Who were you meant to tell? There had to be room for change—there had to be room for a contingency! Like her father: even when Viv was ill once with pneumonia, she had to get up to make his tea. That was no way to live, was it?

"Look at that," she said, gazing into the salad bowl, where Maggie was briskly hurling little fresh chopped-up pieces of things with her sleeves rolled up to the elbows. "You've really made that look lovely and inviting, haven't you?"

Maggie's face darkened with pleasure. That was all you needed, a bit of encouragement! Someone to thank you once in a while and tell you you'd done well—everyone needed that, didn't they? Christine felt warm, weightless with wine. The room revolved in its spangled depths. It seemed to arrange itself around a dense centre, like the petals of a flower. To feel discontent, when you were revolving, warm, in the petals of a flower! It was a worm, a pest, a black blight of feeling! It could never come to anything—it could only blacken you, blacken you where you stood!

"What's eating you, then?" Joe said over her shoulder.

He was standing behind her. His rough voice was in her ear. She was conscious, in the distances of the kitchen, of other men: they sat or stood, dark and imperfect, roughly made. Beneath their clothes their bodies were imperative, full of entitlement, full of a half-forgotten violence. Yet this man had come to her. He had left the others and come to her. Why didn't he touch her? Why didn't he grip her arms, rub the rough bark of his cheek against her throat? She thought of taking off her archbishop outfit. She thought of tearing it off and running through Arlington Park, naked, gyrating.

"I'm fed up with you," she said.

"What've I done, for Christ's sake?"

"Bloody nothing," said Christine. "I'm fed up with it."

"They're your friends," he said indignantly. "I didn't invite them."

Was that what Dom Carrington said to Maisie, in the middle of a dinner party? She didn't think so.

She saw Maggie, the Amazon, still chopping away at the sideboard.

"Look, it's Maggie that's doing all the work!" Christine exclaimed. "Seven months pregnant and she's doing the work in your house!"

Joe looked sullen.

"What do you want me to do?" he said.

"Just get them sitting down," Christine said wearily. "Decide where they're going to sit and sit them there."

Behind her Joe was gone. She took the chicken out of the oven. The little lumps were sizzling away in their fat. They seemed full of helpless agitation: they seemed unhappy in their world of scorching heat.

"That'll do," said Christine, kicking the oven door shut with her heel.

Christine was sitting next to Dave, after all. Joe had positioned himself at the other end of the table, as far away from her as he could get.

"You're not eating much," Dave observed.

"You don't want it, once you've gone to all the bother of cooking it," she said, pushing away her plate.

"You eat it," he urged. "Go on. It'll do you good."

Oh, she could have wept! Dave, so solicitous, despite having problems of his own, a seven-months-pregnant wife of his own! Since when would Joe have even noticed if the woman sitting next to him at dinner had dropped dead into her food?

"Listen to you," she said. "Going around making sure everyone's all right."

"It's lovely," he said, chewing.

On her other side was old bandy-legs Benedict, but he had his hands full with Maisie Carrington. She didn't know what they were talking about, but Maisie looked worried. Or perhaps she always looked like that. Christine gazed at the people talking and eating. Wasn't it strange, to invite all these people to your house and then serve them like they'd be served in a restaurant? Why did they all have to do it? What was the point? She didn't want to be knocking up bloody dinner for eight and then serving it. She didn't want to be passing the butter, and clearing away the starters. She wanted to be living—living!

One minute she was looking at the back of Benedict's head and the next he'd sort of spun around and there was his face, six inches from hers. He had a funny little tipping-up nose and two red dots on his cheeks, and his little blue eyes sparkled like tiny furious fireworks.

"Having fun?" he said.

"I was just thinking what a lot of frigging hassle it all is," said Christine.

He gave a strange bark.

"Do you know what I mean?" she said. She upended the wine bottle over her glass so that the wine came gushing out and made a foaming whirlpool that sent a wave over the rim. "I mean, why aren't we all dancing? Why are we sitting here like the district council discussing a frigging planning application?"

He smiled and folded his arms and looked down into the fold. He was a funny little bloke. He looked like a little elf, with his pointy ears and his red cheeks and his sparkling eyes. Where on earth had Juliet dug him up from?

"Do you know what I mean?" she said.

"I do."

"I mean, talk about being old before your time. Why don't we just push the table against the wall and dance?"

"I don't know," he said amusedly.

"What are we so frigging worried about?"

"I don't know. Making fools of ourselves."

Christine was amazed. "Do you think so? I don't think it's that at all."

"What is it, then?"

The room rested in its destructive beauty, candlelight gilding the table laden with spoiled dishes, the smeared glasses and crumpled napkins, the scattered cutlery and discarded brown remains of food. She saw faces, intricately contoured. Darkness seemed to stand expectantly in the corners, a great expectant darkness whose relationship to the struggling, intricate light expressed itself in these faces, so that they seemed to arise from the commingling of two things, darkness and light. The faces were the manifestation of this destructive beauty: they were so intricate, so full of detail, and yet so precarious. If you blew out the candles they would be gone.

"We're worried about what we might do," said Christine. "And what's the point of that?"

She looked at her husband at the other end of the table. He was talking to Dom, leaning right across Juliet Randall to do it, so that Juliet was pressed back in her chair with a tight, resigned little expression on her face, as if she was stuck in a tunnel with people always pushing past her. He looked big: he looked colossal, the block of his head on the beam of his shoulders, his arms like girders, his hands like shovels. You couldn't get past Joe. You had to reckon with him or quit the field. She wasn't going to get past Joe into a new field of life. She studied his blue shirt: he filled it out nicely with the beam of his shoulders. You'd have to run away, into the rotten places. You'd have to go where a stealthy, insidious rot ate its way through all the solid things. You couldn't come up against him and win: you'd have to go elsewhere, far from Arlington Park and the colossal fact of Joe.

But what you did get from Joe was a feeling of certainty, she thought. She didn't know what it was like to be married to a little bandy-legged elf—but with Joe you got certainty, straight up. She thought of a harbour wall with the sea hurling itself against it. Her parents took her to Lyme once, where the sea hurled itself against the Cobb and made great glittering arabesques in the air. She had thought it would come right over. They had stood there in the lee of the wall, terrified, while the sea tried to throw itself over and the spray soaked them to the skin. They had gone too far out, to where the sea was like a beast hurling itself against the wall, fighting it, fighting to get over and engulf the orderly little town that lay along the shore; and they'd had to wait to get back, wait while the spray soaked them to the skin, wait for the boom and the angry splat of water at their feet. Then they'd run a few yards and and wait again. They thought they'd never get back. They thought they were done for. That was how you got yourself swept out to sea, her father said afterwards. It was that easy.

They were all so lucky in the end, weren't they? Lucky to be here, alive—warm and dry and alive, fed and sheltered, helping each other out when they could. And nothing was perfect. Nothing! You could eat your way through the world like rot, looking for perfection. The point was, you set yourself challenges. You worked with what you had and tried to improve it. Look at Dave and Maggie, look at Juliet: look at Maisie if you wanted, trying to make a new life for herself, giving them her own individual perspective on things. Look at Juliet, bringing her skills and qualifications to the table. Look at Maggie, just being generally inspiring, keeping herself together and inspiring them all. They all had a contribution to make, didn't they? They all did their bit, did their best to make life interesting. And what, Christine wished to know, was life meant to be, if not interesting?

"What would you do?" the little elf Benedict said beside her. "Do you know?"

She felt confused: she wasn't sure what he meant.

"What's the point of all this worrying?" she said indistinctly. "Where does it get you in the end?"

He seemed to be looking at her enquiringly.

"Maisie!" she said loudly, so that Maisie jumped in her chair and turned a troubled face towards her. "What are you looking so worried for? What's the point of it, all this worrying?"

"What do you mean?" said Maisie.

"Only that you looked like you thought the world was about to end," Christine observed morosely.

"Sometimes I think it already has," said Maisie, with a kind of tentative dignity. "Or our bit of it, anyway."

" 'The shadows, the meadows, the lanes,' " said the elf. " 'The guildhalls, the carved choirs.' "

"What's that?" said Christine. "What's that you're saying?"

"It's a poem," said the elf.

"Say it again," said Christine. "Say just what you said then."

The elf recited it with his head tilted slightly forward and to the side, as though the words were coming in by a very narrow thread through his ear and then going out through his mouth.

> *And that will be England gone*
> *The shadows, the meadows, the lanes*
> *The guildhalls, the carved choirs.*
> *There'll be books; it will linger on*
> *In galleries; but all that remains*
> *For us will be concrete and tyres.*

"Look at that," said Christine, in admiration. "Aren't you clever, knowing all that off by heart?"

The elf acknowledged her with a nod and a little smile.

"What does it mean?" she said.

"It's about what's beautiful being destroyed," said the elf.

"Is it? Oh."

"Specifically England," said the elf. "But I suppose it could be anywhere."

Christine considered it, there in the revolving room.

"I never understand why people get so worked up about that," she said.

"You don't?" The elf seemed surprised.

"You can't live in the past, can you? Your happiness can't depend on things staying the same. You've got to embrace change! You've got to embrace the future!"

"In that case," the elf said, "I suppose you *are* the future."

Christine liked that. He really put it in a nutshell for her. She wanted to give him her vision then and there. She wanted to explain to him the importance of steering a course. It was a combination of stewardship and navigation. You had to protect what was worthwhile, while at the same time moving forward. You had to look after what you had, while at the same time getting everything you could out of life. That was why it never did any good worrying about things that had nothing to do with you. You had to steer a course and get what you could, never forgetting what the limitations were.

She wanted to explain it to him, but she couldn't be bothered. She was too drunk.

"We're all building the future in our way, aren't we?" she said instead. "There's Joe, building the flats and offices. There's Dave, doing his bit, making things that make life easier. There's all us women, carrying the future generations, nurturing them, bringing them up. There's you"—she tried to think of a polite way of putting it—"preparing them to go out into the world."

She put her hands around the stem of her glass and tried to stay upright in her chair. What a day she'd had! What a day! She was nearly all talked out. She'd come almost to the bottom. She needed the spring of life to bubble up again, bubble up through the floorboards and fill her to the brim with tomorrow.

"What about love?" said the elf.

She thought she hadn't heard him right. "What about it?"

"Is it important? Does it have any importance, in all this future-building frenzy of activity?"

Christine lifted her glass and saw there was nothing in it.

"I don't know why you're asking me," she said.

He shrugged. "I thought you might know, that's all."

She put her glass down on the table and it fell on its side. She watched a last little dark drop, like a tear, run out and over the rim.

"You've got to love life," she said blearily. "You've got to love just—being alive."

"But how will anyone know you loved it?" said the elf.

The room took a great tilt. It turned on its axis with all its ill-fixed clutter, its plates and people and furniture, its painstaking, ill-fixed record of time. Christine righted her glass, but the room remained tilted.

"Why would anyone need to know that?" she said.

People were standing up. Suddenly there was upheaval, as though the evening had been turned over, like a clod of earth turned over by a spade. There was a kind of exhalation of the used day. People were standing up and pairing themselves, joining together like so many pairs of hands. It was beautiful, in a way, to watch them joining, clasping together like hands. She looked at the clock. It was midnight. Dave and Maggie were standing by the door and Maggie had her shawl on.

"You're not leaving, are you?" said Christine. "Not you two! I was just about to start rolling back the rug—I was getting the music on and dancing."

There was no music, but she danced anyway. She danced in front of them. She raised her arms above her head and snapped her fingers and moved her hips from side to side.

"Sorry!" Maggie said. She squeezed her eyes shut. "I know it's really boring."

"Oh come on," said Christine, grasping Maggie's hands and dancing.

Awkwardly Maggie danced. Self-consciously she shook back her shining hair and danced to the inaudible music. Christine shrieked with laughter. Dave looked at his watch.

"Come on, love," he said.

"The lemon tart!" Christine exclaimed. "I forgot the lemon tart—it's still sitting in its box in the fridge! You can't go till we've had the lemon tart," she said, spinning Maggie clumsily round in a circle so that Maggie stumbled against a chair.

"That'll have to wait, then," said Dave, sententious as a policeman, taking hold of Maggie's arm.

"Oh, listen to him," said Christine. "Listen to him being all boring and sensible. Joe, listen, I forgot the lemon tart!"

Joe was out in the hall with the others. The electric lights were on. They were getting their coats.

"I forgot my lemon tart," she said. "It's still sitting in the fridge."

Joe put his arm around her.

"You're a right handful," he said into her ear. "A right bloody handful, that's what you are."

"There was I, thinking I'd be all posh with my lemon tart," murmured Christine, leaning against him. "I just can't get it right, can I?"

The front door was open. A cold, fresh wind was blowing

through it. It blew into the hall and made the pictures rattle in their frames and bits of paper fly off the hall table. They all went senselessly in different directions. They followed their crazy trajectories. They somersaulted: they made loop-the-loops as they glided to the floor. People were leaving, going out on to the path. Through the door she saw the great dome of night pulsing with stars. She saw the black treetops waving wildly in the wind. When Maggie passed her, Christine did a little dance and snapped her fingers above her head and Maggie giggled.

"Goodbye!" boomed Joe, his arm still around her shoulders. "Goodbye!"

They were going down the dark path. They moved in a body, out into the street, into the night. And then she saw them scatter and break apart, calling, going this way and that, like an armful of birds released into the sky. She stood on the doorstep and watched them until she couldn't see them any longer. Then she went inside and closed the door. Joe was still standing in the hall. His face was full of expression. It was like a little stage with all sorts of things being acted on it. It was as if everything had made its way there, everything she knew: it had all found its way to Joe's face as a form of safekeeping, the whole world of herself concentrated on this little stage.

She did her dance again, snapping her fingers. Joe looked at her with bottomless eyes.

"Come here," he said.